THE CUSTOM HOUSE MURDERS

CAPTAIN LACEY REGENCY MYSTERIES BOOK 15

ASHLEY GARDNER

JA / AG PUBLISHING

CHAPTER 1

London, 1819

I pondered the package that reposed on the dining-room table for a long time.

It had been delivered by a thickset man in a long woolen coat as I was descending the main staircase in the South Audley Street house in search of breakfast on a foggy September morning. From the dining room, I watched the man scan the front windows, and Barnstable, my wife's cool, dark-haired butler, venture out to discover his business there.

After exchanging a few words, our butler stiff with hauteur, the man handed Barnstable a small, paper-wrapped package. Barnstable took it gingerly between his fingers and carried it inside through the front door.

The man remained in place, staring intently at the windows as though trying to watch Barnstable move through the house. Once Barnstable entered the dining room, where I had filled my plate from the sideboard, the man turned away and vanished into the fog.

Barnstable deposited the parcel on the table's edge, as though it contained a tin of horse manure. Next to it, he laid a letter. I sat down with my plate, broke the seal on the heavy paper, and read:

Deliver this to Mr. H. Creasey at Number 11, Hill Lane, off Lower Thames Street, near the Custom House. To be done by the end of the day. J. Denis

I was growing used to James Denis's brevity. He'd used an entire sheet of paper for this message, as usual. Also as usual, I tore the clean part off for my own use, a habit from the days I'd had little money for such luxuries as foolscap.

Barnstable, who would never profess interest in a gentleman's correspondence, had discreetly departed. I was alone in the room, only the crackle of a fire on the hearth as my company.

After regarding the package with deep misgivings, I carefully slid it to me and unwrapped it. The parcel was not addressed to me, but the last time I had delivered a message for Mr. Denis I had become embroiled in a tangle that had nearly killed me. Ironically, it had nearly been the end of Denis as well.

Inside the wrappings, which were clean and crisp, I found a wooden box, about four inches by four and three inches high. A fine piece, made of mahogany, varnished and polished.

The box had a clasp but was not locked. I imagined Denis knew I'd want a look inside and hadn't bothered with a lock I'd only break.

I opened the lid. Inside, nestled on a bed of black velvet, lay a chess piece. A queen, made of ivory.

The piece was perhaps two and a half inches long, carved in a simple shape. I lifted it between thumb and forefinger and held it up to the gray light from the foggy window.

It was an ordinary piece, the sort sold in shops. No costly

gilding or gems adorned it, and nowhere was there any indication of cavity inside, perhaps to smuggle something small and exotic. I examined the queen thoroughly for telltale cracks or hidden catches but found none.

I contemplated the piece for some time then laid it back into its box.

It meant something—why else would Denis insist *I* deliver it when he could have any of his lackeys, such as the man who'd brought it to me, run such a simple errand?

Denis had told me, at the end of my holiday in Brighton this summer, that he expected me to perform a task for him in return for his help during that sojourn. I'd expected an onerous chore, one dangerous or distasteful. Instead I was being instructed to carry a chess piece to an unknown man on the docks.

Very likely the task was dangerous, but I knew Denis would never impart the details to me. He was the sort who expected obedience without question.

However, I refused to let forebodings of doom spoil my breakfast. I returned to my plate and tucked into a hearty if cooling portion of our cook's best offerings.

I INQUIRED OF BARTHOLOMEW, MY VALET, WHEN HE entered to see if I needed anything, whether Thomas Brewster was in the house.

"Indeed, he is, Captain," Bartholomew answered. "In the kitchen, come to have his breakfast."

It was a rare day that Brewster, my hulking bodyguard, did not come to breakfast to supplement his wages with food. My lady wife, whose house this was for her lifetime, had given the kitchen staff orders to feed him. If Brewster's job was to keep me safe from harm, she said, the poor man ought to gain some reward for it.

My wife's servants, proud of their status as staff to a viscount and his mother, had been coolly distant at first to Brewster, a ruffian and thief who did not hide his past, but they'd begun warming to him. Brewster could be blunt and rude—he was to me, always—but he was also loyal, friendly, and even kind in his own way, when he wished to be.

Brewster turned up at my home almost every morning to escort me on even the most trivial of errands. He no longer worked for Denis, who had employed Brewster to keep me alive and useful, but he continued to watch over me because, in Brewster's opinion, I needed a minder.

He came up from the kitchens after I sent Bartholomew down to him, wiping his mouth on the back of his hand, and met me in the ground floor hall. A sweeping staircase, paneled in white, its niches filled with statuary, wrapped around this hall to the next landing. The decor was beautifully elegant, reflecting the taste of my wife, the former Viscountess Breckenridge.

"Should let me deliver it, guv," Brewster said after I told him my errand.

"I doubt Mr. Denis will thank you. This is the task that will release me from my debt to him for saving my life."

"Seems I did my share of the saving." Brewster shoved his hands into the pockets of his square-cut coat. "'Tis one reason I got the sack."

"He asks that I go to this Mr. Creasey and hand him the box," I said. "That is all."

"Huh. Creasey's a right evil bloke. No good will come of it."

"Well, I did not expect the errand to be mundane. Why

would Denis send Mr. Creasey a chess piece?" I lifted the box, which I'd rewrapped in its paper. "A white queen?"

Brewster pursed his lips then shrugged. "No idea. Is it solid gold?"

"No, quite ordinary."

"Then it could mean anything, guv. Right. We go, me one step behind you. You throw the box at Creasey, and then you run the other way. Understand?"

"I will hand it to him politely, or better still, leave it with whomever answers his door. I agree we should not linger."

"Good." Brewster sent me a doubtful glare, but he at last ceased arguing, and we were off.

It was a foul day, too cool for summer and too warm for winter, the fog hanging in thick patches that grew denser as we approached the river. I'd acquiesced to letting Hagen, my wife's coachman, drive us in the family carriage. I did not relish the idea of rolling into the docklands with the viscount's coat of arms blazoned on the coach's door, but the carriage did move us quickly through the crush.

Mayfair had been quiet, as most families that leased houses there had retired to the country for the remainder of the year. As we traveled through Piccadilly to Haymarket and into parts of London where residents lived year-round, the traffic increased. Not all had the means to escape the hot, stinking London summers, and laborers were needed throughout the year. Commerce did not cease because Parliament wasn't sitting and the *haut ton* had departed for more salubrious climes.

Hagen drove us along the Strand to Fleet Street and then around the bulk of St. Paul's to Cheapside. From that busy thoroughfare we inched down lanes until we reached the Thames and its many wharves. I was alone inside the coach, but I imagined Brewster, sitting on a perch on the back, watching the teeming masses with a sour eye.

At London Bridge, Upper Thames Street became Lower Thames Street. London Bridge had occupied this spot since the Middle Ages, although about ten years before my birth, the last of the houses built upon it had been pulled down, and the bridge widened and shored up. No more did heads adorn pikes at its end, just as hangings were no longer a public spectacle at Tyburn. Men and women were executed behind the walls of Newgate, in private, with other prisoners for their audience.

The Custom House stood at the end of the row of docks, with its wide frontage facing the Thames. To the east, the street ended in the wall that surrounded the Tower of London.

Hagen halted in front of the Custom House, and we found Hill Lane, a narrow artery that led north. The street was too large for the carriage, so Brewster and I descended and made our way on foot.

The lane was narrow, inky in the fog. I was now thankful Brewster had insisted on accompanying me. I'd have had to think long and hard before entering that passageway alone.

"Lacey? Good Lord, it *is* you."

I turned at my name and gazed, mystified, at the man who strode toward me from the arched doorway of the Custom House. He wore the black of a fashionable gentleman, with a tall hat slightly askew, his coat tightly buttoned. He had no walking stick and approached with a swift, easy gait.

As he drew closer, memory cleared, and I went gladly forward to meet him.

"Captain Eden," I exclaimed.

The man grasped my hand and shook it hard. I faced Miles Eden, a fellow officer of the Thirty-Fifth Light

Dragoons. "It's Major now," he said breezily. "Was promoted after Waterloo."

"Well deserved." I stepped back to study him. Miles Eden was a tall man, standing an inch or so above me, with a thatch of light-colored hair that had grown thicker since I'd last seen him. Thin sideburns curved along his cheeks to a mouth that was prone to smiles. His eyes were brown, like strong tea, and his skin had tanned to a shade of butternut, a thin scar from Peninsula days white on his cheek.

Eden had been one of the few officers I'd respected. He'd gained his commission through family connections—his uncle was a baron—but he'd proved competent in leading men and thinking quickly in battle. He'd also been good-natured and likable though not a soft touch. His sergeants and men had respected him as well.

"Is it still *Captain* Lacey?" he asked. "I've been away—Antigua, actually. I sold my commission, and since then have heard little of the Thirty-Fifth."

"I indeed bear that title. I took half pay after Vitoria and came home."

"After your injury." Eden glanced at my walking stick in sympathy. "Waterloo would have gone quicker and not been so bloody if you'd been there, I'm certain."

I had to laugh at the exaggeration. "I doubt that very much. Have you returned to England permanently? Or have you become a colonist in truth?"

"No, no, I am home to stay. In fact ..." Eden stepped closer to me, bending to me as men and carts teemed around us. "I would not mind speaking to you about a thing, Lacey. You're just the man to advise me."

"Of course. I am happy to help, if I can."

Eden relaxed as though he'd been afraid of his reception. "Would now be convenient? Or do you have business?"

He trailed off with a glance at the Custom House, where men flowed in and out, shippers paying duties or trying to collect goods held there. I'd heard that the Custom House regularly had plenty of brandy and other seized smuggled goods like gunpowder in their cellars. Indeed, the previous building, only six or seven years before, had exploded like a fiery volcano when it had caught fire. The building I faced now, built a little to the east of the original site, was quite new.

"I do have a man to visit, but my errand should not take long," I explained. I gestured with my stick to the foggy lane. "Just there."

Eden blinked. He regarded Brewster, who hovered at my back, then the small street, then me. "There? A more menacing track I've not seen in a long while, and I have been to some terrible places, Lacey." He squared his shoulders. "Perhaps I ought to accompany you."

Brewster gave him a slow nod. "Another pair of fists might not be amiss."

"I think you are both making heavy weather of it," I said. "I do not intend to linger. But very well. This is Thomas Brewster. He is …" I could not think of a word to describe his position. "He works for me."

"I'd say a good thing he does. Well met, Mr. Brewster." Eden stuck out his hand.

Brewster gazed at him askance for a heartbeat then conceded to the handshake.

"Getting darker by the minute," Brewster said once introductions were finished. "Storm must be coming in."

"Rain will clear the fog," I said with optimism. "Shall we, gentlemen?"

I led the way, my walking stick tapping. Truth be told, I was glad of my friends' presence, both stout fellows, as we reached the mouth of the Stygian lane and plunged inside.

CHAPTER 2

og packed the alley. It roiled around us, reaching with cold, damp fingers. Above the tall buildings at the end of the lane rose the steeple of St. Dunstan's-in-the-East parish church, by London's hero, Christopher Wren. The steeple was ghostly pale, a mere outline in the gloom.

None of the dock workers trundled goods here, the passageway empty of all but us. Our footsteps echoed in the muffled silence.

Number 11 Hill Lane looked no different from the brick buildings to its right and left, and in fact shared a common facade wall with them. Only the number differentiated Mr. Creasey's abode from the doors on either side. The doorstep was crumbling stone, the door itself a black paneled slab.

I stepped up to this door and rapped on it with the head of my walking stick.

Time ticked past, giving us no response. From the end of the lane came the rumble of wagons, the clopping of horses, the shouts of men, but here, in the blanket of fog, all was eerily quiet.

As I was about to tell my friends I would give up and call another time, a bolt slid ponderously back and the door creaked open. A pair of bloodshot eyes under a blotch of greasy dark hair peered out.

"What you want?"

I removed the package from my coat but did not hand it to the apparition in the doorway. The man was thin, dressed in worn and stained clothing, and smelled rancid. I doubted Mr. Denis would thank me for leaving the package with this specimen.

"I have a delivery for Mr. Creasey. Is he at home?"

Home was not the word for this place, but I could be polite.

"What delivery?"

"One of a personal nature." I tucked the parcel into my pocket and drew out a card. "Will you be so kind as to give him my name?"

The man sneered through the crack at the card. "What you fink this is? A palace?"

"Now, look here, you." Eden took an indignant step forward with the air of command he'd turned on insubordinate soldiers. "You fetch your master as you've been told."

The man didn't budge. He was not impressed by gentlemen officers annoyed at his slowness.

Brewster rumbled behind me. "Get him, and right sharpish. This is from Mr. Denis."

The man's dark eyes widened a fraction, and the door slammed shut, the bolt scraping into place. I turned to Brewster in mild annoyance.

"We may never see him again, Brewster. I want to be shot of this errand, my obligation finished."

"Obligations are never finished with His Nibs. You know that."

"Good Lord, who *is* this Mr. Denis?" Eden asked in bewilderment.

I was happy Eden had never heard of him. James Denis was a ruler of the London underworld, with his fingers in many pies from smuggling to theft to forgery. He also procured legitimate artworks for connoisseurs who might not have the connections to obtain what they wanted. Sometimes he did this legally, sometimes not. His clients never asked too many questions. He had connections in high places that kept the magistrates from looking too closely at him, and MPs and aristocrats in his pocket. Denis was unapologetic for his dealings and quick to sort out those who stepped in his way.

"No one you ought to meet." My acquaintanceship with Mr. Denis was too complex to explain. "Necessity makes for strange bedfellows."

Eden's face creased with a weary smile. "Well do I know that. As a matter —"

The bolt rasping back and the door opening once more interrupted him. The lackey had returned.

"Inside." The man jerked his thumb behind him. I trudged forward, Brewster and Eden following. The man growled at me. "Just you. Not the others."

Before Brewster could protest, Eden preempted him. "We'll not let our friend enter such a place alone. We accompany him, or your master speaks with us outdoors."

Brewster folded his arms and became a bulwark, not about to let me enter without him. The lackey muttered a few foul words but dragged the door all the way open.

We entered a long, narrow space that was clearly a warehouse, but no goods filled it. Empty shelves ran along the walls, and thick wooden pillars lining the center aisle held up a lofty ceiling.

Our guide took us through the cold, echoing room to a

door in the very rear of the house. This opened to a winding stair surrounded by brick walls. Brewster mumbled under his breath as I followed the guide, steadying myself with a hand on the cold and mold-streaked walls. Bartholomew would not be happy about the state of my gloves when I returned home, but I less still wanted to fall against that surface.

Eden, directly behind me, said nothing, but I found his presence reassuring. He'd been an excellent soldier, unafraid to ride straight at armed French cavalrymen to ensure that his fellows escaped.

The top of the stairs opened to another long room, very much like the one below, but this ceiling was lower. At the end of the aisle lay yet another door, closed.

"Jove," Eden said. "You'd think with all this space, they could fashion an office a little closer to the stairs."

Brewster guffawed behind him.

The lackey tapped on the far door and opened it after we heard a gruff, "Come."

We entered a large room that was indeed an office. In contrast to the rest of the building, this chamber radiated luxury. Soft woven carpets covered the floor, and tapestries in bright blues, yellows, and reds hid the rough brick of the walls. The tapestries were not modern copies, I could see—my friend Lucius Grenville had a piece of tapestry from twelfth-century France, a hand-woven masterpiece. These were similar.

Furniture ranged from a desk of rich mahogany to a settee in the latest Egyptian style—carved ebony upholstered in gold-and-cream striped silk with small ivory medallion studs. Wing chairs exuding comfort sat next to delicate Hepplewhite, shield-backed dining chairs.

Plants took up the rest of the space, from palms to tall grasses, all contained in pots and containers. The room had a cool humidity, like a greenhouse, refreshing after the bleak emptiness of the warehouse without.

A man sat behind a desk at the far end of the room. The desk had been situated facing the door but a bit to the left of the room's center. So that, I realized, if anyone tried to fire a weapon as they burst in, they'd have to sidestep and adjust their aim. This would give anyone at the desk time to take cover or for the lackey to disarm the intruder.

James Denis kept his desk sparse—I rarely saw anything more on it than one piece of paper or perhaps a book. This man had covered his desk's surface with piles of books, ledgers, and papers, some of the papers rolled into scrolls. Pots of ink and several pen trays were in evidence, as though the man mislaid his pens and ink often and called for replacements.

Books filled shelves behind the desk and formed piles on the floor where the shelves ran out. The only piece of furniture not filled with clutter was a table, on top of which reposed a chessboard set up and ready for a game. It was not missing a queen, and the pieces looked to be made of jade, not ivory.

Denis never looked up at me whenever I was ushered into his presence, busying himself with making a note or finishing a letter, or at one time, partaking of a meal. I'd have to wait until he finished whatever he was doing, as though a call from me was of no importance, even when he'd sent word requesting my immediate attendance.

This man stared straight at me as I entered and rose when I approached the desk. Mr. Creasey was of a slight build with slender limbs and older than I'd expected, with a lined face and iron-gray hair.

Nothing elderly or feeble showed in his eyes, however. Those, which were a light shade of gray, regarded me with the coldness of a steel blade, no matter that his lips bore a slight smile.

"You've come from Mr. Denis, have you? I am curious as to why." Creasey gestured to chairs before his desk, two of which were Chippendale style armchairs and one ebony with gilded arms and legs that was supposed to be Egyptian. It was clear its maker had never been to that part of the world.

"Indeed, Denis sent me. I am Captain Gabriel Lacey, at your service, sir." I clicked my heels and gave him a military bow.

"Lacey. Ah, yes." His manner said he'd heard my name, but under what context, he did not say. "I am Mr. Harlow Creasey. Importer. Are these your servants?"

Creasey knew bloody well that Eden could not be a servant. Brewster was not exactly one, but he didn't bristle. Brewster didn't nod either, standing stolidly by, waiting to see what would happen.

Eden made a similar military bow. "Major Miles Eden," he said coolly. "A friend to the captain."

"I see. Please sit. These chairs are my own and not for sale, and I like to see them used."

I decided to be gracious and settled myself on an armchair. Eden took the other armchair—the Egyptian style one looked most uncomfortable. Brewster remained stubbornly on his feet.

Mr. Creasey returned to sit behind his desk and rested his elbows on it, hands folded. If not for his watchfulness, he might have had no worries about this unexpected visit from strangers.

I withdrew the parcel from my pocket and leaned forward to set it before him. "I have looked inside. It is perfectly harmless."

Creasey reached for it without hesitation. "It would be, wouldn't it?"

If I'd received a mysterious box from Denis, and Denis appeared to be my rival, I'd be exceedingly nervous about its contents. Creasey merely set the package on top of a small stack of ledgers, unfolded the paper, and opened the box.

"Ah." The sharp word brought the lackey out of the shadows. Brewster moved to intercept him.

I held up my hand to keep Brewster from bodily stopping the man. "Is something amiss?" I asked.

Creasey's eyes, changed from cold steel to white-hot anger, regarded me over the box's lid. "Do you mock me, sir?"

"I can hardly mock you. I have no idea what that piece is for or what it means."

Creasey lifted the queen with a trembling hand. He held it up to the light, as I had, but he obviously read more into it.

"It means, I can kill you where you stand." Creasey flicked his hard gaze back to me.

"Steady on," Eden said. "You cannot threaten an officer of the King's army. We'd be within our rights to kill *you*, if you try. Do not think we are unarmed."

My walking stick had within its shaft a stout sword. Eden carried no obvious weapon, but he'd likely have a knife or dagger under his coat. Brewster, I knew from experience, carried several small weapons about his person.

Creasey's tiny smile returned. "But I would be foolish to do so." He laid the white queen onto the velvet with care and clicked the box closed. "Please convey to Mr. Denis that I have received and I understand his message."

I was damned if I knew what message, but I hardly wanted to admit this. "I will."

"Under the circumstances, gentlemen, I suggest you depart." Creasey set the box to one side, where it would soon become so much flotsam on the desk's surface. "You are stout fellows, and as you say, armed, but the men I can summon would not fear you or mind that you are of the King's army. I bid you good day."

Brewster, who remained at the shoulder of Creasey's lackey, stood silently, not offering his opinion. I knew what it would be, however.

I rose. "I believe you are correct. Good day, Mr. Creasey."

Eden did not bother with a polite farewell. He bowed frostily, strode to the door, and flung it open, as though ready to face any horde Creasey could summon. No one was on the other side.

Brewster pointedly waited for me to precede him. I started after Eden, and Brewster, without a word, fell in behind me, close enough that any weapon fired or thrown would hit him first.

"Captain Lacey."

Creasey's smooth tones made me turn back. This annoyed Brewster, who scowled at me as I craned around him. "Sir?"

"Do you play?" Creasey gestured at the chessboard.

I hesitated. "I … have played. In the army. Not much lately."

Creasey waved a hand. "No matter. If you fancy a game of an evening, I would welcome the diversion. Under a flag of truce, of course."

An interesting invitation. I nodded at him. "I will consider it."

"Please do. Good day, Captain."

I nodded then turned and resumed my departure.

The lackey did not accompany us this time. He gave us a belligerent stare as we passed, then slammed the office door as soon as we were through, leaving us alone. I heard a key turn in the lock.

"Cheek," Eden declared. "I suppose we know the way out."

"Sooner the better," Brewster growled. He herded me on, again placing himself so that he could protect my back.

Once we were in the enclosed stairwell, Brewster asked, "Why did ye tell him ye'd play chess with him? You come here again, I doubt you'll leave alive."

"If you recall my words, I said I would consider it." I grimaced as my hand landed on a slimy substance, completing the ruin of my gloves.

"But you're a man of your word," Brewster said. "If you decide to play, you'll come back. And it's me what has to follow you and make sure you stay alive, even if *I* don't. I have a wife, you know, what depends on me."

"I'd not put you into danger from this man, Brewster," I assured him.

"You already have. He'll not forget me face. Ah well." He heaved an aggrieved sigh. "I knew what hell it would be when I agreed to work for ye."

Eden said not a word until we were on the ground floor, making for the outer door and freedom. The fogged-in lane outside would be a pleasant garden compared to the chill menace of this warehouse.

"What did he mean about a message?" Eden pulled back the bolt on the door, which thankfully opened easily. "He seemed to believe you'd understand."

"I do not." I caught the door and followed him out, Brewster behind us. "I am as mystified as you are. Brewster?"

Brewster stepped into the lane and let the door slam behind him. "No idea, guv."

He wouldn't look at me as he said the words, and I could not decide if he knew what the queen meant or not. Brewster rarely lied deliberately to me, but he could be frugal with the truth.

Eden accepted Brewster's answer without question, and we strode at a quick pace back to Lower Thames Street.

The road, with its carts and shouting men, the masts of ships rising above the wharves, was soothingly normal. The lane with its strange warehouse faded into the mists behind us.

"Major Miles Eden."

A voice I knew boomed through the fog. Behind it came a large man with thick blond hair, his blue eyes twinkling as he bore down on us. The man wore a black suit that barely fit his bulk, but it did nothing to hamper his boisterous pace.

"Pomeroy?" I greeted him in surprise. Milton Pomeroy had been my sergeant in the Thirty-Fifth Light and had become an elite Bow Street Runner once he'd returned to civilian life. "What brings you to the Custom House?"

"He does." Pomeroy pointed to Eden, whose color had risen until he was scarlet. "Major Miles Eden, I am arresting you in the King's name for the murder of Mr. George Warrilow. Will you come along like a good fellow, or will I have to wrestle you down? Hate to embarrass such a fine officer, so I suggest you walk quietly beside me, and nothing of the sort has to happen."

CHAPTER 3

*P*omeroy tried to dissuade me from accompanying Eden to Bow Street. "Not your business, Captain," he said in his cheerful manner.

He had a point—I hadn't seen Eden in years, and while I believed him to be an honorable fellow, which of us hadn't changed since the Peninsula? He'd gone to Antigua, with its heat, blood-sucking insects, and slavery. Who could say what he'd done there?

But Eden had gallantly walked with me into the dark lane and the warehouse of Mr. Creasey, when it was clear I headed into potential danger, and I could not now abandon him when he was in trouble.

I waved to Hagen, who'd waited down by the wharf, and the carriage moved slowly toward us.

"Are you certain of this, Pomeroy?" I asked. "You know Captain—I mean, Major—Eden."

"I do indeed. Never saw a braver man on the battlefield, sir, except for you. But you're a wanted man, Major. Only doing me duty."

Pomeroy opened a paper and held it up with a dramatic flair. It was a handbill of a sort the Runners printed when they hunted a suspect. The person's description would be put into the *Hue and Cry* newspaper sent to constabularies all over Britain, and flyers like this one posted.

Major Miles Eden, late of the Thirty-Fifth Light Dragoons, wanted in connection with the murder of a passenger from the ship Dusty Rose *out of Antigua. Major Eden is a tall man with light-brown hair and brown eyes, a thin scar on his right cheek. Will likely be armed. Consider him dangerous.*

"Very flattering," Eden said faintly.

"I'm certain there's a reasonable explanation," I argued.

"Could be, sir. Could be. He can tell it to the magistrate." Pomeroy gestured to the carriage that halted beside us. "Are you lending us your coach, Captain? Kind of you."

"No need to come with me, Lacey," Eden said as Pomeroy jerked open the door. "Or give me the use of your coach. I've weathered worse."

"Nonsense," I said. "We'll visit the magistrate together and clear this up in a trice. Please."

"After you, sir," Pomeroy said to Eden.

Pomeroy hadn't come alone to the wharves. Three foot patrollers stationed themselves on the far side of the carriage, so Eden wouldn't simply bolt out the other door.

Eden showed no inclination to do so. He climbed calmly into the coach and sat on the rear-facing seat.

I started for the carriage, to be held back when Brewster seized my arm.

"You're not going to walk into Bow Street nick by choice, are ye?" Brewster demanded. "And face a magistrate what's examined you before?"

"And found me guilty of nothing. Sir Nathaniel Conant is a rational man."

"I'll tell you this for nothing, guv. You go into a courtroom with a mate, trying to help, and the next thing, you're banged up with him, accused of being his accomplice."

I freed myself from his grasp. "As I know nothing of the matter, that is hardly likely."

"Ye hired me to keep you out of trouble, guv. My advice is to leave it."

"I'd listen were I you," Pomeroy put in. He pushed past us and hoisted himself into the coach.

"You make an excellent point, Brewster. However ..." I reached for the handholds on the side of the coach and pulled myself up and inside just before Hagen started the horses. "Go on home if you don't have the stomach for Bow Street."

Brewster's glare was full of fire. His face creased into a snarl but he caught hold of the coach as it passed him and hauled himself onto the seat on the back.

We said little as we traveled from the river to Bow Street in Covent Garden. Pomeroy was pleased, as he'd receive a reward if a judge convicted Eden of murder.

Eden's nervousness at the wharves and his request for advice became clear. He'd realized his arrest had been imminent, and he'd wanted my advice about it. I wondered if he'd seized the opportunity of our chance meeting to ask for help, or if he'd been searching for me. Any inquiry at the South Audley Street house would have told him where I'd gone.

We bumped along Fleet Street to the Strand, and from there north on Southampton Street to Covent Garden, past the opening to Grimpen Lane, where I still kept lodgings, and around to Bow Street.

The magistrate was already sitting, Pomeroy said, hearing cases for the day. He'd dismiss those he felt were trivial and send any criminal he thought dangerous to Newgate to await trial.

Brewster hopped off the coach and faded into the crowd on the street, never liking to be near a magistrate's court. Pomeroy led us inside the tall house and up the stairs to an office I'd visited before. It was a place where the more genteel could speak to the magistrate, instead of being thrown in with the pickpockets, housebreakers, and game girls.

Pomeroy left us, telling us he'd be back with Sir Nathaniel directly.

"Lacey, please accept my apologies."

Eden paced the room while I stood near the door, supporting myself on my walking stick.

"Please explain what you are apologizing for." I tried a light tone. "So I can decide whether to forgive you."

Eden tossed his hat to a chair and ran a hand through his thick hair. "I should have told you straightaway I was suspected of murder. I didn't commit it of course."

"Who was this man, George ... ?"

"Warrilow. A bad piece of work if ever there was one. I had no idea he was dead until this morning. I'd been asked to return to the Custom House today to gather my belongings they'd seized to search—almost everyone's baggage was taken by the excise men when we landed, as there was some worry about smuggling. They found nothing untoward about mine, and the customs officer was ready to hand my things back to me. But then I saw my name blazoned on a handbill, which did not half give me a turn, I can tell you. The custom officer must not have seen the bills, or he or his clerks would have kept hold of me, I am certain. I then heard men from the ship on which I'd sailed saying that some of their cargo had been stolen, and Warrilow was dead."

A chill crept over me as I listened to his tale. Cargo theft, smuggling, murder, and Eden somehow had blundered into it.

"I decided to make myself scarce—my belongings aren't important—and then I saw you—

His words cut off as Pomeroy banged open the door and ushered Sir Nathaniel Conant into the room.

Conant was the opposite of Pomeroy in every way. Where Pomeroy was robust and loud, Sir Nathaniel was elderly and quiet. He'd been knighted several years ago for his skill as a magistrate and contributions to various reforms of London's thief-takers. I'd found him to be careful and intelligent. He reviewed evidence painstakingly and did not simply send a man to Newgate because it was convenient and he wanted his dinner.

Sir Nathaniel waved us to chairs and took a seat behind a table, spreading out a sheaf of papers before him.

"Major Miles Eden." Sir Nathaniel fixed him with a keen eye. "You stand accused of the murder of Mr. George Warrilow. From what Mr. Pomeroy has indicated, you will enter a plea of not guilty to the murder."

"That is correct." Eden sat forward, his breath quick, his eyes animated. "I did not kill Mr. Warrilow."

"Several witnesses have attested to the fact that you came to blows with the man as you traveled on the ship."

"I did." Eden gave him an unashamed nod. "Mr. Warrilow was an unpleasant person to the point of cruelty. He regularly beat his servants for no reason except to satisfy his pique. About halfway through the voyage, I grew tired of his pettiness one evening at supper and remonstrated him for it. He became enraged and actually attacked me with his fists. I defended myself. The captain broke up the fight and asked that we shut ourselves in our quarters. I had little to do with the man after that."

"He was found in his lodgings the morning after the ship docked," Sir Nathaniel went on in his dry voice. His hand trembled slightly as he moved a paper. I'd heard from Pomeroy that the man contemplated retirement as his health was declining, but he spoke with as much vigor as ever. "Two days ago. Dead from a blow to the head. You were seen visiting his boarding house the evening before, not long after you both had disembarked."

Eden flushed. "True. I looked him up but I never saw him. The landlady told me he'd already gone to bed, so I decided not to bother."

"Why did you visit him?" Sir Nathaniel asked. "If you disliked the man so?"

"To ask him a question—about business he had in Antigua. It scarcely matters now." Eden clamped his mouth closed, setting his face in stubborn lines.

"The landlady, Mrs. Beadle, is a witness," Sir Nathaniel said. "She will be asked to verify your story. Did anyone else see you there—and more importantly, see you leave without speaking to Mr. Warrilow?"

"I suppose there must have been." Eden shrugged. "Servants and such. I didn't notice."

"Mmm." Sir Nathanial made a note.

"Beg pardon, sir," Pomeroy broke in. "I've already inquired. The landlady's boy saw Mr. Eden. He seems a sharp lad. He couldn't swear Major Eden left without speaking to Mr. Warrilow, but he's sure he heard Mr. Warrilow snoring sometime afterward."

Sir Nathaniel made another note. "Thank you, Mr. Pomeroy."

Pomeroy nodded. He was zealous in his pursuit of criminals, but he was fair enough to let the truth of the matter be proved.

"You knew Mr. Warrilow in Antigua?" Sir Nathaniel asked Eden. "What business did you have there?"

"The Thirty-Fifth Light Dragoons—my regiment—sent some officers over to advise the defense force near St. John's, but after about six months of this, I decided to sell my commission and become a planter." Eden grimaced. "Couldn't stick it. Plantations are run on the backs of poor unfortunates who have no lives of their own. So then I had a small trade business, taking over from a man who'd died and whose widow didn't want the responsibility. Made a bit of cash, but I missed home." Eden smiled faintly. "The fog might annoy you gentlemen, but I find it refreshing."

Conant fell silent a time as he made more notes. Eden drummed his fingers on his knee, his booted foot sliding a little on the floor.

After a while, Sir Nathaniel cleared his throat. "You visited the cargo hold of your ship a number of times during the voyage, it seems. Several of the crew and other passengers remarked upon it."

"Nervous about my personal affects." Eden's cheeks stained red once more. "With good cause, as we now know, if some of the cargo was stolen."

Yet he'd told me, only moments ago, that he'd fled the Custom House without retrieving his belongings because they were of no importance.

"What were you transporting?" Conant asked.

"Eh? Oh, you know. Clothing. A chair I liked."

"You traveled without servants?"

"Yes, I am very much on my own." This last was delivered with clarity and without hesitation.

It was unusual for a gentleman of Eden's standing, especially one who'd just confessed to have made a bit of money, not to have at least one servant to look after him. I'd gone years without an attendant, but I'd been nearly penniless.

Eden had always been independent, I recalled, not giving

his batman in the regiment much to do. I'd both envied his carefree ways and felt a bit superior, as I'd had a wife and daughter to return to every night, not an empty tent. That was before my wife had decided a steady life with another man was preferable to following the drum, and had deserted me, taking our daughter with her.

"And what do you plan to do now that you've returned to England?" Sir Nathaniel went on.

Eden shrugged. "Find a house to live in. Look up my uncle. See what I can do with myself."

"Marry?" Conant suggested.

Eden laughed heartily, though the laugh was strained. "Not I. Well, unless I stumble over a woman who steals my heart. But I'm a confirmed bachelor, me."

True, while Eden had had affairs when I'd known him—discreet ones—he'd never shown a penchant for chasing a wife.

Conant finished writing, laid his pen in its tray, and folded his hands on the desk.

"Major Eden, you have been arrested for a serious crime. Please tell me what happened two days before this, once you arrived in England on your ship." He sent Eden a stare from eyes that had not lost their sharpness. "Everything, please."

Eden's pulse beat in his throat, and he strained to keep his voice steady. "Well, let me see. The ship was delayed at the end of our voyage. We had to wait a bit far up the Thames for a fog to clear, then up the river we came. Quite a lot of ships waited with us, all of us bottled up. We put in at the London Docks, which I thought astonishing. Huge place, all enclosed by warehouses, with ships jammed in, unloading all sorts. Our ship contained quite a lot of cocoa and rum, well-guarded, so I am surprised it was burgled. The customs and excise men were waiting for us, searching thoroughly. They seized my baggage, what there was of it, and took it away. I was fetching it today when Mr. Pomeroy, ah, intervened."

Pomeroy chuckled.

"Why did they take *your* bags?" Conant asked.

"Oh … er, as I told Captain Lacey, the customs agents searched most of our belongings. I was traveling alone, not carrying much. Excise men are inclined to be suspicious."

And he'd been visiting the hold often. Someone must have reported that.

"Where did you go once you disembarked?" Sir Nathaniel prompted.

"Hired a coach and toddled off to St. James's to find a place to lie my head. I tried at my old club, Brooks's. Hadn't been there in, oh, fifteen years? Never went much during the war. They didn't have any rooms available, but the doorman sent me to lodgings around the corner in St. James's Place. I thought the house quite tolerable, and I moved in."

"But you left these quite tolerable rooms and returned to Wapping, where Mr. Warrilow had found an abode. How did you know where he was?"

"Asked, didn't I?" Eden's flush returned. "Look here, I'll confess. Not to his murder," he added hastily. "Warrilow was a small planter in Antigua. He came to London for an errand he trusted no one else to do, so he said, but he did not tell me what errand. He grew sugar, so I imagine it had something to do with that trade. We did not see eye to eye on the business of plantations. He believed slavery was the most economically sound of practices, no matter how many reasoned counterpoints I gave him, and was quite boastful of how much work he ground out of the poor sods unlucky enough to belong to him. I went to see him because I'd lent him a book on the subject and I wanted it returned."

Eden's color was so deep I feared he'd drop of apoplexy.

Conant studied him, while Eden squirmed. He'd just changed his story from saying he'd gone to talk to Warrilow about business in Antigua—this story was likely also a lie.

He didn't lie about arguing with Warrilow on the ship or about his belongings being seized and released, I didn't think, but about why he'd hunted up the man after the voyage. Eden must have known where to find Warrilow—the docklands was a warren of wharves, taverns, and lodging houses, difficult to navigate if you did not know them. Which meant they must have made arrangements beforehand to meet.

"I see. What time did you arrive at his rooms?"

"Nine-thirty in the evening. I heard the church clock strike the half hour as I arrived. I left not long later, as I said —the landlady told me he was already abed."

"Did you ask her for the book? As it was yours, she might have fetched it for you."

Eden rubbed his forehead. "Yes, yes, she did. And returned to tell me that Mr. Warrilow was fast asleep. He was alive then, and I never saw the man again."

"Did you take the book?"

"Pardon? Oh, yes, of course."

Conant moved a paper, the sound a whisper. "Which is in your new lodgings, presumably."

"Yes." Eden's hands tightened into fists on his lap.

"Very well, then. The coroner's assistant who examined the body has estimated the time of death to be about eleven that night and probably not later than five in the morning."

"That absolves me, then." Eden looked a little more cheerful. "I was well away from Warrilow's lodgings by eleven and I certainly did not go back later."

"Where did you go?" Conant lifted his pen and dipped it into ink.

"To my rooms, of course." In spite of Eden's confident tone, his fists tightened again.

"Witnesses?" When Eden didn't answer, Conant looked up. "Your landlord? A fellow lodger? Anyone who saw you on the street? Did you stop by your club to greet anyone?"

Conant was trying to help him, I saw. He must doubt that Eden killed Mr. Warrilow, but if Eden continued to fidget and blush, he might as well put a noose around his own neck. Juries tended to believe that anyone who acted guilty truly was. What other reason would a man have to be nervous?

"No, no," Eden said breathily. "Saw no one, unfortunately. Slept like a babe. Spent yesterday looking up old friends, seeing to my tailor—will need heavier clothing for this climate. Got word from the Custom House I was welcome to retrieve my baggage, which is where I went this morning."

The room grew silent, save for the scratch of Conant's pen on the paper and Pomeroy snorting through a stuffy nose. Eden's hands loosened, and he returned to drumming them. His gaze fixed on Conant's quill, which moved evenly over the page.

Finally, Conant set the pen down again. When he lifted his head, he looked at me, not Eden.

"Captain Lacey, I assume you have accompanied your friend to speak of his good character?"

He was giving me the opportunity to clear Eden as well. Sir Nathaniel did not want to send him to Newgate, I could see—he was a fair man, and I had been proved right about the innocence of a man he'd charged before. Either Conant now trusted me, or he did not want to get caught out again.

I gave him a nod. "I served with Major Eden on the Peninsula. We were captains in the same regiment. Major Eden was known for his bravery, but he was not reckless. He saved many a man with his prudence. I trusted him."

"Do you trust him still?" The question came in a gentle tone, Conant's intelligent gaze piercing me.

I thought of how readily Eden had walked into the dark alley with me and faced the subtle menace of Mr. Creasey. He'd been trying to ask for my help—I assume about the handbill he'd seen with his name on it—but he'd put that worry aside to assist me.

"Yes," I answered. "I trust him still."

Conant studied me while I hoped I had not made a terrible misjudgment of character. At last he bent his head and made a note.

"Very well. Major Eden, given the lack of sufficient evidence, I will not charge you for a crime at this time. However." He fixed Eden with a severe gaze. "Please remain in London, until I can be confident in the identity of Mr. Warrilow's killer. Retain your lodgings in St. James's Place, and be prepared to answer any further questions."

Eden blew out a breath, his relief apparent. "Of course. Thank you, Sir Nathaniel."

Conant sent him a brief nod, then gathered his papers and rose. We scrambled to our feet, me leaning heavily on my stick. Conant gave us another nod then made his way around us, moving slowly but with dignity, and out the door Pomeroy opened for him.

"Well, that's you lucky." Pomeroy beamed at Eden. "Congratulations, sir." He came forward and shook Eden's hand. "But do remain where I can put my hands on you again if I need to."

"I have already said I would, Sergeant." Eden sent him a wry smile. "I'm pleased to find you in good circumstances. At least, more pleased than I was an hour ago."

Pomeroy laughed loudly. His response was cut off as

another Runner paused outside the door, one whom I did not wish to see.

Timothy Spendlove, of thinning red hair and light blue eyes, could with his very presence cut through laughter and good cheer like an icy knife. He did so now, his lips flattening into displeasure.

"Captain Lacey."

Pomeroy ceased his laughter in annoyance. "I didn't arrest the captain, if that's what you're thinking, Spendlove. He's here as a witness."

Spendlove's gaze flicked from me to Eden without interest. "I was addressing him, not accusing him," Spendlove said calmly. "I thought you'd like to know, Captain, that someone has tried to murder your Mr. Denis. Not an hour ago. He escaped within a hair's breadth of his life."

CHAPTER 4

I was surprised by the flare of concern and alarm that filled me at Spendlove's announcement.

When I'd first met Denis, I'd loathed and distrusted him, and this before his ruffians had tried to kill me. I never liked that he used me for errands and bound me with obligation. He had helped me many times in the years since our first acquaintance, it was true—making my sense of obligation still stronger—but I did not consider him a friend.

Until this moment, when I realized that if Denis were killed, I'd be sorry.

"Almost murdered?" Pomeroy exclaimed before I could. "What do you mean, man?"

"I do not know details." Spendlove appeared most displeased that the assassin had failed to bring down Mr. Denis. "Someone caught him between doorstep and carriage. Pity he did not succeed."

I tamped down my sudden flare of anger. Spendlove, on the right side of the law, had far less honor than James Denis, a man who had committed criminal acts before my eyes.

"Thank you for the information," I said stiffly. "Good day."

Spendlove stepped aside for me. While his expression remained stern, his lips twitched in the corners, in a ghastly parody of a smile. He liked to see me unnerved.

Eden followed me, with Pomeroy behind him. "Mr. Denis and his sort always fight amongst themselves," Pomeroy boomed, voice echoing in the stairwell. "I'd not be concerned, Captain."

I knew Denis had many enemies, but I was most certainly concerned. First, that an assassin had been able to get past his many bodyguards, and second, that I had not an hour ago visited one of Denis's rivals with a message only he and Denis understood.

I continued to the ground floor, those still waiting to be tried, the dejected who were being led away to await their transportation to Newgate, and barristers' clerks in black, seeking clients.

Outside, a gust of wind sent spatters of droplets over my face. The fog was clearing, to be replaced by cool needles of rain.

I turned to Eden, who settled his hat against the wind. "I must return to Mayfair," I said. "You can ride with me, if you like, and we'll set you down in St. James's."

"No." The word was abrupt before Eden softened his tone. "No, I must go once more to the Custom House and wrest my baggage from them. I hope the handbills have been disposed of, and no one tries to arrest me—again."

"Never worry," Pomeroy, who'd followed us out, assured him. "I'll send word that you're not to be touched, for now. Pleased to see you again, Captain—no, Major—Eden. Life in the islands was kind to you, I see. You are brown as a nut and strong as an oak."

"The sun in the Antilles. It bakes into one." Eden clipped

off a salute. "Pleased to see you as well, Sergeant. Good day to you."

A hackney lingered at a stand on the corner of Bow and Russel Streets, and Eden started for it, me beside him.

"You do not need to see me to the hackney," Eden said, with a glance at my walking stick.

I disliked that he assumed me feeble, though I knew I could not walk a long distance without distress. My pride had learned that lesson.

"I happen to be traveling in the same direction. I must find my man, and I know he will be at a bake shop around the corner." I held out my hand as we neared the hackney, and Eden signaled the driver that he'd take it. "My home now is in South Audley Street, at the Breckenridge house. Everyone knows it. Or a message left at the bake shop I just spoke of— Mrs. Beltan's in Grimpen Lane—will reach me."

Eden shook my offered hand. "Thank you, Lacey, for not deserting me."

"You were good to accompany me on my unpleasant errand. I could hardly forsake you on yours."

A gleam of interest entered Eden's eyes as he released me. "Breckenridge, eh? I read of the death of Lord Breckenridge …"

"And I married his widow." I touched my hat. "Well met, Eden, and good day."

"You'll not get away that easily, Lacey. I'll have the story out of you another time." Laughing, he climbed into the carriage, calling to the driver to take him to the Custom House on Lower Thames Street.

I watched the hackney roll away then continued around the corner to Russel Street, making for Grimpen Lane. Despite the rain, the square of Covent Garden beyond teemed with those shopping, bargaining, and calling out wares. The smell of greens, ripe fruit, and baking bread wafted my way.

Before I reached the narrow entrance to Grimpen Lane, Brewster came at me from the direction of Covent Garden.

"Guv, I have some news ..."

"About Denis?" I drew close to him and lowered my voice, though I doubted we'd be overheard above the din from the market. "Spendlove told me. With barely concealed glee."

"I don't work for His Nibs no more," Brewster said, "but I want to know what happened—what lout let a man with a blade close to 'im."

"I am going in the same direction," I assured him. "Shall we find our coach?"

HAGEN WAITED FOR US ON BOW STREET. I INSISTED THAT Brewster ride inside the carriage with me, and he did so with a show of reluctance, though I believe he was happy to get out of the rain. As we bumped our way along the Strand toward Charing Cross, I told Brewster what had transpired in Sir Nathaniel's office.

"Huh," was Brewster's response. "Your man's an officer and a gentleman, so of course he was let off. If they'd pegged *me* for the murder, I'd even now be in a cage heading off to await me trial."

"You are a known criminal," I pointed out. "Eden has no taint to his name. But I take your point. On the other hand, Sir Nathaniel did send Colonel Brandon to Newgate once upon a time, so your argument does not hold true for all."

"Beg pardon, guv—your colonel might be gentleman-born, but he's good at a lie."

I had observed the same thing. "I'd say he was *bad* at a lie, as it only helped him get banged up. His wife sees through him, which is the most important thing."

"Aye, Mrs. Brandon is a canny lady." High praise from Brewster. "What happened to His Nibs today worries me. No one should have come nigh him."

"How did you hear of it? That a Runner was informed — particularly Spendlove — does not surprise me, but there has scarcely been time for it to be printed in the newspapers."

"And it won't be. His Nibs can't let it get about that someone attacked him and nearly succeeded in killing 'im. I heard because Lewis — one of his men — came looking for me to tell me."

"He knew to find you in Grimpen Lane?"

Brewster shrugged. "Don't matter I'm no longer your nanny for 'im — Mr. Denis knows every move you make. He'd have heard you were headed to Bow Street. Happens I was peckish and went out to the market, and Lewis found me there."

"What did he say of the matter?"

"Very little. He was inside the house and didn't see what happened, but His Nibs is angry." Brewster shuddered. "I want to look in on him, but when he's angry ..."

"I know." I had witnessed exactly what Denis could do when enraged. He rarely lost his temper and shouted as I did, but he could quietly cause very bad things to occur.

We fell silent as we went along Cockspur Street and Pall Mall, past the bulk of St. James's Palace then north through the clubland of London to Piccadilly, and up a narrow lane to Curzon Street.

Denis resided at Number 45, a tall house of brown brick trimmed with white. I had seen only the ground and first floors inside the five-story house, whose windows at the top spoke of servants' quarters.

We saw no sign of disturbance as we descended from the coach. I told Hagen to go home—he agreed only after much convincing. He slapped the reins to the horse's back and the dark coach plodded away up South Audley Street, soon lost to the rain and mist.

"Let me, guv," Brewster said as we approached the front door. Drapes had been pulled across the windows, giving us no view inside.

"You think he'll refuse to admit me?" I asked in surprise.

"You never know with His Nibs. But Lewis will let me in the kitchen if nothing else."

The front door opened as we stood debating—only a sliver, I noted. The butler, an elderly specimen called Gibbons, who was as cold and hard a man as I'd ever met, beckoned to me.

"He is asking to see you, sir." The butler's tones were chilling. "Mr. Brewster, you are to go up with him." Gibbons turned on his heel and disappeared.

He hadn't left the door unattended. As I crossed the threshold, four beefy men surrounded me, and one slammed and bolted the door behind Brewster.

Brewster usually waited for me downstairs with his cronies when I visited Denis, or took refreshment in the kitchen, but the stern faces on the men around us told him he'd not be welcome below stairs today. Brewster's countenance turned sour as he ascended the stairs behind me.

The butler led us to Denis's study, though I scarcely needed him to show me the way. We entered the spartan room, so different from the clutter that surrounded Mr. Creasey. I wondered if the state of Creasey's office was a reason Denis kept his study so austere.

Unlike most days when I visited him, Denis was not

seated at his desk. Today he paced in front of the fireplace, pointedly halting before his path took him near any window.

A tall, clean-shaven man in his thirties with dark hair in a finely tailored suit, Denis lifted a hand when I entered, his demeanor as cool as ever. However, I spied fury burning in his blue eyes, a rage that few men ever saw, and lived to speak about it.

"Before you ask for details of what happened," Denis began, "suffice it to say that a man barreled his way past my guards and came at me with a knife. That one." He pointed to his desk, where lay a long dagger with a slight curve to the blade. The metal was dark with age, the leather on the hilt split.

"Where is the bloke what wielded it?" Brewster rumbled.

Denis resumed his pacing. "Not here. The knife is not significant. It is of Ottoman origin but can be found in any curio shop in London. Likely bought for the purpose. My guards were able to thwart the man, and I entered my house unscathed."

"He was waiting for you," I stated.

I kept my chill at Denis's blunt answer, *not here*, from showing in my face. The words were a reminder of why Denis was a dangerous man. The would-be assassin very likely had not lived to report to his master, but I had no doubt Denis had pried from him exactly who that master was before he'd sent the man to be dispatched.

"Obviously," Denis snapped. "I was returning from an appointment. He hid in the lane next to Chesterfield House and darted forth the exact moment I alighted from my coach."

"Then fools were guarding the house while you were out." Brewster's tone held contempt. "He shouldn't have got near."

"He was well hidden, and it was not an impromptu attack." Denis's glacial tones cut through Brewster's bluster.

"He must have watched this house for a long time. The quick actions of my guards saved me, because, I confess, I had let my mind wander to another matter."

More anger flashed in his eyes, at himself, I understood.

"This incident is not why I asked you to come in, Captain." Denis halted his pacing, putting himself squarely in front of the empty fireplace. "You delivered my package?"

"I did." He'd have known I'd set off directly after breakfast.

"Thank you for being so prompt. You found Mr. Creasey at home?"

"If that warehouse is his home, then yes."

"He does, indeed, live there." The words held disdain. "Not many know that, which is what he prefers. Tell me, what did he say when he opened the parcel?"

I did not question how Denis knew Mr. Creasey would unwrap it as soon as I handed it to him.

"He threatened to kill me. No—" I amended. "He told me the chess piece meant he could kill me where I stood and then said he would not."

"Good." Denis closed his mouth, finished speaking. I had not thought he'd bother to tell me anything more.

"He also asked whether I played chess and said he'd welcome the diversion of a game any time," I added.

Denis's expression changed, a hint of amusement entering it. "I would not choose to do so. Mr. Creasey is a master. He entices people into a match and then defeats them soundly, usually after extracting a wager from them, one of long-lasting consequences."

"Ah." I decided I'd been wise to demur. "Have you played chess with him?"

Denis shook his head. "It is not my game. I would not be

foolish enough to put myself into his power in any way. I suggest you avoid him."

"I had not planned to seek him out again." We stood together in the middle of the room. Gibbons had not taken my hat or offered refreshment. "Is that the only reason you summoned me? To ask about Creasey?"

"It is. I would, however, like Mr. Brewster's opinion on the attack and how another like it might be prevented. If you agree, he will linger for a time and speak with me."

I shrugged. Denis meant that the command to attend him had been for Brewster, not me. He'd used the question about Mr. Creasey as an excuse, knowing Brewster went where I did.

"It is hardly up to me," I said. "Brewster is his own man."

Brewster scowled at me as though annoyed I'd say so. But while he worked for me, I hardly owned him body and soul.

"I will see myself home," I told him.

Brewster took a belligerent step toward me. "I'll not have you running about on your own with men with knives lurking in the shadows. You wait for me, guv."

"I agree with Mr. Brewster." Denis gave me a nod. "Adjourn to the dining room, Captain. Gibbons will bring you coffee."

I surveyed the stony faces of Denis and Brewster and understood that arguing would do no good. So, like a schoolboy dismissed by the headmaster, I made my way down the stairs, following the stiff-gaited butler.

It was nearing the noon hour. Gibbons set coffee before me, along with a basket of assorted breads and a small crock of chilled butter. I was not hungry, but I tried a slice of bread and found it stuffed full of olives and seeds. Unusual, but quite tasty.

While I waited, I reflected on my meeting with Eden and his arrest.

His story was that he'd left Antigua after finding civilian life there unfulfilling and traveled to England. He bought passage on a cargo ship, as did many who needed to cross the ocean, one carrying rum and other commodities. During the voyage, Eden quarreled with his shipmate, Mr. Warrilow, and the quarrel had come to blows.

Not only that but, nervous about his belongings—though he professed to travel with little—Eden had made a habit of visiting the hold to check on them.

Once the ship docked, Eden's baggage was seized by the excise men and searched, then found to be of no interest. Had someone on the ship—its captain perhaps—believed Eden was smuggling goods?

Eden had made his way, without his bags, to St. James's and found rooms in a house that took in gentlemen bachelors. He'd spent his day in St. James's until he'd decided to return to the area of the London docks and look up Warrilow, ostensibly for the return of a book. Eden was lying about that reason, it was clear. Sir Nathaniel Conant, a canny man, had recognized that as well.

In addition, some of the cargo of the ship Eden had travelled on had been taken. I wondered if it had gone missing during the unloading, and the theft discovered later? Or whether a warehouse where the goods were stored had been burgled once the ship was empty.

I could ask. I had a friend in one Mr. Thompson of the Thames River Police. Thompson and his colleagues were tasked with the prevention of this very sort of crime—theft from the merchantmen docked up and down the Thames. He might have more information about the missing goods, and perhaps he would share the information with me. I'd have to explain why, of course. Mr. Thompson did not trust blindly.

I doubted Eden had anything to do with the stolen cargo. Thieves regularly worked the wharves, and the goods that went into the new, enclosed London Docks were high-priced imports like brandy, rum, and cocoa from the East Indies.

On the other hand, while I did not want to believe Eden could kill a man outside a battlefield, I could not dismiss the fact that he might have. Eden could be as much of a stickler about honor as I was. If he had good reason to murder an oafish man, he would.

But then, Warrilow had been found dead in his rooms, slain by a blow to the head. Eden might call out a man or best him in a fair fight, but he'd certainly not pick up the nearest brick and smash it over a man's head.

I would have to discover more about this blow, and whether it had been delivered from behind. If so, I would dismiss entirely the idea that Eden had killed him. He might do so if defending himself, but even then, Eden had very firm views on honorable ways to fight. Also, the Eden I knew would then find a constable and confess he'd accidentally killed a man.

Of course, I hadn't seen Eden for more than five years. He'd traveled to the islands where life was difficult, and men could change. I certainly had changed since I'd seen him last.

I wished for pen and paper so I could make notes about my thoughts and what I needed to discover, but I did not bother asking. I finished the bread and coffee, and at last heard Brewster noisily descending the stairs.

I'd been left on my own in the dining room, though as soon as I stepped into the hall, two large men flanked me. Denis trusted me somewhat by this time, but he'd not allow me to run tame in his house.

Brewster reached the ground floor. He said nothing to me but departed through the front door, and I could only follow.

Gibbons had procured a hackney for us. I had become accustomed to walking the few blocks northward up South Audley Street to my new home, but Brewster hustled me into the cab, darting suspicious glances across the sparsely populated street.

"Not safe to walk," he said as we rumbled the short distance. "Matter of fact, why don't you go off to the country for a time? Her ladyship has that great house in Hampshire you could visit."

The house, strictly speaking, belonged to her son, Peter, but he would not run it until he reached his majority.

"They'll be harvesting," I said. "Mrs. Lacey does not want to disturb the steward by opening the house and distracting everyone from that business."

Brewster, not a country man, looked a bit baffled, but shrugged. "Or your own estate in Norfolk. In the back of beyond, that is."

"Why the sudden whim to rush us out of town? What did Denis tell you?"

I expected Brewster to give me one of his put-upon sighs, but his face set in grim lines.

"That chess piece you delivered to Mr. Creasey. It was a signal. Creasey has been interfering in Denis's business of late. They dance around each other, those two, neither wanting to confront the other, have done for years. His Nibs has just told him that their truce is at an end. That's why Creasey said he could kill you where you stood. It means you are no longer untouchable to His Nibs' greatest enemy. None of us are."

CHAPTER 5

*a*s Brewster's words fell around me, my ire rose. "He sent me to deliver a threat? He's given me such an errand before. I did not appreciate it the first time."

That had been in Norfolk, and I'd ended up hastening the threat's recipient out of the country.

"This isn't the same, guv. Not so much a threat as a challenge. His Nibs had no choice. Creasey has been nicking things what belong to Mr. Denis, apparently, costly merchandise he acquires for clients who aren't happy they're not getting their goods."

"Why use *me*?" I scowled out the window at the spattering rain. "He could have sent any of his men to hand over the parcel, or had a delivery service take it, or even dispatched it by post."

"Because any of his lackeys, including me, might have been beaten and sent back on the spot. You, Creasey didn't know what to do with."

I returned my glare to Brewster. He retained his grim expression but his tone was much too calm for my liking.

"Why didn't you explain this before I went to see Mr. Creasey?"

"I didn't know." Brewster shrugged his large shoulders. "I didn't understand what the white queen was about until His Nibs told me just now. He instructed me to look after you, is all."

"I see." I made myself cease speaking lest I rage at him, and this situation was not Brewster's fault.

The coach halted, and I opened the door and climbed to the ground before our footman Jeremy could hasten out of the house to assist me. Jeremy held the front door open for me, reaching for my hat, and I barely remembered to give it to him.

"Is my wife at home?" I asked him as I stumped by.

"Yes, sir." Jeremy blinked at my brusqueness. "Upstairs, sir."

Brewster had followed me inside instead of simply heading down to the kitchen. He seated himself on a chair in front of the main staircase without a word, his scowl daring anyone to argue with him. Barnstable, gliding from the rear of the house, raised his brows in disapproval, but I knew Brewster wouldn't move. He'd not let anyone up the stairs who wasn't above suspicion, and Brewster could be suspicious of everyone.

Barnstable took my greatcoat but I couldn't stop long enough to remove my gloves, still grime-splotched from Creasey's filthy warehouse. I clutched the railing as I went up the stairs and peeled off one of the gloves while I limped down the hall.

Donata's sitting room, as always, was an island of calm. Her most recent portrait, with her two children, dominated a wall, her painted face gazing serenely down at me. In her previous portraits, which had been done when she'd still been Lady Breckenridge, her face had held sharpness, but now it was a softer oval, the eyes showing a woman who'd found peace.

My wife sat at her desk, a delicate thing of mahogany with tapered legs and a rounded top holding a few small drawers and pigeonholes. I paused as I stripped off my second glove, a part of me enjoying Donata's slender form half turned to me, pen poised, as she glanced up at my intrusion. A peignoir, clasped down the front with a line of bows, flowed over the graceful lines of her legs. It was barely noon, and she would have just risen from her bed.

"Did you have an interesting outing?" she asked. "You ran off with Brewster directly after breakfast, looking like a thundercloud, so Jacinthe told me, so I cannot imagine it was anywhere pleasant."

"It was not. Mr. Denis sent me on my task."

Donata knew all about Denis's condition for what he'd done for me in Brighton. She and I had occasionally speculated during the previous months what the task might be.

Her dark brows arched. "Indeed?"

I threw the gloves to a table, where they landed near a vase filled with fresh hothouse flowers. I dragged a chair next to the desk and sat down to face her. "Why don't we go to Hampshire? Peter would love to ride his own grounds."

A pucker appeared on Donata's forehead. "As I explained, we never return home in September. Opening up the household will take too much time, and everyone on the estate is busy."

"Oxfordshire then. To visit your parents."

"Why the haste, Gabriel? We agreed to stay in London to take care of any business and then journey to Grenville's home in the Cotswolds and await Gabriella's visit."

Earlier this summer, we'd planned a trip to France from Brighton with my daughter Gabriella to take her home.

However, her French aunt and uncle had turned up, and they'd escorted Gabriella to her mother instead, with the promise she could return in October. This was to be Gabriella's first Christmas with us.

Lucius Grenville, a famous dandy who was now my closest friend, had invited us to his large new home in Gloucestershire to enjoy autumn revelries and hunting. We'd arranged for Gabriella to meet us there.

"Because Denis has thrown down a gauntlet to a rival." Rapidly, I told Donata what had transpired this morning. "If this man, Creasey, will strike at Denis through his associates, I do not want you in London."

"I am hardly his associate," Donata said, though I knew she was not dismissing my concern. "Even a hardened criminal—a smuggler and a thief, I am assuming—would hesitate to murder the mother of a viscount and daughter of an earl. The consequences would be dire."

"That might be the case, but what if they aim for me—son of a minor gentleman—but hit you instead? Or Peter?"

"I take your point. Peter will go to Oxfordshire at once." Her eyes softened. "Though Peter will object most strongly. He has become quite fond of you."

Peter and I rode in Hyde Park together every day—he'd taken to rising and going out with me early in the morning. The fog had kept both of us indoors today, but I'd planned to take him out later this afternoon, even with the rain. In light of Creasey's threats, I would change my plans.

"You will go with him," I stated.

"I will finish what I need to in London," Donata countered. She was not obedient, my wife. "Most of that I can do from this house, with a few visits from my man of business. I have already accepted invitations for evening outings, but on those I will be surrounded by friends. Many of these friends you do not care for, so you will not be with me to endanger me."

"I hardly want you rushing about London without me at your side," I began sternly.

"If this man will only hurt me if I am with you, as you have declared, then I will *have* to go about on my own." Donata's eyes were an intense blue, framed with black lashes. "I am not a fool, Gabriel. If there is true danger, I will stay home. But I must see to things. There are investments to look after, plans to make for Peter and Anne. You and I have three estates between us, plus the house in Brighton that will be let once the renovations are finished. I cannot allow Mr. Denis and his battles keep me from my affairs. It will be much faster to make arrangements while I am in London, with solicitors and men of business within reach, than wait for letters in Oxfordshire."

"I wish you were an ordinary woman," I said in despondency. "One who meekly tells her husband he has the right of it and lets him take care of her business."

Donata gave a little laugh. "You would have grown hopelessly weary of me by now. *You* traded learning how to run estates to join the army, while I have been immersed in such things all my life, so you must leave them to me."

"Even so ... "

Donata laid down her pen and turned to me squarely. "We are having this argument the wrong way about. It is *you* who should flee to Oxfordshire or to Grenville's so I will not have to worry about you being felled by this Mr. Creasey."

"I would." I leaned an elbow on her desk. "Except I met a friend today."

Donata's expression held wary curiosity as I launched into the tale of Eden and our visit to Bow Street.

"You wish to help him," she said when I finished. "The fact

that you will not turn aside when a person is in need is a reason I am fond of you." Donata patted the arm that rested on the desk. "However, it is most inconvenient at times. I gather from your glumness that you are uncertain of Major Eden's innocence."

"He is vague concerning his whereabouts, as well as his reasons for visiting Warrilow and the ship's hold, and for leaving Antigua at all. I will have to make him see that the truth will help him more than evasion."

"Unless he did kill this man," Donata pointed out.

"It would be unlike him. Miles Eden was always fair and level-headed. Even when others tried to provoke him or start fights—bored soldiers get up to much between battles—he managed to remain above it all, talking others into calm. He's not a man to lose his temper and bash another over the head."

"Yet he admits he came to blows with Mr. Warrilow."

"In a fair fight. Not sneaking into the man's rooms and finishing him off."

Donata patted my arm again, gently. "Perhaps this time you ought to let things alone."

"Possibly." I could take Peter and Anne to Oxfordshire and insist Donata come with us, using my position as her husband to give the command weight. In theory, she had agreed to obey me when she took her wedding vows.

"If Eden is the only person who can be fitted for this crime, Pomeroy will arrest him again," I said. "Sir Nathaniel wasn't certain of Eden's guilt, I could tell, though he had doubts. If I can help prove Eden is innocent, then I can leave London with a clear conscience."

"Meanwhile, Mr. Denis's foes hunt you down?"

Donata spoke the words casually, but I saw worry in her eyes.

"I will find out what this business with Mr. Creasey is all

about. He might have no interest in me at all. I might be an associate of Denis, rather against my will, but by no means do I work for him. I do not smuggle paintings or hire forgers or steal artwork, and whatever else he gets up to."

"You are friends with magistrates," Donata reminded me. "You can tell *them* about Mr. Creasey."

"I intend to."

The magistrate of the Whitechapel house, Sir Montague Harris, was wont to listen to me. Likewise, Sir Nathaniel would be interested to learn of a smuggler who'd threatened violence. I would also alert Mr. Thompson of the River Police, as I'd planned.

I had still other friends with influence on those in power. Denis had not warned me to keep silent, from which I inferred that he wouldn't mind if I told as many people as possible that Creasey would be plotting something and had already struck.

It occurred to me that there hadn't been much time between me delivering Creasey the message and the assassin going after Denis. Had Creasey been able to arrange the attempt in the time Eden and I had been in the Bow Street house? Or had he been scheming such an assassination for the day Denis and he ceased tiptoeing around each other? It was possible, I supposed. Denis had an amazing network of people across London, and I couldn't be surprised if Creasey had the same sort of thing.

"Can you finish your business by the end of the week?" I asked Donata.

Donata, who'd turned back to her letter, sent me a look of exasperation. "The end of the week? It is already Tuesday."

"I will try to make Eden see reason and tell me the truth, and have him tell the full story to Sir Nathaniel. Once he is cleared, you and I can leave for Oxfordshire. We'll send Peter ahead tomorrow, well-guarded."

"Though you will be in the most danger." Donata's eyes sparkled with heat. "I doubt I can finish by the week's end, Gabriel."

"Do what you are able, and then conclude the rest in Oxfordshire. Why not hire a secretary? You should not have to wrestle with estate business yourself."

"I prefer to. I don't mind assistance, but I will not put all my financial affairs in the hands of a secretary or even my man of business. I trust very few with Peter's estates—you would be shocked to learn of the number of people who'd try to swindle a little boy."

"I am sorry to say I am not astonished." I laid my hand on hers. "I will be happy to assist as well. I should take more of an interest in the business end of things."

I hid a qualm as I spoke. I was terrible at figures and financial decisions, which was why my cousin Marcus had taken over running the Lacey home in Norfolk. But Donata was my wife and should not have to slog through the accounts on her own.

She sent me a pitying glance. "I have finally managed to untangle the books of the Breckenridge properties. My late husband left them in an appalling state. I have taken on the challenge of looking into the Lacey estate as well, with Marcus's assistance. I do not need you mucking it all up again."

"I see." I pretended to be stung. "Your father then. He is a man of wisdom."

Donata brightened. "Yes, dear Papa would help if I asked. Very well, I will do what I can and prepare to remove to Oxfordshire by the week's end." Her smile faded and her severe expression returned. "But I am not going alone. *You* will finish *your* business and quit London by that time as well. If your Mr. Eden has not been cleared by then, you will leave it to Sir Montague or Sir Nathaniel to sort out."

I hesitated. My greatest wish was to see Donata and our children safely away. I had been through hell and back around the world in the army, my career ending when French soldiers amused themselves by torturing me. I had survived all that, which made me tend to dismiss personal danger. The things I'd gone through since returning to London to convalesce had hardened me further.

Donata's eyes narrowed. "I'll not go without you, Gabriel. That is my condition."

I drew myself up. "I am your husband, Donata."

"I believe you recall how obedient I was to Breckenridge. I at least respect you, but not when you are being a fool. We both leave on Saturday morning."

I usually lost arguments with Donata. Sometimes it took longer for me to admit defeat, and sometimes I had to admit it directly.

I gave her a decided nod. "Very well. The end of the week."

She made me give her my word before I left her.

———

I RETIRED TO THE LIBRARY DOWNSTAIRS AND WROTE TO SIR Montague and to Sir Gideon Derwent, a reformer. Sir Gideon was always interested in what criminal activities I pursued, and he'd been much help in the past. I also told him of Eden and how I wanted to help him.

I addressed the letter to Sir Gideon to his country home in Kent. I had heard that his wife, who was consumptive, was not well. That kind lady had proved more robust than most thought, but in the end, she would succumb, which saddened me. I sent the letter to Sir Gideon anyway, knowing he used good works to divert him from his sorrow—his wife encouraged him in this.

I preferred to speak to Thompson of the River Police in person, so I wrote him a note that I would travel to Wapping and call on him this afternoon. If I would keep my promise to Donata, I'd need to begin right away. I handed the note to Bartholomew, who'd brought in a tray with bread, cheese, fruit, and coffee as I worked.

After finishing my letters and the brief repast, I found Brewster—still sitting in the downstairs hall but now slurping coffee—and set off.

"Going straight back to the docks, are we?" Brewster asked as he followed me out. "Where His Nibs' enemy lies in wait?"

"Mr. Creasey could have made good on his declaration that he was able to kill me, but he did not. Perhaps he doesn't think me worth the bother."

"He's biding his time," Brewster said darkly. "Mark me words."

I had asked Hagen to drive us once more, knowing Donata would not be happy if I took a hackney, even with Brewster to guard me. Hagen, always competent, had the carriage quickly prepared and at the front door.

Brewster refused to ride inside this time and took his seat on the back of the coach. I had wanted to ask him more about Creasey, but I would pin him down later.

We traversed the streets back to the City and continued around the large bulk of the Tower, its golden crenelated walls and round turrets shutting out the common folk.

From there we passed the Royal Mint and threaded our way back to the water, where masts of ships gathered like a leafless forest. The warehouses surrounding the London Docks rose in a bulwark around which Hagen steered the coach. On Wapping Dock, not far from there, we halted at the offices of the Thames River Police.

I'd ventured to this house before, when Mr. Thompson had asked my opinion of a case he had wanted to solve, one that had long grown cold. I had been pleased to help, and together we'd discovered a killer.

Peter Thompson, a long, lean man whose frayed clothes grew more threadbare as the years passed, met me outside the coach once I descended.

"Captain Lacey," he greeted me in his slow and careful way. "I received your message. Though you never said so, I suppose you want me to show you the body of Mr. Warrilow. If you'll come with me."

Light-brown eyes twinkling, Thompson stepped back into the house, and I could only follow.

CHAPTER 6

Thompson took me through the main offices and out the back door to a narrow street that climbed northward from the river.

When I'd visited Thompson a year or so ago, he'd led me to a cellar in an outbuilding to show me a skeletal body that had been fished from the Thames. Today he walked away from the river entirely. Brewster came close behind me, his breath loud in my ear.

We hadn't gone far before Thomson halted in front of a squat, brick abode in a line of similar homes. This house had a door and a window on the first floor, two shuttered windows above that, and two more on the top story.

Thompson stepped up to the door and rapped on it. The road's incline here was steep, so that the window in the room next to the door was almost level with the pavement.

A woman with a long apron covering her gown, her graying hair tucked into a large mobcap, opened the door and peered out. "Oh, it's you, Mr. Thompson. Himself is in the middle of a surgery, but if you'll sit yourself down, he'll be out directly."

She ushered us into the front room, whose window did indeed view the cobbles outside and the boots and horses' hooves that moved along the road.

The woman, who introduced herself to me as Mrs. Clay, waved us to seats and then brought us tea, so weak and watery it could barely be called such. Brewster drank his while he stood at the window, watching the passers-by with a wary gaze.

"Clay is a local surgeon when he isn't assisting coroners," Thompson explained when Mrs. Clay had closed the door and left us alone. He sipped the tea with rapt concentration, as though he drank ambrosia. "Amputates limbs, stitches up wounds, pulls teeth."

From somewhere in the back of the house came a howl of anguish, the cry of a full-grown man in agony. Brewster swung around, and I flinched, memories returning of the surgeon who'd poked at my shattered knee and measured it amiably against his saw. I'd managed to banish most of those recollections, but they occasionally haunted me in restless dreams.

Thompson grinned. "Never fear, Captain. If he's screaming, he's likely all right. The very badly injured make little noise."

This hardly made me feel better. More screams followed, which eventually trailed off into muffled groans. Over this, came a deep male voice. "Keep the poultice on it and you'll be right as rain. Once it heals up, you'll forget all about it."

We heard shambling footsteps in the hall then the house's front door opened and banged shut. A man stumbled past the window, pressing a wadded cloth against his right cheek.

Moments later, Mrs. Clay entered the sitting room,

followed by a small, portly man with a beaming face. He wore a white apron, like a butcher's, which was stained with blood.

"Mr. Thompson," the man said with gladness, his voice larger than his person. "What a pleasure to see you again. Which body did you want to have a look at?"

Thompson and I both rose to greet the man. Thompson indicated me. "This is Captain Lacey. We're here to view Mr. Warrilow."

"Good. His corpse is the less gruesome one in my parlor. The other fellow brought to me last night was nearly cut in half stem to stern, and then the fishes got at him. Not a pretty sight. You are lucky, Captain. Mr. Warrilow died very suddenly and is intact."

With this cheerful assessment, he turned and waved us to follow. Mrs. Clay smiled and nodded at me as though encouraging a child who had to face an unpleasant task.

"An unfortunate circumstance of gin houses close to the river," Thompson murmured as we trailed after Mr. Clay. "Sailors come to shore, drink themselves insensible, fight like savages, and dump the losers of the fights into the Thames for me and my lads to find."

Nothing in this small house, painted a lighthearted white with colorful rugs on the wooden floors, betrayed that corpses were cut up and teeth extracted in the back rooms. That is, not until we entered a small chamber in the rear of the house, in which stood a heavy wooden chair. Leather straps for holding a patient immobile hung from its arms, and a basin full of bloody water rested on the floor next to it.

Clay led us through this unnerving room and out a back door to a small yard behind the house. Here reposed a stone shed, its walls thick—to keep the bodies cool, I surmised.

The atmosphere inside the stone building was damp and proved to be far cooler than the outside air. Four pallets lined a long wall, and on an adjacent wall sat a bench strewn with grim-looking tools—saws, picks, knives, and what appeared to be giant tongs.

Two of the four pallets were occupied, both corpses covered with sheets. The other two pallets were empty, stripped down to the wood, awaiting the next set of unfortunates.

"This is Mr. Warrilow," Mr. Clay said moving to the first pallet. "Are you a relation?"

"No," I confessed. "I am interested in discovering who killed him."

Mr. Clay's eyes twinkled. "After a reward, are you? Well, I wish you luck. There's not much to see." He slid back the sheet to reveal the hapless Mr. Warrilow.

Stripped of clothing, his skin gray, Warrilow was a pathetic sight. He'd been of medium height, neck and forearms burned by the Caribbean sun. His stomach was paunchy from middle age and too much rum, or whatever he'd liked to drink. The face was not handsome but not ugly either, just an ordinary man.

However, I could see why Eden had found him unpleasant. Warrilow's jaw was hard, set even in death, as though his obstinacy followed him into the afterlife. Though his eyes were closed, a frown puckered his face. Whiskers shadowed his jaw, and long sideburns, much in fashion nowadays, traced thickly down his cheeks. His hair had been dark brown going to gray, much reduced on the top of his head.

"The blow that caused his death is here." Mr. Clay lifted Warrilow's shoulder from the table and turned him on his side with surprising strength.

The wound lay on the right side of the head where it met Warrilow's thick neck. A great gash had been opened at the base of his skull, Warrilow's hair matted with blood there.

Brewster moved forward, studying the wound with professional assessment.

"A clean strike," he said.

"'Tis true," Mr. Clay agreed. "Felled him hard, killed him quickly. Pieces of bone went right into his brain." He touched the wound, depressing the skull an inch or so inward.

I'd seen far more grisly corpses than this on the battlefield, but the way Mr. Clay prodded him made me shiver. Thankfully, he soon lowered Mr. Warrilow carefully to the table and covered him with the sheet as gently as he'd tuck in a child.

"I can't tell you much more than that, Captain, Mr. Thompson." Clay took up a cloth lying on the bench and wiped his hands. The cloth was already smeared with blood, and I could not see that it did any good. "Whoever struck him was strong, but if a man has a decently heavy weapon, he doesn't need to be extraordinarily strong. Just enough to wield it well. Warrilow must have turned his back and then …?" Mr. Clay swung his arm with an imaginary cudgel in demonstration.

"What sort of weapon, would you say?" Thompson asked.

Brewster spoke before Mr. Clay could answer. "Cosh can be made of anything. Stout stick, its head rounded, stone tucked into a stocking, any sort of bottle."

"Your large friend has the right of it. I'd say this wound was made by something about this big." Mr. Clay made a circle with his forefingers and thumbs four or so inches wide.

"Could be the bottom of a pitcher," Brewster speculated. He held up an imaginary one by its handle. "From a wash basin. Seized in the moment."

"Was a pitcher or anything of that size found in his rooms?" I asked Thompson.

"Not that I know of, but my house didn't investigate. The crime was committed in an area that falls under the jurisdiction of the Tower Liberty, though their magistrate put the word out for the Runners to assist."

I wondered what he meant by the Tower Liberty, but this explained why Pomeroy had been quickly on hand to arrest Eden.

"What happens to his body now?" I asked.

Mr. Clay shrugged. "Inquest has already been held, but no family has come forward. From what I understand, Mr. Warrilow recently returned from the Antilles."

"From Antigua, yes. Will he be shipped back there?"

"If someone stands the cost," Mr. Clay answered. "Probably he'll be put into a burial ground here with a plain marker. He's not a pauper but no one knows much about his family."

"Where were his lodgings?" I asked Thompson.

"Wellclose Square. Not far from here. Shall we go there now?"

I was in agreement. Mr. Clay bid us a happy farewell. As we left him, he was approaching the second body in interested anticipation, but we were mercifully out of the room before he lifted the sheet.

Mrs. Clay saw us to the front door, and I thanked her for the tea. "Not at all, Captain." She showed tea-stained teeth in a wide smile. "Makes a change to have living men in me parlor, whole ones at that." She chortled at her joke, and we left the pleasant little house.

The hill ended at the top of the street, and we took a level road farther north before turning onto Ratcliffe Highway, which ran not far north of the London Docks. A small lane from here took us to Wellclose Square.

The place had once been affluent, I could see, and many fine houses still existed on the street where we walked. In the center of the square lay a lovely white church in the baroque style, reminiscent of ones I'd seen in Portugal. Arched windows lined the church's pale peach sides, and round windows flanked those. The steeple was a graceful flourish of curves rather than a straight spire.

"The Danish and Norwegian church," Thompson told me. "Architect was the father of Colley Cibber, the famous actor, in fact."

"Never 'eard of 'im," Brewster said behind us.

"Dead these fifty years," Thompson answered in his thin voice. "I've only heard of Cibber because I live in these parts, and people come to look at the church. A charity runs it now."

"You said this was the jurisdiction of the Tower Liberty?" I said, gazing around the large square. "What is that?"

"The Crown annexed these lands close to the Tower, which once belonged to monasteries, long ago, and are now known collectively as the Tower Liberty. The Constable of the Tower is in charge of policing the area, and his coroner holds their inquests. Mr. Clay assists, as he's a skilled surgeon—he also assists the Whitechapel coroner. After the recent expansion of the docklands there's been a bit more crime, and the Constable of the Tower welcomes help, especially from the Runners of Whitechapel and Bow Street."

It sounded like a complicated arrangement, but many of the parish divisions in London were left over from centuries of conquest, regime changes, fire and rebuilding, and the natural expansion of the metropolis.

Wellclose Square contained more than private abodes, I saw as we strolled it—several theatres graced the long sides of the square, along with a gin hall or two, but those looked quiet and subdued in the daylight.

Thompson took us to a house in the middle of the square's north side. This house taller than Mr. Clay's, with a mansard roof and large dormer windows, which reminded me of the house in which I'd lodged in Paris during the Peace of Amiens.

This residence had once been grand, but the grandeur was fading. Paint flaked from the stuccoed walls and the black front door, and bare wood showed through the green paint on the shutters. An old bird's nest peeked from the sill on a higher floor, and bird droppings decorated the arches over the windows.

Before Thompson could tap on the door, it was wrenched open, and a thin, harried woman with a lined face, her mobcap askew, stared out at us.

"Pardon us for disturbing you, madam," Thompson said formally. "I am Mr. Thompson of the River Police—"

"Are ye another here about Mr. Warrilow?" the woman snapped. "He's dead, and I'm sorry for it, but tramping into my house day after day won't bring him back."

"But it may help us find his killer," Thompson said smoothly.

"I thought that tow-headed officer did it." The woman's rabbity brown gaze darted to me then Brewster. "Who are they then?"

I made her a bow. "Captain Gabriel Lacey, at your service, madam. Why do you say the officer did it? You mean Major Eden?"

She regarded me as though I were a simpleton. "Saw the papers saying he were wanted for the crime."

"Yes, but he has been able to convince the magistrate he was not here to commit the murder. You are Mrs. Beadle, correct? You yourself saw him at nine-thirty the evening Mr. Warrilow was killed. You told Major Eden that Mr. Warrilow was already abed."

"So I did." Mrs. Beadle came out onto the stoop, folding her arms. "Your major came at the time you said. He stood in the hall at the foot of the stairs while I went up to tell Mr. Warrilow he had a visitor. Mr. Warrilow called through his door that he was abed and wouldn't get up, and he said this exactly — *not for the likes of a self-important army officer who doesn't understand what's what.*"

"You conveyed this message to Major Eden?"

Mrs. Beadle's thin smile creased her face and showed me she once had been pretty. "Not in those words, sir. I told him Mr. Warrilow had retired and was seeing no one."

"Did Major Eden ask you about a book?" I ventured. "He'd come to retrieve it from Mr. Warrilow."

The smile faded, and the blank stare returned. "I don't know about no book, sir. The major — he had very nice manners — bowed to me, told me not to distress myself, and off he went."

"You never saw him again?"

"Never. When the constables came tramping all over yesterday I told them about the major, but they only nodded as if it were of no import. I was surprised, I confess, when I saw the printed bill for his arrest when I went out to market this morning. As I say, I never saw the major again, but I suppose he could have come back to the house later that night, after I went to bed."

Thompson took up the questions. "Do you lock the doors every night?"

"'Course I do. But a few of my lodgers who've been here for years have their own keys. They might have let in Major Eden, as he was so nice-spoken, or they might have forgotten to lock the door behind them when they came in. I run a good house, but one never knows these days. I suppose a ruffian of some sort broke into Mr. Warrilow's room and knocked him down." She let her glance linger on Brewster, who, with his large hands and habitual scowl, was the very picture of a ruffian.

"May we speak to the boy who works here?"

"Boy? Oh, you mean me grandson." Mrs. Beadle did not look old enough to have a grandson, but she might have married very young. "He only stays with me sometimes. But he'll say the same—Major Eden came at nine-thirty or thereabouts and left a quarter of an hour later."

"Do you mind, madam," I began, "if we looked over the room Mr. Warrilow stayed in?"

Mrs. Beadle shrugged thin shoulders. "I've had constables from the Tower, and then a giant Runner, what's another set of gents? The Runner was quite friendly, happier than he ought to be. Laughing and loud."

"That would be Mr. Pomeroy," I said quietly, and Thompson's lips twitched in amusement.

"Well, at least he were cordial. Come in, gentlemen. Wipe your boots, please. I just done the floors."

The house was narrow, like the Clays', but taller and deeper. The staircase was rather grand, with a wide handrail and a double row of twisted spindles of polished walnut. The proprietress must be proud of it, because unlike the exterior of the house, the staircase shone with varnish, the steps in good repair.

Warrilow's single chamber resided in the front of the house, two stories above the ground floor. My knee ached by the time we reached it, and I braced myself on my walking stick.

The room's one window looked out over the square to the aging jewel box of the church, the trees around it aglow with fall leaves, a welcome contrast to the bricks and stones of the city.

The view was the finest part of the room. The rest was

spartan in the extreme. One narrow bed was pushed against a wall, with a tall washbasin in the opposite corner. A table with one hard chair reposed on the other side of the room, piled with Mr. Warrilow's baggage and a stack of papers.

The bed had been stripped of linens and pillows, revealing a hard mattress. That, coupled with the absence of rugs on the floor, made the room chill and barren.

Mrs. Beadle ushered us inside but remained in the hall. "Will anyone be around to collect his things?" she asked.

Thompson turned to her. "No one has come forward to claim him, it seems."

Mrs. Beadle considered this. "Well, I suppose I'll keep them a few more days, in case. After that, I'm selling the lot. I need the room, and the extra cash from his clothes and boots wouldn't go amiss."

"Would you mind if I looked through them?" I asked, moving to the table.

"Suit yourself. If no one wants the things, it's none of my concern, is it?"

Brewster had made his way to the washbasin. It was a simple piece with three legs, a shelf on top, and a second shelf that rested about a foot from the floor. The top shelf had a round hole carved in the center to receive the porcelain wash basin, which was absent.

"Did you take the pitcher?" Brewster asked Mrs. Beadle.

She nodded. "Yesterday. After the coroner's men carried away the body, I took the bedding and the pitcher and basin downstairs and washed everything. I have to ready this room for the next guest."

"Pity," Thompson said. "Had the pitcher been moved? Or damaged in any way?"

While Mrs. Beadle stared, confused, Brewster said, "It might have been used to kill the bloke."

Mrs. Beadle started. "How could it have been? The pitcher and basin were in the washstand, dry as a bone."

"No blood?" Thompson asked.

"No. Basin hadn't been used—he hadn't called for water. The only blood was on Mr. Warrilow. And the bed. I had to throw away the linens." She swallowed, folding trembling hands together.

"Please, do not be distressed," I said quickly. "It was a terrible thing."

"Girl that chars for me found him and screamed something fierce," Mrs. Beadle said. "I came in and ... I tell you this for nothing, gentlemen. I won't soon forget what I saw."

"Were he face up? Or face down?" Brewster asked.

"Face down across the bed. The covers had been turned down. Blood all over his clothes. He must have swung away from whoever it was and been struck. Poor lamb."

The epithet did not describe the man I'd seen lying on the pallet in Mr. Clay's room. He'd been a hard man, and from what Eden had said, decidedly unpleasant.

"You say he was dressed," I said. "Yet, he told you he was abed."

"Indeed, sir. He might have meant he was readying himself for bed. Probably hadn't had a chance to put on his nightshirt."

But the boy, her grandson, had said he'd heard Mr. Warrilow snoring. Perhaps Warrilow *had* gone to bed by nine-thirty, hence the turned-down bedclothes, and then rose again and dressed. Why? To go out? To meet someone? Or had he expected a visitor? Had he admitted his own killer?

"Go ahead and rummage through his bags, love," Mrs. Beadle said. "They're just things, ain't they? If you find anything what points to his family, they're welcome to have them."

My respect for her rose. Mrs. Beadle lived simply—the money she'd obtain for selling Warrilow's clothing and whatever trinkets he'd had to a secondhand shop would be helpful, as she'd indicated. However, she was willing to be fair and return them to his heirs, if they existed. The fact that she hadn't sold the things the moment Mr. Warrilow's body had been found spoke well of her. Many a landlord would have.

I slid a half-crown from my pocket and pressed it into her hand. "Thank you, Mrs. Beadle."

She stared down at the coin, her face flushing in gratitude. "Thank *you*, sir. I'll leave you to it then, shall I?"

As she departed, I tapped my way to the table, my knee still protesting the two flights of stairs. I heard Mrs. Beadle enter the next room, no doubt straightening it for its occupant or a new guest.

Thompson approached the table with me, though Brewster remained at the empty washstand, examining it thoroughly.

"The Tower constables have been through this," Thompson said. "And Mr. Pomeroy had a snoop, I'm sure."

"Yes, but they must not have found anything significant." I opened the portmanteau of stiff leather that sat on the table. "They arrested Eden on the facts that he visited this house on the night Warrilow died and that the two men had quarreled aboard ship. Pomeroy would have mentioned anything he'd found to support the arrest at Eden's hearing."

As I spoke, I lifted each item from the portmanteau, and Thompson and I examined them together. Warrilow had traveled with only a few changes of clothing—two frock coats, two pairs of trousers and one pair of leather breeches, several shirts, underthings, and thick socks that had been carefully darned. No heavier coats or gloves, but he'd not have needed warm clothing in Antigua.

Other than these, and a pair of cracked leather boots, the luggage contained nothing else. Whatever the man had been wearing when he died, I imagined the coroner, or perhaps Mr. Clay, had stored or tossed away.

We went through the pockets and found nothing. No watch, purse of coins, no snuffbox, no pipe or pouch of tobacco. The clothes were simply pieces of cloth with nothing inside them.

"The Tower constables might have taken everything already," Thompson remarked. "Or he had them in the pockets of the clothes he was wearing."

I had to agree. The bag and everything inside had been tidy and undisturbed, however, nothing that suggested a robbery. But usually a man traveled with more than what he could carry in his pockets.

"This room is sparse." Thompson scanned the wall in front of us, where no picture hung, not even a ribbon or souvenir from some faraway place. "Not much to leave after a life."

"Unless his things are back in Antigua. He might have come to London for a short stay only."

"No," Brewster's voice came behind us, "you gents just don't know how to search hard enough."

We turned to see that Brewster had moved a corner of the heavy bedstead, and had pried up a floorboard there, revealing a hollow cavity, an excellent hiding place.

*a*s Thompson and I crowded near, Brewster dipped his hand inside the cavity and removed a pocket watch, a small pouch that clinked, and a gold ring. He handed each of these up to me, and I examined them and passed them to Thompson.

The pocket watch was cheap, made of brass not gold, with the letters G. W. engraved upon it. The watch had wound down, the hands pointing to ten minutes past eight. Inside the pouch were exactly seven shillings. The ring was a plain gold band, a man's wedding ring.

"He didn't trust anyone in the house," Brewster declared. "So decided to hide his valuables. Many gents choose a loose floorboard—you'd be amazed what they tuck in there."

Trust a thief to know exactly how to find a hidden cache.

"There's more." Brewster stretched out flat, his big legs causing Thompson and me to move aside. "He pushed it onto the other joist. It's heavy."

Brewster grunted as he struggled with whatever he'd found. Thompson and I bent to him, hands on knees. Metal clanked, and finally, Brewster dragged out a canvas bag. Instead of passing it to us, he sat up and opened the bag's drawstring, peering inside before he reached in.

He pulled out several tubes of metal and smooth pieces of wood, one with a wide, rectangular end. There was no mistaking the circle of metal with the pan and mechanism for striking it.

"That's a carbine," I said in surprise. "A cavalry weapon— looks to be British. One stripped down for cleaning or repair."

Brewster laid out the pieces on the bag. "'Struth. What's a bloke in the middle of London doing with a cavalry shooter?"

"A very good question," Thompson said as he gazed at the disassembled gun. "Perhaps the last guest hid it there, not our man?"

"Bag's hardly worn." Brewster inspected it with a practiced eye. "Hasn't lain in the dust down there any time."

"Is this the murder weapon?" I lifted the heavy end piece, the stock, grooved to take the firing mechanism.

No blood showed on the wood or on the weapon's barrel, plus the gun wasn't wide enough for what Mr. Clay speculated had clubbed Warrilow.

"Doesn't seem likely," Thompson said.

"Why would a killer shove the gun under the floor but then not snatch up a watch, a ring, and seven shillings for his trouble?" Brewster demanded. "No, depend upon it, Captain, the murderer never knew this was here. Probably took whatever he used to kill the Warrilow cove away with him. Will be at the bottom of the Thames by now."

"I am inclined to agree with you," I said.

"This I will take." Thompson waved at the carbine. "Will you pack the pieces up for me, Mr. Brewster? I'll present it to the magistrate and see what he makes of it."

Brewster set the carbine back into the bag without argument. "Guns are fiddly things," he said as he climbed to his feet and handed the canvas sack to Thompson. "There as like to blow your fingers off as hit your target. Knife or a cosh, much easier."

"There is something to what you say," I told him. In the cavalry, I'd carried a carbine, but I'd preferred my calvary sword and the skill of my horse to shooting. The accuracy of the weapons had not been laudable.

We'd found nothing in the baggage or among the clothing, or indeed the carbine, to tell us whether Mr. Warrilow had family or friends in England, or even Antigua. A wedding band spoke of marriage, but Eden had not mentioned that Warrilow had a wife. A married man usually wore his wedding ring, but a widower might carry it in his pocket, or put it under the floorboards for safekeeping.

When Warrilow's death was reported in the newspapers, with his name, family, if he had any, would surely come forward. Solicitors would need to locate his heirs in any case.

We left the room and went downstairs, Thompson with the carbine in its bag, into which he'd also placed the watch, ring, and coins. Mrs. Beadle waited for us at the foot of the staircase.

"Will this be the last time anyone searches that room?" she asked Thompson. "I have a boarding house to run."

"I will tell them to stay away," Thompson assured her. I doubted there'd be anything left to find. I trusted Brewster's thoroughness. "If no one comes forward, you are welcome to sell the clothes."

"Thank you." She brightened. "Can get a nice price for decent garb. Good day to you, gents."

I tipped my hat to Mrs. Beadle and followed Thompson and Brewster out into the road.

Traffic filled the street, carts bringing deliveries to the gin houses and taverns, women with baskets over their arms perusing the shops, men walking purposefully on whatever business they were attending. A few sailors lingered, probably waiting for the gin houses to open, assessing the streets for later revelry.

As we were on the north side of the square, we walked through a narrow lane to emerge on Cable Street. From there we went east and south again toward Wapping Docks.

I turned to the other question I wanted to ask Thompson as we walked. "I heard an amount of cargo was stolen from the ship Eden and Warrilow traveled on. The *Dusty Rose*. Perhaps that was a motive for Warrilow's murder—he might have seen the thieves or known who they were."

Thompson swung one thin arm, the other burdened with the sack. His coat looked in danger of sliding from his shoulders at any time, but remarkably, it never did.

"It hasn't been the only theft." His usually good-natured expression creased into a frown. "It's buggering me something fierce. Cargos are being robbed, half gone by the time they reach the warehouses. Only part—never all of it. Some ships are only missing a few things, but I'm damned if I know how the thieves are doing it. When the ships come in, the cargo masters check the manifests, and all is well. The laborers are watched carefully as they unload and put the goods into carts to be trundled to the warehouse. When the cargo reaches the warehouse, usually all appears to be well again. But—when the goods are to be packed up and shipped to whoever ordered them, they've vanished."

"You said *usually* all appears to be well."

Thompson scratched his head under his battered hat. "Sometimes an entire cart never turns up at the warehouse. A search is put out but cart, horse, and driver are gone."

"Someone pays the driver to take the cart elsewhere," Brewster suggested.

"Presumably," Thompson said. "But the driver is never seen again. Even if the drivers are innocent victims of robbery, they make themselves scarce, probably fearing they'll be held responsible for thousands of pounds of goods."

"Or the poor buggers are killed," Brewster said.

"I believe we'd find more bodies turning up, if that were the case. Plus we never find the horses or carts again either." Thompson shook his head. "Most of the time, as I say, the goods reach the warehouses. The warehouses are well guarded, and there is never a sign of a break-in. But again, when the time comes for those goods to be moved on, they're gone, as though they never existed. I have men stationed to watch houses where we know stolen goods are traded, but they have nothing to report. It is a true mystery."

"There is a man who lives not a stone's throw from the wharves that deals in that sort of thing," I said. "Name of Creasey. From what I understand, he's a thief and a smuggler."

Thompson gave me a wise nod. "Thief, smuggler, murderer, dealer in stolen goods ... I know all about him, Captain. I have eyes on him, but he hasn't lifted a finger in months."

"James Denis claims he's responsible for stolen merchandise," I said. "Denis's network is thorough."

Brewster snorted. "Aye, I'd say it is."

"Would that I could have a quarter hour to ask Mr. Denis all about it," Thompson said with a meditative glance at the warehouses around us. "What has he told you, Captain?"

"Very little. Only that Creasey is extremely dangerous."

"I know that as well." Thompson sighed. "I have no

evidence on him, unfortunately. If I did, I'd be making many arrests and laughing as loudly as your Runner, Pomeroy."

"If I discover anything more about him from Mr. Denis, I will tell you," I promised.

"Thank you." Thompson gave me a brief smile then sobered. "I would stay clear of Mr. Creasey, Captain. He dislikes anyone poking in his business, and those who do often end up in the river."

"That's what I tell 'im," Brewster said. "Not that he'll listen."

"I'm not as heedless as all that," I said. "I have met Mr. Creasey, and I am not in a hurry to face him again. He's a cold, hard man. I'll not go poking him, as you say."

I discerned by Brewster's and Thompson's expressions that neither man believed me.

BEFORE I LEFT THOMPSON AT THE WAPPING DOCKS, I asked to look at the carbine once again. Thompson relinquished it to me, and I studied the pieces of the gun on a table in a dim room inside the River Police quarters, with Brewster hovering beside me.

"It's fairly new." I brought up the barrel and sighted down it. "It's rifled, as you can see." I peered inside the metal barrel at the spiral grooves. "In very good condition."

"Warrilow was a small planter?" Brewster asked. "Maybe he kept it to keep birds off his land. Or his laborers frightened into working harder."

"A farmer would carry a different sort of gun," I said. "This is a military weapon. It makes me wonder very much indeed where he obtained it."

Thompson cocked his head. "He bought it from a former military man, perhaps?"

"Possibly. Antigua is British. The many forts there are used to fend off attacks on the fortified harbors. Lord Nelson himself had a naval command there. The army forts could have sold off surplus weapons, but I somehow doubt that."

"Maybe one in the King's army purloined the gun," Brewster offered. "And sold it to Warrilow."

Many possibilities, none of them pleasant.

I returned the weapon to Thompson, thanked him for his time once more, and Brewster and I departed.

We hunted up Hagen, who'd remained with the coach near the watery entrance to the London Docks. He chatted with a drover but kept an eye on his surroundings. This was not the most agreeable area of London, but Hagen was a large man with ham-sized fists and a stern gaze. Men scrutinized the luxurious coach but gave it a wide berth.

"My guess is Mr. Warrilow stole that shooter," Brewster said as he boosted me into the carriage. My leg hurt even more now, and I didn't reject his assistance. "Found it on the ship he was traveling on or came across it while kicking about in Antigua. He wanted to sell it and chucked it under the floor until he could find a buyer."

I stifled a grunt of pain as I settled on the seat. "Someone who wanted the gun but was reluctant to pay might have killed him for it. Except it was well hidden, and not taken."

"Killer never found it." Brewster shrugged. "Warrilow sounds an unpleasant cove. Most like he provoked a gent until that gent coshed him on the head."

"Most like."

As Brewster slammed the door and resumed his perch on the back, I tried not to picture Eden losing his temper and going at Warrilow with the heavy porcelain wash pitcher.

Eden had always been an amiable chap, but every man has his limits.

The ride home was slow, as the streets were now choked with carts, carriages, horses, and wagons. I had plenty of time to think over what I'd seen and learned from Mr. Clay, Thompson, and Warrilow's landlady, and what we'd discovered in Warrilow's chamber.

By the time we arrived in South Audley Street, daylight was fading. I expected to find Donata out, stubbornly making her rounds of calls, but she met me on the stairs.

She'd dressed in one of her well-made ensembles of striped silk, but the gown was meant for dining at home. I was always bemused that her casual clothes were as stunning as her theatre garb.

"Peter was not happy with my announcement that he was to go to Oxford," she said by way of greeting. "Perhaps you could speak to him. He's more apt to listen to you, at his age."

Instead of being dismayed, I felt a frisson of pride at Peter's respect for me. "I would be happy to."

Donata looked me up and down, noting how I used both walking stick and railing to keep myself upright. "Shall you rest first?"

"Better tackle it at once," I said. "Are you going out later? Or will you take supper with me?"

"I have very few invitations tonight, nothing of consequence, and I have already sent my regrets. I will tell Barnstable the two of us will be dining."

I looked forward to it with pleasure. Most nights, Donata went on endless outings to soirees, the theatre or opera, musicales, or lectures. I often joined her, but many evenings she moved in her own circles, which she had been doing since her debutante days, while I sought Grenville for conversation or brandy, if he too was not out in the social whirl.

I preferred to be with my wife, which was why I'd married her, after all. However, we were not staid, comfortable Captain and Mrs. Lacey, but an aristocratic lady and a used-up military man. Donata enjoyed her social existence, and I did not have the heart to demand she stay by my side at all times.

The nursery was on an upper floor of this very tall house. I scarcely felt my aching leg as I climbed, because at the end of the journey I'd find my daughter and stepson.

Peter, who was seven years old now and growing sturdier by the day, turned from books piled before him on a long table with a look of gladness. He assumed I'd come to take him riding, as I'd promised.

I postponed the disappointment I had to give him by seeking out Anne. She reposed on a pile of rugs on her side of the room, able now to sit up unaided. She bounced a few times and let out a loud screech at the sight of me.

I was convinced she understood every word I said and could speak herself, no matter that it to us sounded like gibberish. I dropped my walking stick to sweep her up, making her squeal even more shrilly as I lifted her to the ceiling.

The nanny, Mrs. McGowan, hovered nearby, always certain I would drop Anne. I would do no such thing, holding her as though she were the most precious object in the world, which she was.

"How are you, my girl?" I said, resting Anne in the crook of my arm. She reached for a button on my waistcoat with both hands, declaring, "Bah!"

"She has eaten much today," Mrs. McGowan said. "Very robust. Stood up several times, using the chair for support."

"Isn't she clever?" I bounced Anne, who let go of my button to clap her hands.

"Are we going riding, Papa?" Peter asked eagerly. He'd taken to calling me *Papa,* rather than *Sir,* after our sojourn in Brighton this summer.

"Afraid not, lad. I've even convinced your mother to remain indoors tonight. There's bad men about. That is why your mother wants you to go to Oxford." As Peter's face scrunched into the scowl that made him look much like his true father, I added, "We will join you by the end of the week."

Donata and I had decided that Anne was too small to travel without us, even in Mrs. McGowan's care. She would stay here, protected in the nursery, until time for us to leave.

"Why can't we go at the end of the week together?" Peter stuck out his chin, manfully attempting not to cry.

"Because the danger is real. Mr. Brewster says it is, and I believe him. Mr. Denis says so as well. Mr. Brewster will be staying the night." So he'd informed me before I'd come inside, not giving me a chance to argue.

Peter had much respect for Brewster, and his stubborn look softened a touch. "If it is so dangerous, we should go together now."

"I will stay and make sure the danger is taken care of," I said. "And then join you."

Mrs. McGowan had listened in alarm. "You really do mix yourself up in too much, Captain. Begging your pardon, sir."

As she was right, I could hardly admonish her. "Oxford-shire is beautiful in this season," I told Peter. "You'll be able to ride and run in the gardens. Your grandfather will look after you."

More softening. Peter liked his grandfather.

"But you and Mama will come on Saturday?" he persisted.

"We will. And then we'll ride every day."

Peter balled his fists, scowl returning. "Very well, but I

don't like it. You should tell Mr. Denis to kiss his own arse."

"Your lordship!" Mrs. McGowan's voice rang. "That is not the sort of language a viscount uses."

Those were exactly the sorts of words I heard aristocrats use all the time, but I forbore from saying so. I wanted to laugh, but as a good father, I frowned at Peter in admonishment.

"My obligation to Mr. Denis is finished. I will have nothing more to do with him."

So I hoped. I had never lied to the children about Denis and my acquaintanceship with him, but I did not tell them the whole of it. I hoped by the time Peter grew to manhood, Denis would have turned his attention from me.

Peter's expression was skeptical, which meant he knew more about Denis than his mother and I had relayed. But Peter was expert at roaming the house, finding out information his irritating parents would not pass to him.

I bounced Anne again. "Mr. Denis himself would suggest you go to Oxfordshire. Brewster, as I've said, agrees. I am sorry about today's ride, but the weather was bad this morning, and it is too dark now. I will be home all this evening, and I'll read to you later. And see you off myself tomorrow."

Peter remained sullen. "Will I have to take all my books?" He gestured at the table, where a pen dripped ink onto a blot-filled sheet of paper.

"Not at all. It is time for a holiday. Take the rest of the week to enjoy yourself. Too much work is bad for the constitution."

Peter brightened considerably, though Mrs. McGowan frowned.

"Thank you, Papa!" he shouted. Anne, liking the noise, squealed with him in excitement.

"But Mr. Roth will join you and continue lessons next

week." I named his tutor, trying to sound stern and fatherly.

Peter took no notice. He'd won himself a holiday from boring Greek and Latin and mathematics, and next week was a long way off.

I kissed Anne before passing her back to Mrs. McGowan and gave Peter a rough hug. He allowed it, though he'd started not liking too many affectionate gestures. He preferred shaking hands instead.

I reluctantly departed and went downstairs to my own chamber to wash and change for the evening.

Supping with Donata was pleasant. We were served in the dining room, she forgoing her place at the foot of the table to sit close to me at the head. Barnstable directed the service, keeping a watchful eye on the two footmen who carried us dishes of clear soup, fish, salad, capons in white sauce, beef, a savory tart, and several sweet ones. All this accompanied by fine wines that Grenville had advised Donata to acquire.

It was far too much food, in my opinion, for two people eating alone, but when I recalled my sparse existence in the cold rooms in Grimpen Lane, I decided to enjoy.

Donata and I, for once not surrounded by guests, conversed amiably. I told her about my visit to Thompson and all I'd discovered, and she relayed the various tasks she was undertaking to settle Peter's affairs and prepare him for school, which he would begin in the spring. We also spoke of our journey to visit Grenville in Gloucestershire and specu-lated on how Marianne Simmons, a former actress, would do as hostess.

After supper we adjourned to the sitting room, with Barn-stable bringing in coffee for Donata and brandy for me. He was delighted to serve us, I could see, revealing a plate of chocolates as a surprise, and asking us repeatedly if we needed anything more.

"How is Brewster?" I asked him. "Have you found a corner for him for the night?"

Barnstable gave me a nod. "He is a surprisingly agreeable guest, sir. There's a cubby off the kitchen with a pallet we keep for emergencies. Mr. Brewster says he won't use it much, but it will do for him. Cook's feeding him, and he's sent word to his wife."

Barnstable had unbent toward Brewster a good deal in the last year. When Brewster had first shadowed me at Denis's behest, turning up to wait for me, Barnstable had quietly locked up the silver.

All was well in our domestic bliss tonight. I would later keep my promise to Peter and read to him, but meanwhile, Donata and I enjoyed each other's company.

After Barnstable departed, my gaze strayed to the chessboard reposing on a delicate Hepplewhite table near the window. I moved to it, studying the black and white marble squares of the board. I opened a box resting next to it and observed the rows of intricately carved ivory queens, kings, rooks, pawns, knights, and bishops.

"Do you play?" I asked Donata.

"Not much at all." Donata sipped coffee and managed to be languidly elegant. "Enough to keep a guest entertained, but I am wretched at it. Though guests enjoy winning. It makes them feel clever."

"Did Breckenridge play?"

Donata huffed a laugh. "Heavens, I don't know."

The answer cheered me. If she'd known all about how well her late husband had or had not played, that would mean she'd paid attention, had cared. She'd given up on the man not long into her marriage, and I liked finding signs that she'd not allowed him to lodge in her heart.

I lifted the white queen. The one I'd given Creasey had

been abstract, while this was intricate, the queen's face etched precisely into the ivory. I set it on the board and lifted out a black knight—this one a horse with a tiny armored man astride it.

"Are you asking me to have a game?" Donata inquired. "It will be very quick, I assure you. It will hardly pass any time at all."

"I am reminiscing. I played in the army, but I'm rusty." I set down the knight in a square that would threaten the queen. "Do you have any books on the subject?"

"I imagine so. Barnstable would know."

Donata's library, purchased in its entirety by Brecken-ridge, contained a vast number of books on a variety of subjects. Breckenridge had never read one of them, but Barn-stable kept them lovingly. I would peruse the shelves with his help.

For now, I had an appointment with another book full of harrowing stories that Peter adored. I put away the chess pieces, excused myself, and went to the nursery to keep my promise.

IN THE MORNING, I DECIDED TO VISIT EDEN. I WANTED TO ask him more about Warrilow, and about the other passengers on the ship. Warrilow must have quarreled with more people than Eden, or perhaps someone from Antigua followed him to London on purpose to kill him.

I was in a lighthearted mood, in spite of the danger and my anger at Denis for putting my family into said danger. Donata had joined me in the nursery, and we'd read to Peter and Anne—who'd mostly wanted to chew on the book—and bade them goodnight. Donata and I had adjourned to our bedchamber and found a way to celebrate being together, warm, and content.

Brewster's night had not been as comfortable on the tiny room off the kitchen. He was peevish, but still determined to protect me. My suggestion he go home and rest was met with a silent scowl.

"As you like," I said, too buoyant to argue with him. "I am making for St. James's Place, to hunt up Eden."

Brewster nodded with a grunt. "That gent knows more than he's saying."

"He does indeed. Shall we walk?"

"Carriage is safer."

"Perhaps, but I don't want to announce that I am arriving. I'd rather see what Eden has to say when caught unawares."

Brewster considered that and finally agreed. He did insist on a hackney to take us as far as St. James's Street, which I decided was wise. My ebullience did not mean my leg would thank me for tramping so far.

The hackney drove south to Curzon Street, where Denis's house lay quietly, the blinds pulled down over all the windows. A short street led to Piccadilly where we rolled past Green Park then south again on St. James's Street to the narrow cul-de-sac called St. James's Place.

St. James's Place ran east from St. James's Street, then bent around a sharp corner to go back north. It was quiet, another fog settling on London to dampen my sunny mood. We left the carriage there and tramped the rest of the way.

As we turned the corner to the far end of the deserted lane, running footsteps rang behind us.

Instantly Brewster pushed me out of the way, pulling a long knife from his boot, ready to defend me.

When the attack came, however, the assailants, three of them, didn't try to cudgel *me*, but made directly for Brewster.

CHAPTER 8

I shouted as the men surrounded Brewster, murder in their eyes. Surely an inhabitant of one of the houses around us would hear and either hurry to help or run for a foot patroller.

No doors opened, and no one appeared. I shouted again, this time running at the men. They took no notice of me as I staggered toward them, as though I were a mere bystander in this drama.

The men had clubs, but Brewster already held his wicked-looking knife. Two of the assailants were beefy, like Brewster, the third a willowy man with wiry strength. They raised hands and struck with the grim determination of those intent on killing.

Brewster blocked blows and stabbed out with his knife, making the men dance back. He swept his arm, his hand on the blade steady, eyes darting as he held his assailants at bay.

They circled him, more cautious now, but not backing down. Brewster was a good fighter and a former pugilist, but he could only take on so many attackers at once. When one got behind him, he was done for.

I drew the sword from my walking stick, the steel ringing. I charged in, ignoring my protesting leg, another shout issuing from my lips. So I'd yelled in battle, pounding across the field at my enemy, heart racing, blood surging.

I slapped my blade across the back of one attacker, slashing through his coat. He turned in surprise, and I thrust the sword up under the arm that raised a cudgel, the tip of my sword sliding through his armpit to his shoulder.

He screamed in pain and rage and dropped the cudgel, his nerveless fingers refusing to hold it. He swung his other, massive fist at me, but the strike was weak, and I slashed the inside of that arm.

The man howled, clapping his hand to his bloody sleeve, and whirled from me. He ran out of the lane, leaving his friends to fend for themselves.

The second burly man and the thin one circled Brewster, the larger one taking more chances. Brewster burst forth with his knife, managing to nick both men before they leapt away from him.

I flipped my sword in my hand, gripping it so the blade rose into the air, and brought the heavy steel of the hilt down behind the burly man's ear.

He stumbled, though didn't drop as I'd hoped. Brewster took the opportunity to aim a deadly thrust at the man's chest. The man sidestepped to avoid it, and I hit him again. This time, he crumpled to the cobblestones.

The wiry man attacked me while I danced out of the way of the heavy falling body. I found myself fending off a swirl of blows, his strikes coming fast and strong. My grip on my sword was awkward, and I could only use it to block the cudgel coming down.

Brewster tackled him from behind, but the man fought furiously. He kicked my left leg, correctly knowing my weak point. I fell sideways, catching myself painfully at the last moment to keep to my feet.

I took a better hold of my sword and waded back into the fight. Brewster and the wiry man were striking each other without remorse, no pugilism here. They were fighting to kill, blood spattering to the pavement.

The man's cudgel landed on the back of Brewster's fist, knocking the knife from it. Brewster swooped his other hand into his coat, no doubt for a second weapon, but the wiry man moved in before he could retrieve it.

He raised his club to land a blow that would fell Brewster forever. I grabbed the man from behind, slipped my fingers under his chin, and laid my sword across his throat.

Brewster, armed with a fresh knife, lifted it to plunge into the wiry man's chest.

"No." I dragged my captive aside, Brewster's blade narrowly missing his thick wool coat. I jerked the wiry man closer to me, my sword drawing a tiny sliver of blood on his neck. "Go back and tell Creasey he failed. Brewster and I are no threat to him. He is to leave us be."

The wiry man glared up at me with derisive blue eyes and gave me his very foul answer.

"Let me kill him, Captain," Brewster said, breath grating. "He'll not stop 'til I do."

"No. I want him to take Creasey a message."

Brewster yanked the cudgel from the man's hand. "His dead body will be plenty for a message."

I spun him out of Brewster's reach and addressed the man directly. "Tell Creasey he will keep his fight with Denis away from me and mine."

I shoved him aside, releasing my sword at the last minute. The man sneered his scorn and loped off down the lane.

A door slammed open, and Eden hastened down the street toward us, cavalry saber in hand.

"Good Lord." He stopped to watch the wiry man vanish around the corner and turned his gaze to the attacker who lay motionlessly on the ground. "Did they try to rob you?"

"To off me." Brewster strode to the unconscious man and kicked him. "Because I work for Mr. Denis."

"Mr. Creasey sent them," I said.

Eden's face darkened. "The blackguard. I thought I'd left rivalries like this in Antigua. Forgive me for not hastening to your rescue sooner, gentlemen. I looked out of my window and saw you and then could not remember where I'd put my blasted sword."

"The captain felled two," Brewster said with admiration. "While I couldn't come nigh them. Saved me life." He gave me a curt nod. "Thank ye, guv."

"They disregarded me." I inserted the tip of my sword into the walking stick and slid the blade home. "The lame former army captain you are paid to protect."

Eden nudged the fallen man, but he didn't move. "What do we do with this one? The Watch are rather useless, as I recall."

"Send for a Runner," I said. "Pomeroy will find something to arrest him for even if Brewster chooses not to prosecute for assault."

"Prosecute?" Brewster shook his head. "What good will it do? Creasey will dismiss the bloke or even kill him before he comes to trial, and it won't matter. Why not give him to His Nibs? Mr. Denis can use him to find out what Creasey is up to."

I imagined the cold satisfaction in Denis's eyes as he turned to interrogate Creasey's fallen soldier.

"I rather think he will be safer in Newgate," I said dryly.

Eden listened to this in growing concern. "I'll send a lad from my lodging house for the Runners—as long as Pomeroy doesn't arrest me again into the bargain." He grinned weakly. "We can tend to this poor chap's wounds in the meantime. Wouldn't want him to simply expire at our feet."

THE BOOT BOY WHO WORKED FOR EDEN'S LANDLORD rushed to Bow Street and was back with Pomeroy in a remarkably short time. Other residents had emerged from the houses on the close, mostly servants, as the hour was early and the fashionable often didn't rise until after noon.

The ruffian was groggily coming around under our ministrations by the time Pomeroy arrived. Pomeroy took in the scene, listening in delight as Eden told him how Brewster and I had been attacked but defended ourselves valiantly. Pomeroy stepped over to the fallen man, who hunkered against a railing, massaging the back of his head where I'd struck it.

"Billy McCann, is it?" Pomeroy inquired in his ringing tones. "Bashing Billy, as I live and breathe. I've been after you a long time, son, for doing in a woman in Blackfriars. Thank you, Captain. Major Eden, Mr. Brewster."

He hauled up Bashing Billy and strode him off around the corner. The fire in Billy's eyes had died a sorry death.

The excitement over, the footmen and curious maids drifted back into their houses.

I explained to Eden that I'd been on my way to see him.

Catching him unawares was now impossible, but Eden brightened.

"As it happens, I planned to look you up today." He gestured to the tall house two doors down from where the fight had taken place. "Please, come upstairs."

Brewster pulled his hat down on his head. "I'll keep watch. First attempt failed, which means Creasey will only send more next time."

"It was *you* they attacked, not me," I pointed out. "It is better for you to be indoors."

"Indeed, Mr. Brewster." Eden made a sweep of his arm. "There is plenty of room, and my landlady can find you some ale if you wish it."

Brewster scanned the street, brows lowering as he considered. "Just as you like. But I'll need to be by a window."

Thus agreed, we followed Eden into a fine house with bow windows in the first three floors above the front door, and large square windows at the very top. Eden greeted the landlady breezily as he led us inside, she a plump woman who shook her head at the goings-on of ruffians in the street. She did not like the look of Brewster, but Eden assured her he was my trusted servant, and upstairs we went.

Eden's lodgings were on the third floor, up a polished staircase with an oriental carpet runner and twisting balusters. Tables with curved legs on the landings held silver candlesticks and clocks, I supposed so gentlemen lodgers could find their way upstairs in the dark and also know what time they were stumbling home from their clubs.

The front room of Eden's chambers contained one of the bow windows I'd seen from below. Brewster immediately strode to it and sat himself on a chair there.

The rest of the room was pleasantly furnished with gold upholstered settees, a shelf of books near the fireplace, tables for snuffboxes and the aforementioned books, and a desk with a curved lid supplying a stack of paper and a pen tray with quills and a pot of ink. Through an open door I spied a bedchamber with another fireplace and a bedstead hung with brocade curtains.

The contrast between this elegant abode and the rooms I'd occupied above the bakeshop in Covent Garden was marked. When Eden began apologizing for the cramped space, I was hard-pressed to hold my tongue.

"Think nothing of it," I said tightly. "I've been looking into the matter of Warrilow, if you do not mind my prying."

Eden gestured me to a chair. "Not at all. I'm happy for any help to untangle me from this snarl."

Before either of us could continue, a footman entered with a tray of coffee and a few small cakes, and ale for Brewster. Brewster took the glass with a nod of thanks but barely pulled his eyes from the street below.

Once the footman had departed, I sipped the coffee, which was quite good. "I've come to know magistrates and one of the River Police since I've been living in London these past five years," I told Eden.

Brewster's snort was soft, but we heard it. Eden raised his brows, but I shook my head. Brewster was not the sort who would efface himself and hide his opinions.

I told Eden about my visit to Wellclose Square and the little I'd discovered about Warrilow. "We found a wedding ring. Was he married? Did he have a family?"

Eden's face smoothed as he sipped coffee. I watched him think through his answers, choosing his words carefully, and wondered why the devil he'd need to.

"Warrilow was a small planter, as I told you." Eden set his cup into its saucer with precision. "He is—was—a widower. I don't believe he had any children. He'd lived in Antigua a long time, thirty years, I think I heard him say."

"And he was returning to London for business he didn't trust any other to do?"

"Eh? Oh, yes, I suppose that is what he said."

"It is what you told the magistrate."

Eden's face reddened. "See here, Lacey. Did you come to interrogate me or help me?"

"I came to get to the truth of the matter." I sipped coffee and took in my surroundings. Eden had mentioned he'd transported a chair he liked, which was one reason he'd visited the cargo hold, but I saw no chair here that did not match the decor. These sofas and armchairs had been purchased as a set. I suppose the customs men could have kept hold of it, but Eden seemed to have forgotten all about it.

"The truth of the matter is I went nowhere near Warrilow the night he was killed," Eden said firmly. "Mine is not the hand that struck him down."

"I'm inclined to believe you, for many reasons. His landlady told me the same tale of you turning up at half past nine and Warrilow being abed. She considered you a fine gentleman."

"What a relief. Exonerated by an East End landlady." Eden took a sip of coffee, eyeing me coolly over the cup. "I hope that is enough for Pomeroy and his magistrate."

"Please do not take offense. I do want the truth. I must warn you that if I discover you truly did kill the man, I will have to let Pomeroy take you."

Another soft snort from Brewster. I heard a mutter of *thickheaded pride and honor.*

Eden didn't seem to notice. "I'd expect no less, Lacey. Likewise, if I discovered *you* bashed the man over the head for some reason, I would haul you before the magistrates myself."

"Then we understand each other. Truth is our best chance."

I saw Brewster shake his head as though fed up with mad army officers.

Eden opened his hand. "What do you wish to ask me?"

"Did you know Warrilow in Antigua? You said you tried your hand at planting. Did your paths cross?"

"Unfortunately. Let me explain about Antigua, Lacey. There is much money to be made in sugar—if you have the right connections. The island is dominated by large planta-tions, the owners of which bring in fortunes. The navy and the dockyards where Lord Nelson commanded before he went off to chase old Boney were put in place to protect the merchantmen hauling rum to the rest of the world and supplying the planters when they returned. The business runs the island."

"Is that why you tried planting? To make a fortune?"

Eden shrugged. "I needed to do something with myself. The threat from the French had died once Napoleon was defeated." He trailed off. "Think of it, Lacey. Nelson, one of the great naval captains, and his foe, Napoleon Bonaparte, another astonishing man. We'll not see their like again. One dead, the other withering away on an island prison."

"And here you and I, who bloodied our hands in the thick of the battles, sit in comfortable chairs drinking coffee." I took a sip. It did make one think. "Wellington survived. He's as confident as ever."

"So I have heard." We reflected for a moment on all we had seen and done in the long, long fight to defeat Napoleon. "In any case, you are waiting for me to answer your question," Eden went on. "Yes, my path and Warrilow's crossed. He was known for his brutality and actually twitted me for being soft with my workers. I can't look the other way at slave labor—

it's an archaic and barbaric practice that should have been banished centuries ago. In any case, I freed the twenty slaves who worked for me and settled them into paying posts or sent them to acquaintances in Canada for the same. After that I turned my hand to shopkeeping." He chuckled. "I was horrible at it. My employees were relieved when I sold the business and decided to return to England."

"Did you and Warrilow clash over anything in particular?"

I studied the gilded carved plaster of the fireplace as I waited for his answer.

"No." Eden sounded uncertain. "No." This was more firm. "He simply put my back up. He did with everyone."

When I turned my gaze to Eden once more, he'd lifted his coffee cup as though hiding behind it.

"Did he clash with anyone else in Antigua? I mean more than irritating them in general."

Eden shook his head. When he lowered the cup, he had more command of himself. "Not that I heard. I wouldn't be surprised if he annoyed someone enough to kill him, though. He was unpleasant in the highest order."

"You are saying anyone could have done it? That is not particularly helpful."

"You didn't know him." Now Eden's eyes held grim anger. "I do not think any man deserves to be struck down without being able to defend himself, but it does not amaze me that someone did."

"What about Mrs. Beadle, his landlady? She was there all night, on the spot. Would know where to reach for a weapon."

Eden paused. "I'd hate to say yes. I'd land her in it, wouldn't I? She seemed a good soul when I met her, but if he upset her enough…"

"He was coshed extremely hard." I recalled Mr. Clay

probing the wound on the man's skull. "I will be charitable and say I think it unlikely Mrs. Beadle is the culprit. She must have had many an unpleasant lodger, and killing them would put her out of business."

Eden nodded somberly. "You jest, Lacey, but Warrilow truly was a bad person."

"Yet, he married."

"Yes, pity the woman. Dead these ten years, poor thing."

Compassion swam in his eyes. If Warrilow's wife had been gone ten years, then Eden wouldn't have met her. Ten years ago, he and I were slogging through mud in the Netherlands before heading to Portugal. That meant Eden wouldn't have quarreled with Warrilow when gallantly defending his wife or blaming Warrilow for her death. His sympathy for the lady was fellow-feeling only.

"Well then, let us turn to the others aboard with you," I said. "Could Warrilow have enraged his fellow passengers enough for one of them to follow him home and strike him?"

"I think it highly likely." Eden set down his cup and tapped his fingertips together. "Let me see, there were seven of us traveling to England. The captain of the ship didn't like to fraternize with the passengers. He was congenial and a reasonable man, but not a conversation maker. He was busy most of the time, in any case."

Eden paused to sip more coffee.

"As for the passengers—there was a missionary couple. Kingston was their name. Very earnest. You know the sort. They'd been traveling through the islands, converting the heathen. They were also abolitionists, which did not sit well with Warrilow, I can tell you. It was when he was busy hurling abuse about that at Mrs. Kingston that I became incensed and we nearly came to blows."

I could easily picture Eden abandoning his affability to defend a lady, even a zealous missionary.

"What did Mr. Kingston do during this exchange?"

"Smoldered. He was the weaker of the couple. Mrs. Kingston was quite spirited." Eden grinned in remembrance.

"Did anyone else witness this quarrel?"

"Of course. It happened at the supper table—that's how gauche Warrilow was. Couldn't keep quiet even to let us all dine in peace. The other passengers were there—a Mr. Laybourne. Small man, rather threadbare, soft-spoken. An accountant for a merchant in St. John's, he said, though I hadn't met him before. The other man, I knew slightly. Mr. Orlando Fitzgerald. A gentleman in his fifties, rather grand, went on about his connections to the Carlton House Set when he was younger. I gather his father sent him to Antigua to separate him from said Carlton House Set and their rakehell ways. Or perhaps Fitzgerald never knew the Prince of Wales at all and glorifies his past. Easy to do when you are among countrymen far from home."

"My friend Grenville might know of him," I said. "He's acquainted with the Carlton House Set of old."

Eden's eyes widened. "Lucius Grenville? Good Lord, Lacey. You sit and speak off-handedly of befriending magistrates and marrying the beautiful Lady Breckenridge, and now you claim friendship with the most famous man in Britain? You are a wonder, my friend."

I flushed. "Accidents all. They took a liking to *me*, though I'm damned if I know why. I have a foul temper."

Eden studied me in amusement. "You intrigue people with your honesty. They never know what to make of it. I remember this happening quite frequently during our army days."

I shifted, uncomfortable with this change of topic. "What other passengers were with you?"

"That is all. The missionaries, Laybourne, and Fitzgerald."

"You said seven."

"I was including Warrilow and myself."

"Which makes six."

Eden's flush returned. He counted on his fingers. "Jove, you have the right of it. Well, I misspoke. There were six of us."

His blush was so furious and deep this time, that I knew he lied, and fervently so.

CHAPTER 9

I remembered that whenever Eden grew discomfited, whether because he had to hide an opinion at an officer's supper or explain his rash actions on the field to Colonel Brandon, he'd become as pink-cheeked as a debutante when asked for her first dance.

I eyed him now, wondering what the devil he was hiding. When he'd claimed innocence of murdering Warrilow, Eden's face had been clear, but at the moment, he was beet red.

To give him time to compose himself, I returned to the passengers he'd named. "Do you have an idea where Mr. Fitzgerald or Mr. Laybourne might have gone once they disembarked? Did they mention where they were staying in England?"

"Laybourne, no." Eden drew an easier breath, relieved I didn't press him about his slip of the tongue. "He seemed the penniless sort of clerk, so he'd find an inexpensive boarding house in the City, I'd think, and search for a post. Fitzgerald regaled us with descriptions of his large home in Surrey and another in Hampshire. He claimed to have much business in

London to see to, so I'd guess he'd use his house in Surrey, or is staying at his club. White's. He boasted of that as well."

"Then Grenville will be even more helpful, being a member of every fashionable club in existence. I will write to him."

Eden grinned, his face having regained its normal color. "You do move in high circles, Lacey."

"Your uncle is a baron," I countered.

"Ha. Which means I dine on gold plates and wear silk next to my soft arse?" Eden shook his head. "Uncle Reg is out of pocket most of the time. He inherited a nice plot of land he doesn't know what to do with, and his sons, my cousins, run up plenty of debt. I went to the colonies because I knew I could expect nothing from that branch of the family. No idea what I'll do here. But it's good to be home." He let out a contented sigh.

Eden must have *some* money, I reflected, to be able to afford these elegant rooms.

"The missionaries?" I asked. "Mr. and Mrs. Kingston. Did they mention where they were from?"

"A parish somewhere in London. Let me think …" Eden tapped the arms of his chair. "Oh, I remember. Lambeth. Warrilow twitted them about people who swanned around Lambeth Palace rushing off to convert impoverished sinners. Idiot."

Lambeth Palace housed the Archbishop of Canterbury, the head of the Church of England. I doubted common missionaries from that parish were allowed into its hallowed halls.

"I take it they are from an eager parish church, ready to carry Bibles to the unfortunates of the world?"

"Indeed. Not Methodists or others of that ilk—they are C of E—but as I say, quite earnest. I don't agree that reading a

Bible to an illiterate slave will help his lot very much, but they mean to be kind."

"They were abolitionists, you said."

"Yes, fervent ones. They don't simply sit and spout indignation about the evils of the world, but actually work to fix them. The Kingstons have cornered MPs and put their muscle behind bills to end slavery in the colonies forever, or so they say. I respect them for that—it is a struggle. Their fights for laws will be much more effective than all the singing and praising that fills up their days."

I knew quite well Eden's feelings on established religion, which bordered on the atheism of the French revolutionaries, though he did not condemn any man for his beliefs.

"What about your chair?" I said into the lull in conversation.

Eden jerked. He'd just lifted his cup, and liquid splashed into his face. He coughed, set down the coffee, and reached for a handkerchief.

"Bloody hell, Lacey." He mopped his chin. "What chair?"

"The one you said you transported because you liked it."

The flush reappeared. "That was something to tell the magistrate, as he was keen for a reason for me to go into the ship's hold. Keeping an eye on my meager belongings wasn't convincing him. Which reminds me, I never did manage to collect my baggage yesterday."

"I thought you went to the Custom House after you left Bow Street."

The redness deepened. "Meant to. Was distracted, and it takes a blasted long time to move through this town. I gave up and came back to St. James's. Looked in at Brooks's but saw nobody I knew there. I think everyone's forgotten about me."

"Most of London are in the country riding after foxes and preparing to shoot game," I said, pretending not to notice how he'd deflected the topic. "If you'd arrived during the high Season, you'd have plenty to do. Not now. My wife told me last night she only had three or four invitations, none of any consequence."

I contrived to look amazed at this, and Eden burst out laughing. "Jove, I have missed you, Lacey. You can look at a thing and see it for what it is. The only time you were a soppy fool was over your wee daughter ... Oh ..." Eden trailed off. "I forgot. Please, forgive me. *I'm* the fool."

"Not at all." Eden had been in Paris with us when my wife had taken Gabriella and deserted me for a French officer. I'd been hauled in front of high commanders to assure them that Carlotta hadn't been a French spy all along.

"I have found my daughter again." My pride surged. "She is a beautiful young lady, already engaged to a young man I will meet soon." I stifled a growl—I was still not happy about her engagement and had yet to form an opinion about her suitor. "I ended my marriage to Carlotta, which is how I was free to marry Donata. Lady Breckenridge."

"I'd assumed you'd claimed abandonment," Eden said lightly. "I truly am sorry for bringing up such a painful subject. You ought to call me out."

"As everything has turned out happily, I will spare you meeting me at dawn."

"Good." Eden held out a hand, and I shook it. "I say, why don't you come with me to the Custom House? I still need my baggage, and perhaps you and your well-wielded sword can convince the customs fellow to hand them to me without delay. Quite a handy weapon you've made that walking stick into."

"It has proved useful." I set aside my coffee. "Now, if we discuss our troubles any longer, we will head into melancholia, so let us make for the Custom House at once. Perhaps we can discover where Mr. Laybourne has taken up lodgings."

"Do you suppose *he* killed Warrilow?" Eden rose at once, ever ready to make words actions. "He seemed a quiet, harmless little chap, more interested in numbers than conversation."

"One never knows." I'd met plenty of harmless-looking people who'd turned around and committed murder when provoked.

"He should be the first ye nab then." Brewster drained his glass of ale and joined us. "I can have an ask about, while you hunt up the major's bags."

Eden pronounced this an excellent idea, and off we went.

———

BREWSTER SCRUTINIZED THE HACKNEYS AT THE STAND IN St. James's Street, letting a few be hired while we waited, until he pronounced one safe.

"I know this bloke. Doesn't belong to Creasey or His Nibs." Brewster lifted a hand to the coachman before he more or less pushed me inside the hackney. He then proceeded to scramble to the top of the coach while Eden took a seat across from me.

During the ride, Eden and I studiously did not speak about the murder, the attack, Eden's actions regarding Warrilow, or any such harrowing topic. As do most army men who are suddenly reunited, we reminisced. Along Piccadilly and down into the Strand, we relived the tedium, mud, blood, fear, triumph, and exhaustion of the war with France, letting the safety of the years between us and battles paint the scenes with misty colors.

Eden spoke of a few ladies he'd known, with fondness.

Eden's affaires de coeur had tended to be less intense than mine, he flirting with all the wives and having true affairs with a few Spanish ladies who flowed away from him as happily as they'd come to him.

I told him of my life since I'd last seen him just before the battle at Toulouse. I made light of the hardships I'd experienced—I knew all about having land but a bankrupt estate. I danced over my meeting with Grenville and Donata, and ended with my delight in becoming reacquainted with my daughter.

"Bravo, Lacey." Eden clapped when I'd finished. "I worried about you greatly when you came in from that mission with your leg shattered, but you've landed in the pink of things. I must meet Lady Breckenridge. Her husband was a dolt and a knave, if I may speak ill of the dead."

"You may," I said. "I loathed the man, and so did she. The only good thing Breckenridge did in his life was produce Peter, my stepson."

"He sounds a grand lad. Ah, we have reached the Custom House."

The hackney stopped at the busy space before the wide building, which teemed with even more people than yesterday. The wharves were crammed with ships, men busily trundling barrels and crates up and down gangplanks or hoisting cargo via ropes and pulleys. More ships anchored in the river, awaiting their berths.

Brewster climbed rapidly down from the top of the coach to land on the pavement as soon as we alighted. He darted his gaze everywhere, hand inside his coat on his knife.

"Don't forget Creasey's squatting in his lair not a block away," Brewster told me. "I'll see ye inside, then do my asking."

"His men attacked *you*, remember," I told him. "Take care."

"I know how to, guv." Brewster tramped directly behind us and did not turn away until we'd opened the great wooden doors of the Custom House and stepped inside.

Noise flowed down as we climbed a flight of stairs to take us above the ground-floor warehouses. The din grew as we reached the long room at the top, where the cacophony was deafening.

A hundred or so men thronged the huge space, lit by a row of arched windows that looked out to the Thames. A counter lined each long wall, behind which a row of men faced the crowd. They were the customs clerks, with their ledgers, quills, and blank countenances, explaining to those who leaned on the counters before them how much they owed.

The shippers speaking to the clerks hunched in bored resignation, growling or sighing as they produced coins or signed documents to prove they had paid the duty on their goods. Those awaiting their turns milled through the hall, shouting to one another, laughing, haranguing.

"Which is yours?" I called over the noise to Eden, indicating the line of counters.

"None here. I'm to go to a private office, yonder." He pointed down the long room to a door under a giant octagonal clock.

"We've done battle with Marshall Soult's best forces," I said. "Surely we can reach the other side of this fray."

Eden laughed and led the way through the throng.

The hats the multitude wore were many and varied I noted as we passed, from the tricorns of naval officers, to the tall hats of gentlemen, short-crowned ones of men of the City, and even turbans from those who had made the long voyage from India. All of humanity must past through this hall, I reflected, as anyone who brought goods into London had to stop and pay the excise.

I also reflected that this would be an excellent place for someone like Creasey to stage an ambush. So many men—and a few ladies as well—swarmed the room that a hand could push a knife into someone's back and vanish before the victim even knew he was dead.

With that in mind, I skimmed sideways past rough-looking men and made as much haste as I could after Eden.

We at last reached the far doorway without mishap. Eden pushed it open to reveal a hall with a staircase.

"I say," Eden called to a passing clerk in black who was rushing down the stairs. "Can you direct me to Mr. Seabrook?"

The clerk's scowl, which he'd assumed when Eden stopped him, became an expression of respect at the mention of Seabrook's name. "Oh, aye. He's one above. Fourth office down when you come off the stairs. To the right."

"I thank you, sir. Shall we, Lacey?"

We climbed the flight and followed the clerk's directions. Or attempted to. The fourth office was not as easily found as all that, as the floor was a maze of rooms that led to other rooms. After several more inquiries, promptly answered, we stood before a door that looked the same as all the others we'd passed.

A clerk hurried around us and directly into the office. "Mr. Seabrook. That army gent from Antigua to see you."

"Yes, yes," came a growl. "Please come in, Major Eden."

We entered to find a small chamber with a large desk and shelves piled with reams of paper and ledgers. A man rose from behind the desk, setting aside a pen, the stacks of papers piled on either side of him like a castle wall.

"Delighted to see you again, sir," the man greeted Eden.

He was rather tall and a bit spindly but had a wiry strength, similar to that of the ruffian who'd attacked us earlier this morning. The resemblance ended there, however. This man had a narrow face, dark hair slicked back from his high forehead, a pointed chin, and eyes that had seen plenty of smugglers striving to outwit him.

His words were delivered with sincerity. I wondered if he were simply congenial, or if it had been a pleasure to deal with the affable Eden instead of surly captains annoyed that they'd been caught trying to sneak in extra barrels of brandy.

"This is Captain Gabriel Lacey," Eden said. "An old friend. I have at last come to collect my baggage."

"You will stay this time while it is retrieved?" Seabrook's dark eyes held a twinkle.

"I had a pressing matter to attend to yesterday," Eden said glibly.

"I hope that matter has been cleared up. I noticed no more handbills with your name on them this morning."

"Yes, that was a relief. Nothing to do with customs and my baggage."

"No, no." Seabrook called to the clerk who'd shown us in. "Fetch Major Eden's things and be quick about it."

"Sir." The clerk saluted and disappeared.

"I have half a mind to take myself to the colonies," Mr. Seabrook said after the waft of the young man's passage had faded. "To warm my bones after a lifetime of working on the Thames." He trailed off wistfully.

"It's hot and musty most of the time," Eden told him. "But the shores are beautiful. Still, England is home."

"Ha." Seabrook's melancholia faded. "Says a man with the means to travel. Here I sit in the cold dampness of London. Men from all across the globe come through these doors, and I rarely leave the City." Seabrook shook his head, then clicked his tongue against his teeth and grinned. "I have a decently paid post and am glad of it. Are you a traveler, Captain?"

"I do enjoy it," I admitted. "The little I've done that wasn't to fight a war, that is. Do you see much cargo from Egypt?"

"Egypt? Not I. I have the shipments from the Antilles and the Americas. Rum, cotton, spices, cocoa, that sort of thing."

"Ah." I sought any excuse to talk about Egypt, but I tamped down my eagerness. "I have heard about shipments that have gone missing." I continued to wonder if they were connected to Warrilow's death, in spite of Eden's belief that the man had been killed by someone he'd enraged. "Were those from the Americas?"

Seabrook's dark eyes went cold. "I'll thank you not to speak too much of it, sir. The thieves have confounded us, and yes, much of what is stolen is from the Americas. Valuable cargo that disappears as though it never existed. Someone making fools of the excisemen."

"You check all the ships as they come in, don't you?"

"Indeed. No one goes ashore or offloads cargo until my men have gone over the ship, and the captain and cargo master have signed the forms."

"Why did you take Major Eden's belongings?" I asked. "Surely you did not suspect him of smuggling."

Seabrook slanted me a wise glance. "You'd be surprised, Captain, what innocuous persons like Major Eden try to slide into the country. My lads were being thorough. We waylaid about half that cargo, as we'd had a hint that it was poached. Good thing we did, as some of the rest of it vanished from its warehouse. Fortunately, Major Eden's things were found to contain nothing but what a man needs to keep himself, and we have no reason to hold them."

As he finished, the young clerk returned bearing two

valises and a large wooden box with a lock. The clerk handed Eden a key.

The collection represented very little for the years Eden had spent trying to earn a living in Antigua. Nothing that would warrant him visiting the cargo hold as much as possible to check on his belongings. He could have stashed these under his bunk, and the box could have made a decent night table.

Then again, space was tight aboard ship, and perhaps he'd been commanded to stow his things below.

Eden rose. "I thank you, sir." He held out his hand, and Seabrook shook it. "Hopefully, we shall not meet again, at least not under these circumstances."

Seabrook chuckled. "I understand you, Major. Happy to have made your acquaintance, Captain." He shook my hand as well, then I reached for a valise to assist Eden to carry his things out.

"No, no," Eden said. "I'm used to hoisting them around." He tucked the box under his arm and lifted a valise in each hand.

The clerk opened the door for us. I gestured Eden out first, as he staggered under his burden. I'd relieve my pride for not being allowed to help by asking Brewster to tote things, once we found him.

I glanced back before I departed for a final farewell and caught Seabrook gazing after Eden with an expression of vast suspicion. He smoothed out the look when he caught my eye and gave me a half smile.

I departed, wondering very much what was on the man's mind.

I caught up with Eden who navigated the stairs awkwardly, but he landed without a mishap. We pushed our way through the long room, which, if anything, had grown more crowded, and back down to the street.

Before I could mention Seabrook's odd reaction, or suggest we find Brewster to carry the box for him, four large men surrounded us.

One pointed a thick finger at me. "Mr. Creasey wants to see you. *Now*."

CHAPTER 10

I faced the man who'd spoken, his broad finger almost touching my nose. "I'm very busy at present," I managed to say coolly. "Mr. Creasey may write for an appointment."

The man curled his hand into a fist. "He don't make appointments. You come with me, now."

"Steady on," Eden broke in. "Captain Lacey can go where he pleases and do as he likes."

"Not if he don't want his nose broken. This way, guv."

I glanced about for Brewster but saw him nowhere. Meanwhile, Eden and I were surrounded by four toughs, larger still than the ones who'd attacked Brewster and me in St. James's.

Eden and I could possibly fight them, if Eden dropped his luggage. And, in this crowd, surely passers-by would jump in to assist, though whose side they'd take I could not guess.

"What does he want?" I asked the fist.

"T' have tea." The bully bared blackened teeth in a foul grin. "He says t' bring ye for a talk, for an hour or so. Not t' kill ye."

"How polite of him," Eden said. "And if we refuse?"

"I'm t' bring the captain don't no matter what. Not you, guv."

"I'll not desert my comrade," Eden said stoutly.

"It's all right." I shot Eden a quick glance. If I went alone, Eden could go find a patroller or Runner to rescue me, or better still, Brewster. "I'll see what he wants. You lug your things home."

Eden opened his mouth to protest, then understood my look, and nodded. "Right you are. I'll hunt up a hackney, shall I?"

The four men closed around me.

"Go on, then," the ruffian said, finally lowering his fist and waving Eden off.

I concluded they didn't mean me any harm, at least not at present. If they'd wanted to kill me, they'd not have let Eden go—they'd have herded us both to Creasey's warehouse and murdered us together, so Eden would not bring the law down upon them later.

Eden gave me a nod and tramped away, balancing his luggage, reluctance in every step. As soon as he faded into the crowd, the four men stationed themselves around me and marched me toward the lane in which Creasey lived.

His empty warehouse looked the same as it had yesterday, with dust-filled corners and blank walls. As I hoisted myself up the stairs, the ruffian who'd spoken to me seized my elbow and half-lifted, half-pushed me onward, impatient with my slow pace.

They hurried me across the upstairs floor of the ware-house, more blank walls and darkness, the only light leaking in through a single dirty window above the staircase.

The man who held me opened the office door and thrust

me into the room. Creasey was seated at the table with the chessboard, the only uncluttered area in the place. An unmatched chair rested on the other side of the chessboard, and the pieces had been set up in their rows.

"Captain Lacey," Creasey said without rising. "Welcome. Do sit. We'll have our game."

I made for the chair—a maroon-upholstered Hepplewhite delicacy—but only because my leg was aching from all the stairs I'd gone up and down today. I sank onto its seat, finding it stiff and somewhat uncomfortable, but my knee was grateful for the relief in pressure.

"I have not played in years." I laid my walking stick against the table, near enough that I could easily grab the sword inside. "I have heard you are a master at the game. You might be disappointed in me as an opponent."

"Not at all," Creasey said in his thin, dry voice. "Any game is instructive. You do know the moves?"

I inclined my head. "I do."

"Excellent." Creasey gave me a smile that could have graced a gargoyle. "You have white, so may begin."

The player who made the opening move had an advantage, it was true. However, an experienced player would be able to best anyone, no matter who went first.

I studied the board, reminding myself of the pieces and recalling the games I had played in Paris. These chess pieces were not as detailed as the ones in Donata's sitting room, but they were made of polished jade, one set a deep green of the ocean, the other so pale it was almost milky white.

Creasey would win the game, without a doubt, and from the smugness in his eyes, he knew it. He didn't want to face a good opponent. He wanted to gloat, to revel in his power.

Well, I could let him. I did not have much pride when it

came to chess, which had dismayed the fellow who'd taught me the game. The fact that I could take it or leave it had bothered him greatly. I made a note to write to the man and express my gratitude to him, if he were even still alive, for his training. It had been some time since I'd seen him, and I'd rather forgotten about chess.

I decided on a simple opening of sliding my bishop's pawn two squares forward.

Creasey laughed, a sound like dry paper. "I did not call you here simply to demonstrate my ability at the game, Captain. I truly do enjoy playing for its own sake, and I rarely have a partner anymore. No, I summoned you to explain how things stand."

He moved out a knight, and I scrutinized the pieces, trying to decide what to do next.

"The rivalry between you and Denis, you mean?" I moved another pawn, which would allow one of my bishops to stride out.

"There is no rivalry. James Denis is an upstart. I have tried to pay him no mind. When he first came to London, he was nothing." Creasey spat the word and moved his second knight. "He had to scramble to build up loyalty, which he did by stealing clients from me and from others. I could have had him snuffed out at any time, but he interested me."

I lifted my bishop and let it come to rest on a square diagonal to Creasey's first knight, threatening it. Creasey immediately took my bishop with his second knight.

"Ah," I said, acknowledging the hit. I was concentrating more on his words than the game. Creasey meant that he'd watched Denis, letting him do the work that brought in wealth, probably intending to either take it at some point or sweep young Denis into his own fold. "Did he refuse to join you when you proposed it?"

Creasey's eyes went flat. "I did offer him quite a good position in my order, but Denis was too sure of himself. He refused me, all but spit on me. Fool. I let him go. He could build his empire all he wanted, and then I'd take it from him."

I thought of the empty warehouse on the other side of the door and the emptier floor below. "But you never did?"

"He armed himself well. By the time I was ready to overthrow him, he'd grown very powerful. I'd have had to fight hard—I'd win, of course, but I'd lose much money and many loyal men in the process."

Creasey brought out his queen, taking one of my pawns in an elegant sweep.

"Is that why you agreed to a truce?"

Anger stained Creasey's cheekbones. "*I* suggested it. As long as Denis stayed away from my business—my clients, my employees, my profits—I would leave him be. We did not cross paths much after that. I work mostly in the East End, and he has decided to be a man of Mayfair, moving in circles I won't touch."

"Mmm." I did not point out that Denis's work encompassed all classes, from the Prince Regent to boys who swept the streets. He'd taken over most of the west side of London, and had MPs and aristocrats dancing to his tunes.

I was not certain how Creasey wanted me to respond, so I kept silent and moved my remaining bishop to guard my king.

"We have rubbed along like this for years," Creasey said. "It has been tolerable, mostly. Then he sent me the white queen." He reached across the board and lifted my queen from the square it had not left, studying the light jade piece closely.

"Which meant the end of your truce?" I asked.

Creasey frowned at me and returned the queen to her place next to my king. "He told you that, did he? What it means is that he intends to move into my territory. All agreements are nullified. He is warning me. He will try to overthrow me, possibly to murder me, and destroy everything I have." He lifted his rook and his king in the castling move, slamming them to their new squares.

"Your men attacked Brewster," I pointed out. "They did not seem interested in me."

"The man called Thomas Brewster is one of Denis's foot soldiers. They are fair game. You, I know, do not work for Denis by choice. He has entangled you in his mesh with promises, lies, and obligations."

A chill crept through me. For years I had been repeating almost the same words in my head.

"I am not certain he has lied to me." I do not know why I hastened to defend Denis, but spoke before I could stop myself.

"He has a way of dancing around the truth," Creasey said.

I remembered when Donata had hidden Peter away from her treacherous cousins. Denis had known exactly where the boy had gone and I did not, and Denis had refused to tell me.

"Perhaps," I said.

Creasey snorted as he moved his queen to threaten my bishop. "There is no *perhaps*. He has used you abominably, which is why I've spared you thus far. You are guilty only of being a fool. I know you saved Denis's life when an incendiary device went off in his house—I hear you warned him of it in time."

Another memory—this one of smoke, noise, and confusion, Denis snarling at his lackeys for not searching the man who'd made the device thoroughly enough. That man, Ridgley, had vanished, and I'd never learned what had become of him. Another body for Thompson to fish out of the river, I supposed. I'd saved Denis's life another time, in Norfolk, but we had been alone, with no witnesses. I decided to keep that adventure to myself.

I brought out one of my knights. "I hardly could have stood by while the entire room blew up with me in it."

"Of course not," Creasey conceded.

"To be fair, Mr. Denis has saved *my* life a time or two."

"Well, he would, wouldn't he? You are useful to him. Why let you be killed?" Creasey's queen swooped in to capture my knight.

In his zeal, he'd left one of his pawns unguarded, and I took it with my bishop. "Is there a point to your narration, or did you simply bring me here to tell me you dislike James Denis?"

"My intention is to explain the situation to you. You are in many ways a competent young man, but you have a blindness. Your unflinching fervor to keep your own word and do what is most honorable makes you commit foolish acts."

"Such as saving Denis's life."

"Precisely. You did that because you felt obligated to him, because letting him die would mar your sense of honor. No matter that you know he is a hardened criminal. A thief and a murderer."

I'd also once thought Denis a procurer. He'd absolved himself of that, which is when I'd begun to respect him slightly. I'd taken a long time to acknowledge that respect, but I had.

Creasey was telling me nothing I did not already know. His words echoed the whispers in my own mind.

"You know much about me," I said. "While I only learned of your existence yesterday."

"Because I make it my business to know everything regarding Denis and whom he recruits. You intrigue me. Such an unusual sort of man for him to trust."

"Because he knows of the honor you twit me about," I suggested.

"Ha. He plays you like a fiddle. He knows exactly what you will do in any situation. This is why he has not let you out of his web."

"Does he know what I will do at this moment?" I moved my remaining knight. "Here in your warehouse?"

Creasey chuckled, his thin body rocking. "He likely has heard by now where you are. You are well watched. And yes, he knows what you will do. You will scold me for trying to kill the man assigned to guard you, but you will not try to hurt me. You will play chess with me because I insist, even though you are not a strong player."

He took the bishop I'd used to capture his pawn.

"It has been some time since I have sat down to this game, yes." I made another move that would gain me nothing but wouldn't lose me a piece. "As I told you."

"So you did." He too made a neutral move, one that would coax out my queen while he set a trap.

"No matter the reason you brought me here, I would like you to leave Brewster alone," I said. "He is not simply the man assigned to me—he is my friend."

I might have also argued that Brewster had a wife who depended on him, but I decided not to bring up Mrs. Brewster. Creasey doubtless knew about her, but I did not want to put her in any more danger than she already might be.

"He is not your friend," Creasey snapped. "He is as tangled in obligation to Denis as you are. A former pugilist and thief, who escaped the noose by the skin of his teeth. It is Denis's influence that has kept him out of the dock all these years. He follows you at Denis's command to pay off his debt."

I forbore to point out that Denis had sacked Brewster,

who now worked for me directly, but I chose not to. Either Creasey already knew this or he was fishing for information.

"Even so, Brewster does not deserve to be punished for Denis's sins."

Creasey's brows went up. "So you admit Mr. Denis is a sinner? I am happy to see you are not misled by his smooth facade. Very well, I will tell my men to spare Mr. Brewster. Only him. I will be so kind to do so even if you refuse my proposal."

"I take it you brought me here to ask me to work for you instead of Denis." I slid my queen a few squares. If he did not block her, I could at least check his king in a few moves before I lost the queen. "I am afraid I must refuse. I will work for neither of you."

"Captain." Creasey not only blocked my queen with his rook but the position pinned my king without mercy. "You are wrong. You must work for one of us. You will not be allowed to continue otherwise. Check and mate."

"Ah." I peered at the board. "I did not see."

When I lifted my head, Creasey was, as I'd guessed he would be, preening himself for besting me so easily. I laid my king on its side and rose.

"I apologize for my poor skills," I said.

"Actually, you are a competent player, if a bit clumsy. I would be delighted for another game at another time."

Implying I could depart without hindrance. "Perhaps."

Creasey climbed to his feet. Although I topped him by many inches, he did not seem in the least intimidated by my height. He rested his hands on the tabletop.

"I will take this *perhaps* to mean you will return. I look forward to it. Good afternoon."

I bowed. "Good afternoon."

I took up my stick and walked to the door, trying not to

hurry. I wanted Creasey to believe me calm and composed, though my heart was beating rapidly and sweat beaded on my forehead. I expected any moment to feel a knife slide through my ribs or at least one of the toughs to give me a beating to remember him by.

"Captain."

I'd reached the door. I opened it, pretending to ignore the two ruffians stationed on either side of it as I turned back. "Mr. Creasey?"

"You intrigue me." His momentary triumph at winning the game had passed, and the steel in his eyes returned. "But do not take too long to decide where your loyalties will lie. When I strike, I do not miss."

He closed his mouth, finished. I gave Creasey a cool nod, as though merely taking in his words, turned, and left him.

His men followed me through the upper floor, down the stairs, through the warehouse, and out into the lane. As soon as I stepped to the cobblestones, they shot back into the house, slammed the door behind me, and threw home the bolt.

I dragged in breaths of London's clammy air, stinking of the river, dead fish, tar, and heavy smoke. It was perfume after the confines of Creasey's office, with its scent of exotic wood overlaid with a miasma of evil.

A HAND GRABBED ME AS I EMERGED FROM THE LANE. It was attached to Brewster, who dragged me aside, the crowd before the Custom House parting for us.

"Explain to me why the bloody hell ye went into that devil's lair without waiting for me," he yelled into my face. "Why ye went in at all. Ye should have made use of your handy sword and then legged it. I always thought you daft, guv, but this … "

I backed away a step from his outburst. "I am none the worse for wear." I patted my chest and arms as though checking for wounds. "He only wanted to play a game of chess and boast of how much he knows about me and about Mr. Denis."

Brewster's eyes narrowed. "And what does he know?"

"Nearly everything. He must have spies who follow Denis and note who he meets, what he does, who his associates are. Denis does the same to Creasey, doesn't he?"

"I don't pay much mind what His Nibs gets up to," Brewster growled. "I only do what I'm told."

"You are a poor liar, Brewster." I brushed off my coat, as though I could rub off the disquiet Creasey had given me. "I did make Creasey promise to leave you alone, however."

"Oh, did ye? For what price?"

I shrugged. "He asked none. I think he was perplexed by me."

"Everyone is, guv. But you're wrong. He might not have named a price, but he'll have one. We should visit His Nibs, tell him all."

I followed Brewster as he pushed through the crowd in search of a hackney. "I thought you no longer worked for him."

Brewster threw me a scowl over his shoulder. "It ain't that simple, guv. It's like you with the army. You don't have to obey your commanders no more, but you'd tip them the wink if someone was after 'em, wouldn't you?"

He had a point. I admired him very much in this moment, for choosing not to wash his hands of Denis.

"By the bye, did you discover any gossip about Mr.

Laybourne?" I said as we hurried along Lower Thames Street. "The clerk from Eden's ship?"

"'Appen I did. Here's a coach. I trust this driver, as much as I trust any of 'em."

"Wait a moment." I scanned the street. "I can't desert Eden."

"Major Eden found me, told me what happened. I was coming to yank you out of that house when you emerged, much to me relief and surprise. The major was worried about you but had to rush off to an appointment." Brewster paused as we reached the hackney and he opened its door. "If you like, you can go to His Nibs, and I can stay and follow the major, see what he gets up to. I know what road he went down. I can find him."

"No." I said the word abruptly. "Leave him be."

I climbed past Brewster into the coach, and he watched me, brows rising. "He strands you with a bloke like Creasey, he lies to you about all sorts, and you're not curious what he's about?"

"A man's business is his own."

I thought I had an inkling about Eden's evasiveness and lies, though I could not be certain. But Eden had the same honor Creasey had sneered at me about. If Eden disobeyed orders or broke the law, it was to protect another. In battle, his rashest moments had been acts to save others. His measures had earned him a dressing down from his superiors on more than one occasion, but as he'd already saved the lives in question, the rebuke never upset him.

"We'll learn of it soon enough," I told Brewster. "I am more interested in clearing him of murder than condemning him for lying to me."

Brewster stared at me as though I'd run mad. "It might all

have to do with the same thing, guv. The lies and murder all mixed up."

"Possibly, but I do not think so. Now, are you coming in the coach, or riding above?"

"Up top." Brewster slammed the door. "Where you won't drive me spare. The accountant, if ye want to know, is rooming in Cable Street. Very near to where the dead man lived. I call that interesting, even if you don't."

CHAPTER 11

I did find it very interesting that a fellow passenger from the *Dusty Rose* had taken rooms close to those of Warrilow. I would have to hunt up this Mr. Laybourne and have a long chat with him.

Meanwhile, the hackney conveyed us across the metropolis, as it had yesterday, to the home of James Denis.

It was now that I missed Grenville. He'd been gone from London some weeks, excited about his new house and bringing Marianne to it as his wife. She'd never be accepted fully in his circles because of her background—or lack thereof —but deep in the country, away from the crush of London, she might find a place for herself. Grenville was no fool, and he'd have chosen an area where they could have a modicum of peace.

If Grenville were here, we would discuss the mysteries put before us, dividing up the tasks and interviewing those close to the crime. I would write to him of all this tonight, including asking about the Mr. Fitzgerald Eden had mentioned.

We would visit Grenville soon, I told myself. I looked

forward to viewing Grenville's home, and cursed Denis again for deciding to bring danger down on us all. Though Creasey had promised to spare Brewster and to leave me alone, I certainly did not trust the man to keep his word.

When we reached Curzon Street, Brewster climbed down from the top of the coach, helped me descend, and sent the driver onward.

Denis was not at home. The butler, Gibbons, opened the door a crack and informed us of this.

"We'll wait," Brewster said.

Gibbons scanned the street before he condescended to pull open the door. Behind it, four men were poised, I suppose to make certain we'd not been sent by Creasey as decoys to get us inside Denis's house. When no one swarmed down the road to push in behind us, Gibbons relaxed a fraction—an expression very difficult to discern—and quickly closed and locked the door.

He led us to a cold reception room decorated in pristine whites highlighted with gold. Denis did not keep his masterpieces of art in this room where anyone might be admitted, but the chairs, paintings, and candelabras were nonetheless impressive and obviously costly.

I perched on the edge of a graceful settee, leaning on my walking stick. Brewster would not sit, but folded his arms and stared at the herringbone pattern of the wooden floor, still annoyed with me.

"They did not give me much choice," I told him. "I sent Eden off in the exact hope that he'd find you, which he did. If Creasey had wished to harm me, his men would have killed me the moment they took me inside."

Brewster lifted his head, his eyes flashing in a glare. "He's a snake in the grass. Never have truck with him again."

"Yes, sir," I said, snapping off a salute.

"You joke, but I'm not wrong. He'll lure you in, then snap you up." Brewster brought his hands together in a loud clap.

"I'm not as naive as all that, Brewster. I know he's a bad man, and I won't forgive him for sending men after you. I'll not go to him tamely."

"Not tamely, but you will. He's got ice in his veins, that one. He doles out violence as easily as he sips his breakfast tea."

I'd thought the same of Denis many a time, but I believed it more strongly of Creasey. Denis was a thoughtful man, only striking when he had to. Creasey struck for the fun of it, akin to the way he played chess. He enjoyed the game but intended to win.

"He agreed to leave you be," I said. "But like you, I do not trust him. Perhaps Mrs. Brewster ought to also be a guest in our house, for her safety."

Brewster shook his head. "You're house ain't safe, guv. Not with the likes of Creasey knowing where you live. Em knows how to look after herself. She'll keep out of his way."

"Are you certain she'll be well?" I asked in concern. "With you hovering over me instead of home protecting her?"

He snorted. "Em's known the London streets since she were a lass. She's much shrewder than you are, more canny too. She'll be all right."

Having met Mrs. Brewster, I knew that she was most capable. Even so, I would not like to see her drawn into Creasey's machinations.

I wanted to argue further, but under Brewster's warning stare, I decided to change the topic.

"What did you find out about Mr. Laybourne? Aside from where he resides? Which is immensely helpful. Thank you."

"Don't try to talk me 'round, guv. How your lady wife puts up with you, I don't know. I found Mr. Laybourne easily enough. Fellows at the Custom House know 'im. He used to be a customs clerk then went off to do the same in Antigua. Couldn't stick the heat and caught the ague. Recovered, but it made him sallow and sickly. So he came back here to restore his health. Huh." Brewster glanced upward as though at the gray sky we could not see. The room had no windows.

"Whether you rein in your anger at me or not, this is helpful knowledge," I said. "Not that I can imagine why a sickly clerk would kill Warrilow, or if he'd have the strength to do so. But it's a link, of sorts. I will interview the man."

"As ye like. You are leaving at the end of the week, though, mind."

"Of course. I have said I would."

Brewster sent me a narrow gaze and resumed staring at the floor.

We sat thus as a silver gilt clock on the table chimed out the half hour. After it had gone three rounds of this, I heard a door open in the hall, and then Gibbons entered our room. Without speaking, he gestured us to follow.

Denis had come in but not through the front door. He walked from the back of the house, in his greatcoat, divesting himself of hat and gloves and handing them to a beefy footman.

The butler put himself between us and Denis as he passed us without a word and walked upstairs. As soon as Denis had vanished on the upper floor, Gibbons led us in his wake to his study.

Denis had moved his desk. It no longer sat against the front wall between the windows, but before the fireplace, facing the door. The shutters on the front windows were closed, and blinds had been drawn over the back ones. In this gloom, the butler lit candles, their light joining that of the fire.

A chair was brought to me so I could sit, but Brewster remained standing.

"What did he want?" Denis had seated himself at his desk and now drew a letter from a stack that had been placed there. He broke its seal and scanned the contents while he waited for my answer.

I did not ask how he knew I'd been to see Creasey. Brewster hadn't said a word to any but me since we'd entered the house, but as Creasey had acknowledged, Denis would have sent men to watch my every move.

"To offer me a post," I answered. "At least, so he said. In truth, I imagine he was trying to pry information from me."

"I doubt that." Denis laid the letter aside. "He would have more information from his spies. He summoned you to discover what sort of man you are. To learn what it would take to make you betray me."

"I am not in the habit of betraying people," I said stiffly.

Denis spread his fingers. "He will poke at you until he understands your exact price. Every man has one."

"So you said to me when we first met."

"I stand by my assessment." Denis gave me a slight nod and placed his hands, palm down, on the desk. "I would like to know all he said to you."

I saw no reason not to repeat the conversation and told him all I could remember. "He painted you in the wrong, which did not surprise me. That he'd agreed to a truce he'd suggested and abided by it until you sent him the queen."

Brewster huffed and began to speak, but Denis quelled him with a glance. "The truce was forced upon him," Denis said. "He never liked it. I knew about Creasey long before he was aware of me. I told you once how I grew up on the streets. He was a force then, one I avoided. If anything, I owe my success to him, as I found avenues of business he had neglected. Nothing I did overlapped with what he had—I was very careful about that. But he saw me as a threat, wisely, I think. I offered the truce when it became clear we would soon clash. I promised to keep to my pursuits and leave his alone if he did the same for me. If either of us failed in the bargain we were to send the chess piece to signal that all restraints were off." He shrugged. "Creasey is an old man now, and he has not groomed any lieutenant to take his place on the day he dies. He trusts no one. I could wait."

He finished with the air of one who assumes they have far more time on this earth than those of their grandfather's generation.

"But that is no longer the case?" I asked.

Denis slid his hands together in one abrupt movement. "A ship came in from China. It contained antiquities, very rare and difficult to find. One agent of mine nearly lost his life acquiring them and another actually did. The buyer had already paid a high price up front for the expedition and was to pay me the balance upon delivery of goods. He is a powerful man, more powerful than Creasey, or even me. Creasey stole that cargo. Whether he knew my things were among it, I do not know, but he took all. His actions forced me to return my client's money, bearing the cost of the expedition myself, and make my apologies." Denis's usually cool tones took on a harder note as he spoke. "Creasey overstepped the bounds of our agreement. Even if he hadn't known part of the cargo was mine, upon realizing it, he should have turned that portion over to me. He did not. I sent a man to tell him of my disapprobation, and he had that messenger beaten and returned to me half dead. Thus, I had you deliver the white queen, the agreed-upon signal that the truce was over, that I felt free to take over his empire. Which I will do."

A chill touched the air at his last words. I shivered, wondering that the fire and all the candles couldn't warm me.

"A moment," I said in rising irritation. "Your first messenger was beaten within an inch of his life, yet you sent me straight into the lion's den without a warning?"

Denis's eyes remained icy. "I debated for a long time whether to do so, but in the end decided you were the best person to deliver the package. You are a gentleman. Creasey has no qualms about killing a fellow thief, but he'd hesitate to injure you until he understood who would retaliate against him if you came to harm."

I gripped the mahogany arms of my chair. "My wife and her rather powerful father would, I suppose. I hope so, anyway. Or perhaps they'd be happy to see the back of me." I smiled at my feeble joke.

Denis's eyes didn't flicker. "Just so. You have far stronger connections now than you did when we first became acquainted. You have Mr. Grenville, who is worshipped by most of the *haut ton,* in spite of his misalliance marriage. Sir Gideon Derwent is always poised to wipe out the dregs of London, in his most well-bred way. Even your colonel would charge to your aid, if only to appear loyal to his fellow officer. You also have magistrates who respect you, though Creasey controls some who do not."

A warm feeling began in my chest as he spoke. It was true that I'd been alone for a long time, but I did now have friends and family to assist me.

"You asked me to conduct this task when we were still in Brighton," I said. "Some months ago. Why wait until now?"

Denis forced his hands to return to a calm position. "Creasey had not yet betrayed me when we were in Brighton. When I told you I wished you to do a task for me, I did not have a specific one in mind. I knew that one would present itself. Unfortunately, it did."

"You crafty bugger." I couldn't stop the words. Brewster tensed, as though expecting Denis to signal one of his men to punch me in the mouth.

"Not crafty," Denis said coolly. "Expedient."

"I am rather tired of being expedient for you," I growled.

Denis's brows lifted the slightest amount. "I realized when I first met you that I would have to either use you or kill you —you'd never let me alone otherwise. You have proved to be very useful, so my decision was sound, but if you prefer the other ..." He rocked his hands open as though leaving it up to me.

With any other man, I'd think him teasing me. With Denis, I had to take the words at face value.

"If you believe doing your bidding is my choice, you are wrong." I cleared my throat. "Though I have appreciated your help in the past."

"Just so. We have built an understanding, and each of us will keep our words to the other. I know this. Creasey, on the other hand, does not understand the value of honor."

Denis rose, a signal that he was finished with our conversation. I climbed to my feet and Brewster pried himself from the wall he'd been leaning against.

"Go home, Captain," Denis said. "Play no more chess with Creasey. Please put aside any notion that you can reason with him, beguile him, or warn him off. You cannot. It is best you take your family and leave London while I attend to this business."

"Perhaps you should leave as well," I said. "He's nearly killed you already, if you recall."

"He did not succeed, and now I am on my guard. I will send you word when the business is at an end."

When Creasey was dead and gone, he meant. I thought of the wizened man sitting above his empty warehouse, surrounded by his guards, gazing longingly at the empty chessboard. I could feel sorry for Creasey, had I not seen the hard coldness in his eyes and if he'd not sent three men to kill Brewster in the middle of a Mayfair lane.

I decided to take Denis's advice. I had Eden's reputation to clear, in any case, plus I'd grown decidedly curious about Warrilow and why someone had crept into the house and killed him.

"Very well," I said, giving Denis a bow. "I will keep out of the way. Thank you for explaining. Good day to you."

Denis's eyes widened slightly. I'd never simply obeyed him before. The glance he sent to Brewster told him to make certain I did what I claimed I would.

Denis remained standing at his desk. The butler swung open the door and ushered us out.

By the time I reached home, I was quite hungry, so I paused to have a meal. Donata had gone out, Barnstable informed me, with Lady Aline Carrington, in her coach, to make calls she claimed she could not avoid.

I knew Lady Carrington was looked after by servants as loyal as Donata's and that she'd protect Donata like a lioness guarding its cub. This was not to say I did not worry and would breathe easier when I heard my wife's voice floating through the house.

I convinced Brewster to return home and make certain *his* wife was well. He went, but only because I made a promise not to leave until he returned. I also knew Denis had stationed a man outside to guard me, though he remained discreet.

Peter was to depart this afternoon for Oxfordshire. The lad was still unhappy, Bartholomew reported, but resigned. I decided to remain home for the rest of the day so I could see the little fellow off.

I remembered being shunted away to school when I'd been about his age. The estate's gamekeeper, a bad-tempered man who'd been perpetually half drunk, was the one who'd lifted me into the coach and threatened to thrash me if I made any trouble at school. Enough trouble to get me sent home, he meant. No one wanted me there.

I'd not let Peter remember this journey in such a light. He was not being punished or discarded but sent to safety.

After eating and visiting the children, I retired to the library and wrote to Grenville, telling him about Eden, the death of Warrilow, the ships' passengers, and Denis's battle with Creasey. It took much paper, and once the ink had dried, I folded it into a fat bundle, sealed it, and addressed it to Lucius Grenville at Nutgrove House, the Cotswolds, Gloucestershire.

By then, it was time for Peter to leave.

Donata had returned, Lady Carrington's carriage halting at the front door, and our footmen and Lady Carrington's swarming like bees around their queen to escort Donata indoors. Not long later, she and I walked Peter down from the nursery and took our farewells of him in the front hall.

Donata hugged Peter hard, never caring how it crushed the delicate silk of her gown. "You mind Hagen, now. And Jeremy."

The footman Jeremy, a bright lad, had been trusted with Peter's care, as had Hagen. The coachman would remain in Oxfordshire with Peter and Jeremy, and Donata, Anne, the nanny, and I would travel by a hired chaise and four.

"Yes, Mama," Peter said dutifully as Donata released him.

He swallowed, torn between the sorrow of leaving us and the excitement of being on his own with young Jeremy and Hagen, both of whom Peter admired.

"Have a good journey." I stuck out my hand, and Peter shook it gravely. "We'll be along in only three days."

"Yes, sir." More blinking, but Peter managed not to let the tears leak out.

"You're a brave lad, Peter." I gave in to impulse and swept him into a bear hug. "When I arrive we will ride from dawn to dusk."

Peter brightened at that. He loved to ride. Jeremy, waiting just inside the front door, held his hand to Peter. Peter took it, and the two marched out, Jeremy lifting Peter easily into the waiting coach.

I turned to Donata to find her face streaked with tears. "It was only last week he was no bigger than Anne," she said in a near whisper. "Wasn't he?"

I drew her to me, caressing her, to the further ruin of her silk. "We will join him soon, and then we won't be apart." I went quiet a moment. "I am so grateful to you for giving me a family, Donata."

Donata raised her head. She wiped her eyes with her fingers and strove to regain her usual sangfroid. "You had Gabriella long before you knew me, if you recall."

"True, but I had given up trying to find her—fearing I'd discover the worst—until I decided I wanted to marry you. Being bold enough to hunt for Carlotta to make certain I was free to wed led me to Gabriella. So I thank you for reuniting me with her."

I'd coaxed a watery smile from Donata, which had been my intent. "You do rather well with flattery, you know."

"It is not flattery," I whispered. I pulled her close once more and tenderly kissed her lips.

"Ah." A lighthearted voice came over the sound of Peter's carriage jangling away. "I do beg your pardon. I am rather good at interrupting at entirely the wrong moment."

Donata stepped from me hastily, eyeing the intruder who had entered from the vestibule, another of our footmen fluttering behind him. Donata and I were usually in some other part of the house when visitors arrived, not kissing in the front hall. The guests would be invited to kick their heels in a reception room while Barnstable determined whether they'd be admitted or simply allowed to leave a card.

Today, we were decidedly informal.

"Eden," I greeted him heartily. "My dear, this is Major Miles Eden, of the Thirty-Fifth Light Dragoons. Eden, my wife, Donata Lacey."

"How do you do?" Eden had swept off his hat, and he lifted Donata's hand to his lips in old-fashioned courtesy. "Lacey, you have managed to steal the most beautiful woman in England. The rest of us have no hope."

"Now *he* is a master flatterer." Donata withdrew her hand before Eden could hold it too long, and gave him a nod. "Perhaps you should learn at his feet."

She spoke in her usual cool tones, but I could see she was pleased. Eden knew how to flirt without becoming smarmy, to compliment a lady without angering her gentlemen enough to call him out.

Barnstable floated in from wherever he'd kept himself and took Eden's greatcoat and hat. "Coffee and brandy, sir?" he suggested to me.

"Just the thing. In the library would be best. Shall you join us, Donata?"

"A pair of army officers from the same regiment?" Donata feigned a shiver. "No, indeed. I have plenty of letters to write and will leave you to it. Good afternoon, Major Eden. Delighted to have met you."

Eden bowed to her, and Donata gave him another nod, touched my arm fondly, and glided up the stairs.

"I say, she is quite stunning," Eden told me once we heard her sitting room door close. "Even more beautiful than rumor has it. Congratulations, old man."

"Please return your eyes to your head," I said, not without a note of pride. "But I will accept your congratulations. I rejoice every day that she is mine. Shall we?"

I led him to the high-ceilinged library, which was lined with bookcases, a heavy desk that I'd cluttered reposing in its midst. The tall window that looked out to the back garden lent us some light, though gray fog had once more descended on London.

Barnstable brought in coffee and brandy, taking his time to set out cups, glasses, spoons, and a pot of sugar perfectly before asking if we needed anything more, and skimming away.

Eden gazed about in approval as we took our seats, I behind the desk and he on a Louis XV chair. "A lovely house, a beautiful wife, a perfect butler, reams of books—you have done quite well for yourself, Lacey. Is Brandon apoplectic with fury at you for it?"

"We've mended our fences." I recalled how Brandon had enjoyed himself coming to my aid in Brighton this summer. I shrugged. "More or less."

"How is the beautiful Mrs. Brandon? I should have eloped with her long ago, but I knew you had a tendresse for her, so I gallantly stepped aside." Eden ended with a flourish of his hand.

"Mrs. Brandon and I are friends," I said in a light tone. "If you had eloped with her, as you pretend you wished to, she'd have had you firmly under her thumb from the first moment. Might have improved you."

Eden burst out laughing. "You have the right of it." He trailed off. "I apologize for abandoning you this morning. I found Brewster and told him where you'd gone, but I had a devilish important appointment to keep. Business, you know. It wouldn't wait. I came to see if you'd fared all right against that horrible man."

I gave him a nod. "He released me without damage. Brewster was charging to my rescue even as I emerged from Creasey's lair. Creasey didn't torture me. We played chess."

Eden looked alarmed. "I thought he was a master. What did he want from you?"

"To teach me my place. He won, of course, but I tried to play better than he expected so he'd not become disgusted and have me beaten for the entertainment of it."

Eden shuddered. "I met Bonaparte once. He was a man well confident of his own power, fairly certain he was destined to become a god, but he was also polite and intelligent, courteous to an officer of his enemies. He made me know I was less than nothing to him, but he did not frighten me anywhere near what this Creasey does."

"You will be glad to learn that I have decided to leave him to Mr. Denis. Both Denis and Creasey—and Brewster—are correct that I should step out of the way." I poured a dollop of brandy into my coffee and sipped. Both beverages were excellent, and combined they made a superb concoction. "Which gives me more time to focus on your problem."

Eden gave a heartfelt sigh and lifted his coffee. "I thank you. I will be glad to have Pomeroy not popping up to greet me wherever I turn, with that hearty laugh of his. I imagine every criminal in London is terrified of him."

"They are," I assured him. I set down my cup and folded

my hands on the desk. "But I need perfect frankness from you if I am to help." I leaned forward and gave him an intent stare. "Tell me, Eden. Who is the lady?"

CHAPTER 12

I had expected Eden to splutter into his coffee, cough, and send me a flurry of lies as his face grew crimson.

Instead, he lowered his cup in puzzlement. "What lady?"

Hmm. Either Eden had improved at deception in the last hours, or my assessment was wrong.

"Come now," I said. "There are none here but us, and what you tell me will go no further. You have mysterious errands that pull you from important situations, such as fetching your baggage held at the Custom House, or dare I say it, rescuing me. You cannot explain why you visited the hold of your ship many times though you had no cargo there. You quarreled with Warrilow about the horrors of slavery, came to blows with him defending a woman who spoke strongly against it. Perhaps Warrilow knew your secret, and you went to his rooms that night to make certain he told no one. My conclusion is that you fell in love with a lady, who perhaps was owned by a planter in Antigua, and you spirited her away across the ocean where she could live in freedom. I commend you for it, but others unfortunately, like Warrilow, would condemn you and try to send the lady back to her captivity."

Eden sat in bewildered silence as I put forth my theory, which had made logical sense to me when I'd worked it out. Eden was a gallant gentleman, and it would be just like him to steal away a woman to bring her to the dubious paradise of England and set her free. It would also explain his stumble when Eden had claimed there had been seven passengers, and then spoken only of six.

Eden sipped his coffee with an air of relief. "I say, Lacey, you have a vast imagination."

Damnation. He did have a secret, a reason he'd done all the things I'd outlined, and he was happy I hadn't guessed correctly.

"I have told you, your magistrate, and many others, time and again, that I am a confirmed bachelor," Eden said. "I do enjoy the fairer sex, as you know, and I have had my share of liaisons, but no I did not act the romantic swain you paint. I would help such a woman, of course, but I'd have simply purchased her freedom so she could travel with me openly, and I'd have already introduced you to her. What you have outlined is a superb story for the theatre or a sentimental novel."

My face burned. I'd been sure I was right, and the man was hiding *something*, but I sat in embarrassment. I had grown too enamored of my own opinion, I supposed. "Forgive me. Perhaps my wife's fondness for opera has confounded my thinking. You must admit that your behavior has been odd."

Eden waved a hand in exasperation. "I am trying to settle myself in England once more, a country I have not spent much time in for many years. Like you, I followed the drum across the world, and then thought the Antilles would make my fortune. Now I need to put myself somewhere, doing something. There is not much for a former soldier who knows little about finance or farming, but when opportunities present themselves, I must pursue them."

"I see." I sipped coffee to hide my confusion. I'd been so certain. Eden was usually a straightforward person to the point of vexation, and his evasiveness troubled me.

But his explanation was logical. If he had wanted to rescue a lady, he would have done so in the most candid way possible, to make certain no harm came to her. Helping her run away and stowing her on the ship was romantic, and Eden, as I'd noted, was not. He did enjoy the company of women, but never grew starry-eyed about them.

"I do beg your pardon," I said, my words stiff. "To avoid my flights of fancy, perhaps you ought to simply tell me what you've been doing."

Now his flush returned. "I will. In time. You must trust me that nothing I have done has resulted in the death of Warrilow. I am as confounded about it as you are. Yes, I shouted at him—he was a pompous bully—and yes, I visited him to shout at him again, but as Mrs. Beadle told you, he was abed. I never saw him, never clouted him with a wash basin, did not kill him. I give you my word, as a gentleman and an officer of your regiment."

"I believe you." Eden was not a man who'd promise his word without all honesty behind it. "I will not mention it again."

"I am grateful to hear it." Eden slurped down more coffee. "Now, we should turn our attentions to who *did* murder Warrilow to, as I said, give Sergeant Pomeroy another man to chase."

"Very well." I moved aside the books on chess Barnstable had helped me find this afternoon and laid the notes I'd made on the problem in front of me. "When we searched Warrilow's rooms, we found an army carbine. Did he have such a weapon with him on the ship? I imagine him as the sort who'd show it off at the supper table."

"I agree he would be that sort, but he never did." Eden set down his cup, calming. "I never saw a carbine in Warrilow's possession. Perhaps he acquired it after he landed home to use for protection. The areas around the wharves can be dangerous."

"Then why dismantle it and hide it beneath the floor-boards?" I opened my hands. "When one confronts an intruder, you do not say, *Excuse me a moment,* extract a stripped weapon, put it together, load it, prime it, point it at the intruder, and finally announce you are ready to do battle."

Eden chuckled. "I see what you mean."

"Thompson carried the gun away with him, but he might let me have another look at it, as both of us know much about cavalry weapons. I wonder where Warrilow found it."

"There is surplus lying about now that the Frenchies are behaving themselves and we gave up trying to subdue the Americans. He might have bought it secondhand somewhere."

"It was a fairly new model, not leftover from Waterloo." I mused and made a note. "Brewster discovered that the clerk, Laybourne, let rooms in a house very near Wellclose Square. What can you tell me about him?"

"Not much more than I have already. Laybourne kept to himself most of the time. He was a sickly chap—he had to leave the islands and their tropical diseases behind. He felt very sorry for himself and went on about his delicate health and his lack of fortune a fair bit."

"Sounds an excellent traveling companion."

"We were all ready to see the back of him. The mission-aries assured Laybourne that all his suffering was the will of the Lord. They claimed the same for every cloud that floated by, every bird that rode our wake, every fish that leapt from the water. Each of *those* incidents reminded them of an event in the Bible—we heard about Jonah and the whale until we wished one would rise and swallow our ship."

I smiled in commiseration. "Remember young lieutenant Wheeldon?"

"Preaching Parson Wheeldon? Haven't thought of him in donkey's years. Very certain the word of God would shield him. And it did. Bullet hit him right in the Bible he carried in his coat pocket. He became insufferable after that."

We shared a chortle. Wheeldon had left the army after Vitoria when his father had passed away in Bristol. I hadn't heard of him since.

"What about Fitzgerald?" I asked. "The former Carlton House Set man?"

"Oh, he was quite congenial." Eden leaned back in his chair, lacing his hands behind his head. "I might have found him so only in comparison with the others, but he was a tolerable companion. Come to think about it, he too liked to visit the cargo hold. Said he didn't trust these sailors who barely made two coins not to rifle the baggage."

An interesting fact. I wondered why Eden was only mentioning it now.

"I've written to Grenville about him. I will be curious as to what he has to say—Grenville has made a study of characters in London. His observations are invaluable." I realized I missed that as well. I was glad Grenville had found some happiness, but I also hoped he would not absent himself from London for too long a stretch.

I found Eden staring at me with an infuriating smile hovering about his mouth. "You rub shoulders with the famous and casually tell me you await his opinion. My, my."

I set down my pen. "I believed Grenville would be too pompous for words when I first met him. He has his moments of pomposity, but he really is a clever chap, and can be very kind."

"I read that he'd married an actress. I imagine the mothers of the *haut ton* are weeping over that. They must abandon their dreams of having Mr. Grenville—and all his money, connections, and influence—for a son-in-law."

"They are unhappy, yes." Several ladies had taken Donata aside and made their feelings clear, knowing she and I were Grenville's close friends. We ought to have stopped the match, was their decided opinion. "I have been blamed for intro- ducing the pair, and it is true, I did. Or rather, Marianne rudely pushed her way into my rooms to help herself to candles and intrigued Grenville by not being impressed by him."

"A deadly sin?"

"A puzzling encounter. They danced around each other for a long time, but it was clear a passion had developed. I think them well matched." I lifted my pen again. "I should not gossip. Grenville has been a very good friend to me. He will weather the storm."

"I wish him well," Eden said. "If he can aid me, I will be forever in his debt."

I noted the little Eden had related next to Fitzgerald's name. "I have promised many that I will quit London at the end of the week. This includes my wife and my son, and I cannot break my word to them."

"Which means we must clear up my problem in the next few days." Eden lowered his hands and rested his elbows on his knees. "I say, Lacey, you have no need to help me at all. This is my conundrum, not yours."

Yes, I could retire to Oxfordshire and let Eden sort things

out with Pomeroy. But I would worry and wonder, and before long I'd be back, unable to cease probing until a solution was found.

"I would never turn my back on a fellow of the Thirty-Fifth Light," I assured him. "Plus I am intrigued by the mystery for its own sake. I only meant to warn you that we must work swiftly. And you are most welcome to travel to Oxfordshire with me, as well as on to Gloucestershire. Donata's father's house must have fifty bedrooms, her family is quite hospitable, and Grenville would be delighted to welcome one of my old friends."

I wasn't certain how delighted Grenville would actually be, but he'd politely accept Eden, and I knew Grenville would like Eden after a time. Everyone did.

Eden chuckled. "Fear not, Lacey. I am not in need of charity. I have plenty of funds for my rooms, and I can go rot at my uncle's leaky pile if I truly need a roof—one full of holes—over my head. My trouble is not cash but finding a way to make myself useful. In the army, we never worried about what we'd do day after day. We knew. Once I had no one to command me, I rather blundered about. I must cease."

"I do understand. When I returned from the Peninsula, I was sunk in melancholia. Wounded, with little but my half-pay packet, knowing no one ... that is why I grew interested in helping others when the magistrates could do little."

"Convivial of you. Ah well. I will hit upon something. Please do not suggest I marry, as every other person does. A married man must support a wife, and we have already exhausted the topic."

"Right then." I capped my ink bottle and tossed the pen to its tray. "We will work tirelessly in the next few days to clear your name and then you can return to deciding what to do with the rest of your life."

"Done." Eden lifted his cup in a toast, and I did likewise.

I PLANNED TO SPEND ANOTHER AGREEABLE EVENING indoors with Donata, but Eden, who'd departed some time after our brandy and coffee, sent me word that he'd run Mr. Fitzgerald to earth at White's. Fitzgerald had been pleased to meet Eden again and invited him, and by extension, me, to dine with him at the hallowed club.

I did not like to leave Donata alone, but she told me to go, that she'd enjoy the hours to herself. She never had many, and I know sometimes she found me hopelessly underfoot.

I kissed her, had Bartholomew dress me in one of my better suits, and departed.

Brewster accompanied me in the hackney south to St. James's Street, where we had begun our day, though this time we stopped shy of Jermyn Street, in front of the imposing edifice of White's.

"I'll be waiting," Brewster told me as I prepared to enter. "If you need me, shout out of a window."

"I hope to be safe from Creasey's men *here*," I told him. "I doubt they'd be admitted. The doorman is formidable."

"You joke, as per usual, but you never know. His Nibs has plenty of acquaintances inside White's, and Creasey probably does to. Don't let any of them stick a knife in your back."

With that, he gave me a scowling nod and faded into the shadows.

I realized Brewster gave me good advice. I would take care to whom I spoke.

I was not a member of this bastion of upper-class gentlemen, but I had entered its hallowed halls as a guest of Grenville. Eden met me on the doorstep, and together we went inside. We were greeted by the doorman, who was indeed formidable—none would pass who did not belong. When Eden told him our names, the doorman gave us over to a butler, who led us upstairs and through a vast hall to a dining room.

The elegant room boasted a ceiling of gilded plaster leaves surrounding a large chandelier of glittering crystals. A fireplace graced one wall, the fire built high. A large dining table reposed in the center of the room with smaller tables off to the sides.

The butler led us to one of these private tables where a round-stomached man in a finely tailored suit waited. He vaulted to his feet as we entered the otherwise empty room.

"Major. Thank you so much for joining me." The man's voice was smooth, his smile warm. His face and hands were brown from the Caribbean sunshine, his portly build attesting to his love of meals, but his suit was as well-made as any Grenville wore. His hair, going to gray, had been slicked back with pomade, his watch chain gleamed gold, and the stickpin in his lapel bore a winking emerald.

"Captain Lacey," Orlando Fitzgerald said, shaking my hand. "Well met. I am so pleased you could come along. I love meeting new people. And a friend of Grenville's no less."

His final words told me how Eden had persuaded Fitzgerald to include me in the invitation.

We were seated, and the efficient butler brought red wine, sugar, and a bowl to set in front of Fitzgerald. While he proceeded to make these into punch, I accepted a glass of dry white hock to drink unadulterated. Eden took some of the punch.

"One grows used to sweet concoctions in the tropics," Eden told me apologetically. "It takes the sting out of the torpid weather and the biting insects."

Fitzgerald laughed heartily. "Indeed. Rum is best when mixed with orange, lime, and a dash of sugar. Delightful. To your good health, sir."

He raised his glass to me and took a fulsome gulp. Eden and I sipped more modestly.

"Pity about Warrilow," Fitzgerald went on after he'd dabbed his mouth with a handkerchief, leaving a pink stain on the linen. "He was not the most pleasant of fellows. Downright blistering on occasion. I imagine he startled a burglar, and Warrilow, instead of shouting for help like a sensible chap, snarled at him about the error of his ways. Burglar became fed up and smashed him over the head." He chuckled.

"An interesting speculation," Eden said. "But until we find the burglar, we shall never know."

"Ah, well. It's a terrible thing, and I am certain to tell my valet to lock my door at night. But it makes me all the more determined to enjoy life while I have it." He lifted his glass in another toast.

"What brings you back to London?" I asked.

"A rather creaky ship." Fitzgerald grinned. "It was time. I'm not a young man anymore. My poor old pa sent me out to Antigua to remove me from the danger of becoming a dissipated and useless blight on the landscape. A canny man, was my father. We didn't have a title to keep the family from ruin, and I could have landed him in desperate straits. Look what happened to Brummell, who's now rusticating in France, living on the charity of others. I was furious with my father for packing me off, but it turned out to be the making of me."

Several footmen served us a cream soup as this speech ended, then quietly retreated. I dipped my spoon into the smooth, thick liquid, and tasted a velvety broth with a hint of nutmeg. Some among the dandy set disparaged White's cuisine, considering Watier's, run by a chef, to have the best food. However, I found nothing to sneer at as I imbibed the soup.

"You enjoyed Antigua?" I asked as we slurped.

"I am not certain one *enjoys* Antigua." Fitzgerald swallowed his last bite of soup before Eden and I were halfway through our bowls. "But it was good to me. I made a circle of friends. I was a bit haughty about the plebeian crowd when I first arrived, but soon found genuinely good fellows. I nearly married but came to my senses in time. Ha ha. She wed a better man and bore him a half dozen sturdy children."

"But it was time to come home?"

"Indeed. As I said, I am growing no younger. The heat became more difficult to bear each year, and the storms ..." He shuddered. "They did not come along often but when they did, they were terrifying. Eden, here, knows what I mean. English weather is far more tame. Forever damp, but it's predictable."

Fitzgerald leaned back comfortably as he waited for Eden and me to catch up, not at all chagrined by his appetite.

The footmen whisked away our bowls as soon as I'd scooped up the last drop and replaced them with plates of fish in a butter sauce with plenty of fresh dill.

Eden took over the questions. "What do you plan to do now that you are home? Retire to the country and collect spoons?"

Fitzgerald laughed and thumped the table. Though he ate quickly, he did so neatly, wiped his fingers on a napkin, and only spoke or laughed when his mouth was empty. A gourmand, I decided, rather than a glutton.

"I hope not. No, I shall look up old acquaintance, go to the theatre, join a hunt, enjoy what I could not in the islands."

"A sound plan," I said.

We finished the fish, Fitzgerald inhaling it in several large bites. The footmen removed the plates and brought forth the meat, a roast in an excellent wine sauce accompanied by hunks of crusty bread.

"You did not join me tonight so I could speak nostalgically about my life, Captain Lacey," Fitzgerald said after we'd made a start on the beef. "You want to know if I had anything to do with Warrilow's death. I have heard much about you in the very short time I have been staying at White's. Grenville's captain friend, they say, who makes a nuisance of himself but finds criminals where the Runners cannot. The cavalryman with mud on his boots who stole away the beautiful Lady Breckenridge and has brought down men from on high." Fitzgerald sawed at his roast and paused, a large hunk poised before his mouth. "So, Captain. What would you like to know?"

CHAPTER 13

Fitzgerald's amiable openness was disarming—almost. I decided not to let my fledgling liking for the man cloud my judgment.

"Why were you closely watching your baggage on the ship?" I asked casually. "Eden says you were worried about the common sailors, but if anything had gone missing, the captain surely would have made them turn out their pockets."

"Ah." Fitzgerald finished his mouthful of beef and washed it down with a long swig of wine—the butler had returned and filled our glasses with a hearty red. "Not for nefarious reasons, Captain, and nothing that had anything to do with Warrilow. I came across a curiosity while traveling among the islands, and I'd purchased it for a goodly sum. I was assured by the seller that it was worth quite a bit more, and I believe it. When we finish our meal, I'll show it to you. If my boots or silver hairbrushes had gone missing, that would have been annoying but hardly devastating. However, I would have been quite upset if someone had stolen this prize. It is not large, and a sailor could hide it among his things. But even if the captain would have searched their belongings if I'd reported the item stolen, I did not want to risk it being damaged. It is irreplaceable."

Fitzgerald punctuated his remarks with stabs of his fork. At the end, the fork dove into the last of his beef, and he masticated, mouth closed, explanation at an end.

He had me intrigued by this curiosity, whatever it was, which had been his purpose, I believed.

We finished the beef and turned to the next course, greens that were decidedly limp and a capon in a black pepper sauce that was tough. Perhaps this was why the dandies had preferred Watier's, a lively club that had sadly come to an end.

"What will you do with yourself, Eden?" Fitzgerald asked as the chicken and greens vanished from his plate. "Unless *you* plan to do the spoon collecting?"

Eden shrugged, making patterns in the thick sauce with the tip of his knife. "Who knows? As I was explaining to the captain, I am at a bit of a loss. I'll kick over some stones and see what I find."

"I'm happy to help if you like." Fitzgerald wiped his mouth clear of the peppery juices. "I am dining with the Prince Regent tomorrow. Renewing our acquaintanceship, that sort of thing. The old chap has let his self-indulgence get the better of him, but he is still the Prince of Wales, and standing in for our poor enfeebled monarch. I could find out if there's a place for you in his sphere—as military adviser or counter of royal spoons or whatnot. If nothing else, you might have a stipend while you discover what interests you."

Eden brightened. "That would be kind of you. Thank you, sir."

"Not at all. I am in your debt for preventing the conversation on our voyage from being tedious in the extreme. With the Kingstons preaching, Warrilow snarling, and Laybourne moaning, I welcomed our tales of life on Antigua. As though we were heroic adventurers." He dissolved into laughter once more.

I knew a man who worked in the Regent's abode of Carlton House—he looked after and cataloged the prince's vast art collection and advised him on what to purchase. Such a man might need an assistant. I hesitated to mention this, however, because not only did the gentleman in question have a sharp tongue, he also worked for Denis.

Grenville, on the other hand, had many friends and acquaintances throughout the *haut ton*. Any of them might need a secretary or a steward.

I kept this to myself as well, because I did not wish to appear in competition with Fitzgerald to be Eden's mentor. I decided that if the Regent had nothing for Eden to do or didn't want to bother with him, I would ask Grenville for help.

Our supper continued with another serving of meat, and I felt my waistband tightening. I'd have to ride for a long time to work off this meal.

More came in the form of a lemon tart, a trifle, and French chocolate truffles, finished with a sweet dessert wine from the Rhine valley.

At long last, the final plates were removed, and we were treated to brandy. Fitzgerald produced an enameled snuffbox with the portrait of a smiling, beautiful woman on the cover, and offered it. Eden took a pinch but I declined, as I disliked snuff.

Eden and Fitzgerald inhaled the fine tobacco, then sneezed into large handkerchiefs, Eden more delicately than Fitzgerald. I smiled tolerantly and sipped the excellent brandy.

It was late by the time Fitzgerald rose and asked us to

follow him to his chamber, where he would display the curiosity.

Fitzgerald led us to an upper floor. The rooms he ushered us into were small and rather plain but bore touches of luxury. A fire had been lit, the fireplace faced with gilded pilasters. A clock flanked by bronze lions proclaimed the time from the mantelpiece. A wide window looked out to the street, heavy drapes now drawn over it, and double doors presumably led into a bedchamber. The few chairs strewn about spoke of comfort. The room was lit by a chandelier, a miniature of the one in the dining room, lending the room a soft glow.

"Help yourselves to brandy," Fitzgerald said waving to a table laden with several decanters. He opened one of the double doors that gave us a glimpse of a tall bedstead behind it.

"Lacey?" Eden moved to the table and lifted a decanter, amber liquid sloshing in it. A silver tag on a chain around the decanter's neck told us it held French brandy.

"Why not?" I'd already imbibed plenty of hock, wine, and brandy at supper, but the drink was good and I didn't often indulge this much.

Eden poured. By the time he'd handed me a goblet, Fitzgerald had returned with a box about three feet long and two wide in the crook of his arm. He moved a table out from between two chairs and deposited his burden onto it.

The box was obviously old, its varnished wood worn but polished to a high sheen. It had been well made, with a carved lip on top and bottom, and painted superbly with cherubs who were cavorting, drawing at an easel, or enjoying life as cherubs are wont.

One of the box's sides was completely open. Eden and I bent to peer inside and found the painting of a house's interior. The colors were vivid, the floor a black-and-white pattern, the walls a golden hue, with several open doorways that frame other rooms.

However, the perspective was terrible. I had viewed art at the Dulwich gallery, studied Grenville's collection of master-pieces, and gazed in awe at the few paintings Denis displayed in his house. I surmised that this painting was Dutch, as the interior space was similar to that which I'd seen in the picture of the girl with a cream jug in Denis's home.

This artist had done bizarre things with lines, some of the floor tiles slanting up the other side of the box and a door canted sideways, making the scene beyond it stretch oddly.

Eden straightened. "I can't say much for the artist. He's no Canaletto."

Fitzgerald's smile was broad. "I said a similar thing to the chappie from St. Maarten who sold it to me. They're Dutch there—at least, part of that island is. Then he revealed the secret."

Fitzgerald set another table next to the box, on its open side. On this he placed a small lantern and lit the candle inside. Last, he unfolded a very thin sheet of paper and laid it over the open side of the box, concealing the interior but letting the light glow through the paper.

"Now, gentlemen. Observe." He pointed to a small hole on the short end of the box, an identical hole on the other.

"Captain Lacey? You appear to be skeptical, so why don't you have the first look?"

He positioned a chair near the table. I sat down, having to lean only a little to put my eye to the opening.

I peered inside … and beheld a wonder.

The strange distortions had vanished. I was gazing into the interior of a large home, pleasingly spartan, with wide square tiles and a few pieces of boxlike furniture. Through a doorframe in front of me, I saw a larger room with paintings

Another open doorway beyond that led to an
th a windowed front door. A man with a high-
tood outside, waiting for a small woman who
reached to admit him.

"Remarkable." I raised my head. "It appears to be multiple
rooms. I didn't notice it being divided inside, unless you've
slid in partitions?"

As Fitzgerald watched with glee, I peeled back the paper
on the open side, but the box was an empty cube, painted only
on its walls, floor, and ceiling. Yet when I looked through the
hole again, I'd swear I was gazing at a succession of rooms
and beyond to an outdoor courtyard.

"I understand why you wished to acquire it." I relinquished my place to Eden, who was soon exclaiming in astonishment.

Fitzgerald beckoned to me. "Now try the other side."

I stooped to gaze through the second hole, even while
Eden continued with the first. Now I saw more rooms, but
differently furnished, and which led, one after the other, to a
garden. A dog, sitting upright nearly in front of me, watched
me interestedly.

"Good heavens." I stood up, touching the top of the box.
"It is a masterwork."

"Very clever, these Dutch chaps. Made nearly two
hundred years ago, if you believe it."

"Why did the man sell this to you?" I asked. "I'd not let
this treasure out of my sight."

"He was hard up, poor fellow. I paid him handsomely for
it, never fear. Do you understand now why I feared losing it
to a sailor who'd have no idea what it was?"

"I do indeed." I caressed the box as Eden rose, then I
couldn't help resuming the seat to peer through the hole again.

"The customs agent who came to the ship seized it, of

course," Fitzgerald said. "I had to present a clear bill of sale, which I had. But it spent the night in their warehouse. I didn't sleep a wink, worrying about the thing. Fortunately the customs men didn't mar it. Or steal it."

"It is enchanting." I let myself be absorbed once more in the colors and the amazingly perfect perspective. "My oldest daughter would love this."

I wanted more than anything to show it to Gabriella. Perhaps I could prevail upon Fitzgerald to allow us a visit when he settled so she could see it.

"I will keep an eye out for another if you like," Fitzgerald offered. "These boxes are very old, and not many know what they are. I'll hound the local art dealers, who might have tossed them into their back rooms as badly painted antiques."

I thought of Denis. Much of his business was locating artworks for others, which was why he was so angry at Creasey for looting his shipment. If the antiquities Denis had lost were half as interesting as this little box, I understood his declaration of war.

"You are very kind," I said. "I accept. You can write to me either at South Audley Street, or at the Pembroke house in Oxfordshire if you have any luck."

Fitzgerald gave me a happy nod. "I like to see a keen admirer of art. What about you, Eden? What do you think of my little find?"

"It is dashed clever." Eden lifted his brandy glass and raised it to Fitzgerald. "I suppose the ladies will be intrigued."

"Let us hope." Fitzgerald boomed a laugh. "I will look out for one for you, Lacey. That is, if you don't land me in the dock for Warrilow's murder. Then I suppose I could leave you this one in my will."

"Only if you are guilty," I said lightly.

Fitzgerald found this statement hilarious. "Juries are not

always certain when a chap is innocent. If you *do* manage to have a man arrested for this crime, make sure he's the right one, hey?"

"FITZGERALD IS A CONGENIAL FELLOW," EDEN SAID AS WE walked from St. James's Street to Piccadilly. Brewster strode behind us, having materialized from the shadows as we'd exited White's.

"Indeed." I had ended up liking Fitzgerald, as exuberant as he was. "I've unfortunately met other congenial men—and women—who turned out to be thieves, fraudsters, or murderers."

"I am aggrieved to hear it." Eden shook his head. "I'd like to think that a man's character isn't so easily disguised."

I heard a breathy mutter behind me but ignored it.

"I hope Fitzgerald showing me the box was not to distract me from believing him a suspect," I remarked.

"Interesting that he said the customs agents held it, just as they took my things," Eden mused. "I didn't notice at the time, but I was arguing with them about my own baggage."

"Well, we shall keep an eye on him. I can always ask the customs agent—Mr. Seabrook—whether his story is true."

"I'd rather not go back to the Custom House, thank you very much." Eden shuddered. "Here is a hackney. I will leave you, Lacey, and walk the few steps home. Thank you for joining me on a most pleasant evening."

He stuck out his hand, and I shook it. Brewster hovered a few feet away, and once I took leave of Eden, he fell into step beside me.

"Ye seem chuffed, guv."

I waited for Brewster to approve the hackney driver,

which he did, and I bade him ride inside with me. I told him briefly about the meal with Fitzgerald and what I had learned of him, and also about the magical painted box.

Brewster went thoughtful as I described it. "Sounds like one by van Hoogstraten."

"Pardon?"

"Dutchman from far back. Painted pictures of wine goblets and lemons, that sort of thing, and these boxes with the peepholes. Wrote a book about the tricks of the perspective. Something with a long name, all in Dutch."

I listened in mild surprise. Though Brewster appeared much of the time to be an illiterate ruffian, he was anything but. He could read perfectly well, and he'd learned much about art, rare books, and sculpture, mostly, I admit, by stealing them. He also had acquaintances who moved stolen art and others who forged it.

"It was most fascinating. Was that sort of thing well-known in its day?"

Brewster shrugged. "Could have been. But I do know those boxes are rare now and worth a powerful lot of money."

"Are they?" I rested my hand on my walking stick as we rolled north to Curzon Street and around the corner to South Audley. "Then how did a hard-up Dutchman on St. Maarten get hold of one?"

"Maybe it was in his family, and when his money began to go he had to flog it. If Mr. Fitzgerald promised to find you another, he don't know what he's saying. Or maybe he does, and is trying to put you off the scent, like."

"He might be correct that art dealers could have them lying about in their back rooms and not realize what they are."

"True enough, but the real conno-sooers would ferret them out. If you asked His Nibs to find one for you, for instance, he'd charge every farthing its worth, plus more for the trouble."

"Ah." I deflated. There was a difference between obtaining a novelty for a lark and investing a fortune in rare artwork. I doubted my wife would thank me for spending Peter's inheritance—if I could touch a penny—on a pretty painted box.

"Fitzgerald's family must be more wealthy than he lets on," I said after a moment. "If these are as precious as you say."

"Or he got it for a bargain. Mayhap the bloke what sold it to him didn't understand the worth of it or was so desperate for cash he'd let it go for any price."

"All those things could be true." We neared the house. "Perhaps that is why the customs agent took the box from Fitzgerald for a time. To make certain it wasn't stolen or smuggled. Or that he hadn't smuggled anything else inside it."

"Very like. The customs blokes can't keep their hands off anything. His Nibs has to pay a large sum every time to make sure his goods don't get held up. Corruption is everywhere." Brewster shook his head at the sad state of the world.

We parted, me to stagger inside the front door, Brewster to go below to his bed in the kitchen. He'd insisted on remaining to protect me until I left for Oxfordshire.

Barnstable, who'd helped me upstairs more than once since I'd known him, assisted me to my bedchamber, and Bartholomew undressed me for bed. My partial inebriation coupled with the large meal made me clumsy and sleepy.

I was stretched gratefully in bed with a warmed nightshirt over my bare body, closing my sandy eyes, when the mattress sagged beside me. A soft weight landed against me, and Donata rested her head on my shoulder.

"Mmph," was my enlightened greeting. I ran a tired hand over her hair.

"Mr. Fitzgerald had fine brandy?" she asked in a low voice.

"He did. Plus he gave us wine and a many-coursed supper."

"Rather tedious food at White's, I have heard."

"On the contrary, I found it quite edible."

"Mmm." Her response told me my tastes were not quite as trained as she'd like. "Lady Aline knew Mr. Fitzgerald in her salad days. I asked her about him. He was apparently much the rakehell when he was younger. Cornered her in a few ballrooms, and kissed her, much to her delight. He was the gentlemen mothers warned their daughters about. Very exciting."

I had difficulty reconciling the portly and loud Mr. Fitzgerald with a dashing roué kissing the debutante Lady Aline in a shielded corner.

"Why ladies prefer gentlemen who lie, gamble, and womanize, I have no idea," I mumbled. "Why do you not like them staid and stodgy?"

"We believe we can reform them, of course." Donata snuggled closer. "That ours will be the love that changes them forever. We ladies are fond of this idea and nurture it."

"A foolish one." My words were a mumble.

"Do not worry. I prefer the staid and stodgy." Donata caressed my chest.

I was too tired to respond appropriately. "Fitzgerald seems reformed enough. Or at least finished with his young foolishness. Was he the sort who would murder a small planter for being irritating?"

"In his day, yes, according to Aline. He had a prickly temper and fought several duels. Wounded a man in one, though the young man recovered. However, the gentleman's family tried to sue Fitzgerald's family for the injury. That was

when Mr. Fitzgerald's father sent him off to the colonies. The
ordeal of island life must have frightened him into bettering
himself."

"So he says." I yawned. "I must tell you about what he
showed me."

I tried to describe the box by van Hoogstraten, but sleep
overcame me. I felt Donata's lips on mine, heard her chuckle.

"Tell me in the morning," she whispered, and then I met
oblivion.

I FOUND DONATA BY MY SIDE WHEN I WOKE IN DAYLIGHT.
She was not an early riser by habit, but she stirred when I did,
and then she kissed me and slid her arms around my waking
body.

I did not get out of bed for some time after that.

When I did emerge from behind the bed curtains, I rang
for Bartholomew and began preparing for my day. Donata
dragged the covers over her head and went back to sleep.

I washed and dressed, Bartholomew shaved me, and I
went down for breakfast. My overindulgence at White's last
night slowed me a bit, and the back of my neck ached, but my
morning with Donata had refreshed me.

I was ready to discover who had killed Mr. Warrilow if I
had to wring the information out of every person in London. I
wanted to quit the city and find some peace with my family in
the country.

I summoned Brewster when I finished breakfast and told
him we were off to Cable Street.

CHAPTER 14

*L*aybourne's lodgings, to which Brewster directed me, lay immediately north of Wellclose Square, the house nearly backing onto the one in which Warrilow had taken rooms.

"Discover whether a person can reach that house from this through the back gardens," I said in a low voice to Brewster as we approached. "Perhaps Laybourne slipped out unnoticed, climbed over the wall, or went through a gate, or some such. Mrs. Beadle might never have seen him enter."

Brewster gave the house a dubious glance. "Don't know if I can find out much in this place, but I'll do me best."

The abode was rundown, though it had obviously once been grand. Like Wellclose Square, this street's better days were long gone. Paint peeled from the house's shutters, the stucco was pockmarked, and a layer of grime filmed every window.

"Mr. Laybourne, you say?" asked the thin woman who answered my knock. "He's having breakfast, inn't he? Who are you, love?"

"Captain Gabriel Lacey, madam." I made her a bow. "He does not know me, but I am a friend of Major Eden, one of his shipmates on his voyage from Antigua."

The woman looked me up and down in clear doubt. "Well, I'll ask him."

She shut the door in my face, leaving me in the drizzle that began to coat the street. Brewster, heading down the outside stairs, gave a breathy laugh and disappeared into the dingy recesses below.

I shivered in the rain for some time before the woman yanked open the door and stood aside to allow me to enter. "He's in the dining room, love. Has never heard of ya and didn't like Major Eden, but he's curious why you're here. Go on in."

I thanked her and removed my hat, politely scraping my boots before I stepped onto her tiled floor. Not that my efforts would have made any difference. The floor bore scrapes and smears, bird's feathers, and a coating of dust.

The dining room had a threadbare carpet and one long table surrounded by a few rickety chairs. A small, thin man was its only occupant. He sat at the head of the table and gazed dolefully into a bowl of porridge.

"Mr. Laybourne?" I extracted one of my cards. "Good morning to you. Apologies for disturbing you at your meal."

"Ain't much of a meal." He took a bite and made a face as he gulped down the lumpy porridge. He made no move to reach for the card, and I tucked it back into my pocket. "Don't have any spirits on ye, do you? I'm a sickly man."

I could not place his accent, which was surprisingly neutral, but perhaps he had lost it during his time in the West Indies.

"Of course." I removed my flask, which I kept for warmth on chill autumn days such as this and handed it to him.

Laybourne proceeded to pour a liberal amount over his porridge and another dollop into his tea. "Thank you, young man."

I doubted he was much older than me, but I nodded. Mr. Laybourne had lean limbs in a shabby coat that was too large for him, affirming Eden's claim that he'd left Antigua to better his health. He wore his graying hair pulled back into an old-fashioned queue, was clean shaven, and gazed at me with doleful brown eyes. His skin held the yellowish pallor of one who'd suffered from the ague.

"Did Major Eden send you?" Laybourne asked. "What the devil does he want?"

"No, I wished to see you myself. To ask you a few questions about Mr. Warrilow."

Laybourne's brows went up. "That pestilence? I heard someone offed him. Good riddance."

He did not invite me to sit, but I scraped back a chair and did so anyway. "He lived in the square behind you." I glanced at the window but could not see much through the dirty panes. "Your garden almost backs onto his."

Laybourne briefly turned his head to stare at the window. "Does it? I'd think he'd have more funds, and sense, than to stay in these dregs."

Warrilow's rooms had been faded and worn, but Mrs. Beadle kept her place clean and scrubbed.

"His house is a bit nicer than this one. Perhaps you could move there."

Laybourne scowled at me and jabbed his spoon at the mess in his bowl. "Are you meant to be amusing? Though I suppose they do have an empty room now."

I hadn't been attempting humor. I'd thought that I wouldn't wish anyone to stay in this house. Even my small and cold rooms in Grimpen Lane had been more cheerful.

"I beg your pardon," I said. "Did you know Warrilow at all in Antigua?"

"Never met the man until he stepped aboard ship," Laybourne snapped. "A bad day when that happened. He was a menace."

"Yes, I have heard he was unpleasant."

"Sneering, small-minded, pompous idiot who pointed out the supposed shortcomings of others to cover up his own." Laybourne shoved his spoon into his mouth, stopping his words.

The anger in his eyes struck me. He boiled with it.

"You quarreled with him," I ventured.

"Everyone did." Unlike Fitzgerald, Laybourne didn't bother to swallow before he talked, spitting pieces of oats onto the table. "If you think I climbed the garden wall and then in through his window to—how was it done? Stab him, cosh him, strangle him?—you are mistaken. I am not a well man. Bloody malarial islands nearly killed me. I can barely walk up a flight of stairs and am reduced to eating this mush."

He slammed his spoon into the porridge, spattering the sticky mess. He shoved the bowl away from him.

"I am terribly sorry. I know what it is to be laid up." I hefted my walking stick then tapped my left knee with it. "Took me almost a year to be up on this leg again, and even now it pains me in this sort of weather."

"You were an army man. Injuries are to be expected. I went to the islands to make a bloody fortune. Huh. All I got for my troubles was the ague."

And he was enraged. Had that rage enabled him to march to Warrilow's—using the conventional means of the street and the front door—and kill him? I wondered who all Mrs. Beadle's grandson had seen that night.

"I suppose not everyone can grow rich there." Eden hadn't

been able to find a way to make his life in the islands profitable. Warrilow had been a small farmer only able to afford rooms in this end of London.

"I never said—" Laybourne broke off. He coughed heavily, lifted his teacup, and gulped. The brandy from my flask must have soothed him, for he quieted.

"What exactly did you do there?" I asked when he'd recovered.

His suspicion returned. "Why do you want to know?"

I shrugged. "I might make a go of it myself. Eden said Antigua was beautiful, despite its mugginess."

"Major Eden is a dreamer. Not a very practical bloke, you might have noticed. The only way a man survives in the Indies is through hard work and luck. You need both. I don't think you'd have the luck, Captain. You're already a cripple."

I hardly thought of myself as such, but I nodded as though not offended. "I suppose one needs both to survive in London as well," I said diplomatically.

Laybourne huffed in mocking amusement. "One does. I'll be quit of this place soon enough." He glanced around the room. "Sooner would be better."

"Not all of London is this dingy," I said.

"Yes, it is. Fog so thick you can cut it. Rain and wind when fog's not present. In the summer the river stinks of all the dung washed into it. That is, even more than it does in the winter. No, I'm finished with London."

I had the feeling that if I asked outright where he planned to go, he'd not answer. I tried a more oblique approach. "I too will be heading for the country soon. Oxfordshire."

"Not far enough, in my opinion. Me, I'm for the north. The open green of the Yorkshire Dales."

"Ah." I pretended to lean back comfortably, which was

impossible in this chair. "I have heard of its beauty. One of the soldiers in my regiment came from York itself."

"I'm off to High Harrogate. Right against the Dales." The angry light in Laybourne's eyes faded, and he took on a fond expression. "Cool and green. I think I'll grow well there."

"You don't sound like a Yorkshireman. My soldier spoke in speech so thick I could barely understand him at first."

"I lost my accent in my twenty years in Antigua. Deliberately. A Yorkshireman is considered thick, the judgement rendered as soon as he opens his mouth. Those like yourself couldn't, as you say, understand a word." He shifted his voice to the soft vowels of a northern Englishman. "But no more a' that for me."

"Excellent," I said. "I wish you well. Now, if you can tell me no more about Warrilow, I'll leave you in peace. Do you have any idea who might have killed him?"

Laybourne sent me an impatient look and reverted to his neutral accent. "Anyone who met the man. Who knows? A needle in a haystack, you're looking for. He infuriated the captain of the ship, the quartermaster, the first mate, many of the sailors, all of the passengers, and the customs and excise men who boarded us when we landed. I saw him railing at them, trying to teach them their job. I imagine he angered every person he passed between the docks and his house, including his landlady. *She* did it, I wager."

That was always possible, though Mrs. Beadle seemed too easygoing to lose her temper at a bad boarder. I rather thought she'd be more likely to put up with him for the rent money.

I rose. "So has everyone I have spoken to about him has stated. I am understanding that Warrilow was a foul person."

"He was. Trust me." Laybourne retrieved his bowl and

began stabbing at the porridge, which must be ice-cold by now.

"Again, thank you for your time, and best wishes for your travels to High Harrogate."

"Aye," Laybourne said, the Yorkshireman back.

I paused at the door. "By the bye, do you have any idea why Warrilow should have an army carbine? Did he ever speak of such a thing?"

I turned back casually, rewarded with an unguarded expression from Laybourne. His eyes widened, absolute fear flashing in them, before his face resumed a careful blank.

"He never said nowt about a gun." Laybourne scooped up more porridge. "Talked a lot of rot, but never about that." He shoved in the mouthful, wincing as though he regretted it.

I expected him to ask why I'd posed the question, but Laybourne only chewed and glared at me, finished with the conversation. I gave him a polite bow and left him to it.

I MET BREWSTER OUTSIDE, HE A FEW STEPS DOWN THE kitchen stairs, leaning against the wall. He pushed himself off and leapt up the final steps to join me.

"Couldn't stick it below stairs," he said by way of greeting. "Bad-tempered cook and maids, filthy place. Stingy too. Wouldn't part with a pint of bitter or even a drop of coffee." His frown was formidable.

"Did they have any information about Laybourne?"

"Oh, yes." He fell into step with me as we moved down Cable Street toward Wells Street. "They don't like him. He complains about everything imaginable. Hates the food, hates the lodgings, hates London, hates everyone he meets. Which presumably includes you now."

"Possibly. Any chance that he could have slipped through the gardens and murdered Warrilow?"

"Good-sized wall between them and the square behind. I looked. Garden choked with junk. You couldn't swing a cat there. No gates. 'Sides, Mr. Laybourne was abed at seven in the evening the day he arrived, which is the night Mr. Warrilow was done."

"Can they be certain he stayed there?"

"They can. He swallowed a tonic, for his ailments, he said, before he went to bed. The maid was curious about the tonic and took a sip. Laudanum, she said, very strong on the opium. She slept well all night with that one nip, and Laybourne had taken a full swig. Her brother is an opium eater, she said, so she knows what it smells and tastes like."

"I see." If Laybourne had drunk a good dose of opium before retiring, he'd likely not have waked until late in the morning. I had taken strong laudanum for my aching leg before and knew how solidly a man could sleep on it. "He was a good suspect, near to hand and disliking Warrilow so much."

"You won't have a small number of people who disliked the man, I'll wager."

"That is the trouble. Laybourne was correct when he said almost any Warrilow spoke to could have struck him down. I perhaps should worry less about who actually did and simply find evidence that Eden did not."

"Would help if Major Eden were more forthcoming. I understand he's your friend, but I know a liar when I see one."

"Yes, but about what is he lying? I suspected him of spiriting away a beautiful woman, but he was right when he claimed me to be too romantic. My idea genuinely surprised him."

"Don't mean he didn't spirit away something else. Suppose he helped someone transport goods he shouldn't? Maybe Mr. Warrilow found out and threatened to expose him."

I did not like to embrace the possibility, but I knew I had to. Eden was in a good position to be a smuggler—no immediate family to disgrace, no ties to anyone but an uncle and cousins he was not close to. He had enough money to stay in elegant rooms in St. James's and by his own admission was not worried about cash.

"Eden was surprised about the carbine you found," I said as we turned down a lane that took us to Wellclose Square. "I would swear he knew nothing about it, which relieves me. I'd hate to believe Eden had become a gun runner. However." I paused as we entered the square, the church rising in the open space, surrounded by the welcome sight of trees with their autumn foliage. "Laybourne appeared most upset I'd mentioned it. Was terrified."

"Was he now?" Brewster rubbed his hands. "That's summut."

"Have you ever been to High Harrogate?"

Brewster's brows came together. "Where's that, then?"

"Yorkshire. The West Riding, I believe."

"Well, I wouldn't know about it. Never been to Yorkshire. My family came from near Birmingham, but a long time ago. I spent most of my youth in London."

"High Harrogate is a spa town," I said. "Not as much in fashion as Bath or Tunbridge Wells, but there are hot springs and plenty of visitors. Not that I have ever been either."

"And why are we discussing a spa town in the West Riding of Yorkshire?"

"That is Laybourne's destination, or so he claims. It's a town for retirement and leisure, not for finding work when you're hard up. Laybourne was very angry when I spoke to him, angry at his surroundings—you say he complained about everything."

"According to the kitchen staff."

"Perhaps he is a man used to finer things. Perhaps he was stealing and selling weapons—a lucrative practice, I am certain—and is lying low here until he can collect his money and move to Yorkshire. Perhaps Warrilow discovered what he was up to, taking one of the carbines as proof. But Warrilow was killed before he could show the gun to a customs agent or a magistrate."

"That would tie things up nice and neat," Brewster said with approval. "Have your Runner arrest Mr. Laybourne, then."

"Though I wonder why Warrilow didn't simply show the gun to the customs agents when they boarded the ship. Apparently he was remonstrating with them."

"Maybe he tried to show them, and they didn't believe him."

"Could be. So he took the carbine home with him and hid it, preparing to tell a magistrate about it in the morning? Laybourne knew this, paid a visit, and killed him?"

I began walking again, heading for the house in which Warrilow had died.

"There's another possibility, guv. Warrilow maybe kept the gun to see how much cash he could pry out of Laybourne for his silence. But you're up against Mr. Laybourne going to bed early, dosed with laudanum."

"Unless he only pretended to drink it. Or, he paid a visit to Warrilow earlier, long before he went to bed, and killed Warrilow then. Perhaps telling Mrs. Beadle when he came downstairs that Warrilow said he'd go early to bed and didn't want to be disturbed."

"Then Mr. Laybourne drinks the laudanum to put himself

hard to sleep so he can't possibly be accused of killing the man." Brewster rubbed his nose. "A bit far-fetched."

"We can clear it up easily." I rapped on the door of Warrilow's lodgings.

Mrs. Beadle opened it promptly. "Oh, it's you again, Captain. I'm sorry, love, I've let the room and can't let you search it no more. I need to make a living, you know."

"I have no intention of disturbing you at all, madam." I gave her a bow. "I only wanted to ask you—did a Mr. Laybourne visit Mr. Warrilow the night he died?"

"Thin little man with a face like he'd eaten a lemon? Oh, aye, he were here. But much earlier than your Major Eden. I'd say about six o'clock or so."

"And he spoke to Mr. Warrilow?"

"I suppose so. I sent him up. Came down not long later and went off."

"Did he mention that Warrilow was going to bed? Or did not wish to be disturbed?"

"He said nothing at all, love. I heard the door bang and then spied the small man speeding off down the street in a pique, fists balled."

"After that, did you see Warrilow?" I asked.

"Didn't see him, but he called for some coffee, which me grandson carried up to him. Heard him growling when he took the cup. Not a patient man, was Warrilow."

So Laybourne had been here, but he'd left Warrilow alive. So much for my theory.

"Is your grandson about, Mrs. Beadle? I want to ask him about that night, if it is all right with you."

"The lad is here, as it happens, and he'll answer you. He's a bright boy. Come in out of the damp, and I'll fetch him."

CHAPTER 15

*A*s we stepped inside the boarding house, I was struck anew by the difference between it and Laybourne's lodgings. The house was no longer lavish, but its polished banisters and scrubbed floors shone with care and pride.

Mrs. Beadle left us in the hall while she hurried toward the back. I glanced inside a room to my right and found a pleasant if sparsely furnished sitting room. The ceilings were as high as those in White's, the plastered decorations once as luxurious. Time and chance had let this house and area recede into faded respectability while White's was at the relative height of its grandeur.

Mrs. Beadle returned quickly. "He's in the yard." She waved her hand at a rear door, the top half filled with a windowpane, through which we could see a small space with a gray wall. "Too muddy to come in without a good bath. Perhaps another time?"

"We would be happy to speak to him outside," I said. "And save your floors."

Mrs. Beadle sent me a good-natured smile. "I could get him cleaned up for tomorrow…"

"No, no." Tomorrow was Friday and too near the time Donata would load me into the carriage and steer me out of Town. "I don't mind a little mud. When I was in the cavalry, I fell into it plenty."

Mrs. Beadle conceded and led us out the door into a small yard. I glanced at the garden wall to see it was indeed as high and thick as Brewster had mentioned. I also could not swear to which of the buildings towering over the other side housed Laybourne.

A small figure, liberally plastered with thick mud, waited in the drizzle. He stood stoically, hat, coat, breeches, and boots covered in muck as well as his hands and much of his face. He had scraped mud from his eyes, revealing two pale ovals of skin.

"This is Captain Lacey, Harry," Mrs. Beadle said. "You mind your manners and answer any questions he asks you."

She closed the door but hovered on the other side of it, watching through the glass. A wise woman to not let her grandson alone with two strange men.

I was sorry she had spoken so sternly to him, however, as Harry, about ten summers if I was to judge, looked up at me with trepidation in his brown eyes. I was usually good with boys, but he watched me in dislike.

"Good morning, Harry." I extended a hand. "Captain Lacey, at your service. I was explaining to your grandmother that I grew as muddy as you falling off my horse in the cavalry."

Harry wiped his palm on his breeches, which did no good, before taking my hand in a feather grip. He whipped his arm away just as fast, staring at me with misgivings.

Brewster leaned to him. "What did ye do to get yourself so covered in muck?"

"Boxing." The reply was defiant.

"The other bloke knocked you down, did he?" Brewster asked.

"No other bloke. I was practicing by myself."

"Were you, now? I'm a bit of a pugilist meself. Show me your stance."

I thought Harry would refuse, but he planted one foot behind the other and brought up his fists.

"That's not bad, lad. But you want to hold your forward hand a bit more turned up, like so." Brewster gently turned the boy's wrist, so his closed hand faced the sky. "Then, when you punch, you have more room to turn it for a hard strike." He demonstrated a tight, focused blow to the air.

Harry watched in reverence, then tried to imitate the punch. Brewster put himself alongside the boy. "Shift your weight so one foot is always rock solid. The other gives you a place to go."

He made a few more jabs, while Harry copied him diligently. Brewster had made a name for himself as a pugilist before he'd been a lackey for James Denis, and his technique was still polished and precise.

Harry began to unbend as Brewster showed him more moves. First came a grin, and then Harry started to talk. I stood back and let Brewster work his magic.

Eventually Brewster came around to the reason we were here. "The night the chap Warrilow were killed," he said. "You saw everyone who went in and out that day, didn't you?"

"Aye." The answer came readily. "Mr. Warrilow had a couple of visitors, but he wouldn't see none of them."

"I wager you noticed everything about them."

"I did." The boy gave a competent roundhouse punch at

Brewster, who caught it in his palm. "A tall, thin chap, came a little after five o'clock. Said he was a parson."

"Did he give a name?" I broke in before I could stop myself.

Harry tensed, but Brewster distracted him by showing him another move. "'Tis all right, lad. My friend is curious."

"I think it were King. Something of the sort."

"Kingston?" I asked.

"Mayhap."

Kingston—the missionary who'd been on the ship. Why had he sought out Warrilow?

"And Mr. Warrilow never saw him?" Brewster asked.

"Naw. Told me gran to send him away."

"Anyone else?" Brewster prompted.

"Another chap not an hour later. Small bloke, suit all crumpled."

Laybourne, I was certain. "He went up to Warrilow's room," I said.

Harry nodded. "But Mr. Warrilow only opened the door a crack. They were going on at each other, but I couldn't hear what they said. The small bloke left after only a few minutes, his face all scrunched, stomping his feet all the way."

That fit with what Mrs. Beadle had said. Laybourne hadn't stayed long but had been very angry when he'd gone.

"And then later, the major," Harry went on. "He were a kind bloke. Gave me a penny. Mr. Warrilow was already abed. I had lit a fire in his room not long before that, and he was in his nightshirt ready to climb under the covers. He told me to hurry it up and then leave him. So I did."

"You are very certain Major Eden never went upstairs?"

"He never did. Blokes from the Tower asked me, and so did the Runner, but I said no. Because he didn't. Later, when I was going up to my room—I stay here with my grandmother sometimes—I heard Mr. Warrilow snoring behind his door. Snoring loud. I think that was about ten in the evening. I thought I saw the parson chap lurking out in the street, but I couldn't be certain. I went to bed after that. Then in the morning, Mr. Warrilow were dead," Harry finished with animation.

Harry seemed a clever lad, not one to misunderstand what he observed. In that case, Eden had arrived and departed without going up, as Mrs. Beadle had stated, and Warrilow was alive and asleep at ten o'clock.

Eden might be saved the noose after all—if the boy would swear to Eden leaving well before Warrilow had been killed, and that Laybourne and Mr. Kingston had also been visitors. That is, if a magistrate or judge would accept his testimony. Boys weren't always believed.

I made myself stem my excitement by reasoning that Pomeroy likely had already spoken to Laybourne and Mr. Kingston, discovering that they were elsewhere when Warrilow died. Probably with witnesses, like the maid who'd tasted the tonic. Eden had no alibi, and therefore, Pomeroy had started the hue and cry after him.

"Thank you, Harry." I fished in my pocket for a coin. "For your trouble." I laid a shilling in his outstretched and very dirty hand.

"Thank you, sir." Harry doffed his cap and bowed to me as though I were an aristocrat. Drizzle glistened in his hair.

"You go on practicing," Brewster told him. "And you'll be up to scratch in no time. The trick is, ye pick an opponent what is equal to ye. Too tough, and they'll hurt ye. Too easy, and it's not much of a victory."

"Right you are, sir." Harry happily returned to punching at the air.

Mrs. Beadle opened the door for us. "You ought not to have given him so much, Captain," she said reprovingly.

"Nonsense," I said. "He's been very helpful. He told us a man called Kingston came about. Did you see him?"

"I did not. I was busy in the kitchen at the time. It's part of Harry's job to open the door to visitors when I'm elsewhere. Any rate, he didn't stay, did he? Mr. Warrilow didn't much want to see anyone."

But he'd seen someone after ten that night. Had dressed himself, admitted them, and been killed for his trouble.

I thanked Mrs. Beadle, and Brewster and I departed.

My next destination was the Custom House.

Brewster halted in dismay. "You have an uncanny knack for going exactly where it is most dangerous. Mr. Creasey dragged you off to his lair yesterday when you went to the Custom House."

"This time, I will have you at my side. I want to alert Mr. Seabrook that a potential smuggler of guns is living near where Warrilow did, and possibly killed him—or at least arranged for him to be killed. Laudanum and illness provide a good smokescreen."

"Send Mr. Pomeroy to tell him. We're too near Creasey's even now for my comfort."

"We will have a hackney stand by so we may flee as soon as I am finished speaking to Seabrook. Who knows? I might not even be able to see him. I am certain he is a busy man."

So speaking, I turned my steps back toward Cable Street, which would, if the map I'd consulted this morning was correct, take me more or less around the Tower and south again to the Custom House.

When we reached the Mint, Brewster signaled for a hackney. He was tired of walking in the rain, he said, plus he didn't want me nabbed by Mr. Creasey.

I'd been flagging and pretending not to be, so I let him help me into the coach with feigned reluctance. I admitted to myself that riding was preferable to tramping in the rain, but I so feared becoming what Laybourne had called me, a cripple, that I pushed myself to keep to my feet as much as possible.

The coach wound through a warren of streets north of the Tower and then back toward the Thames. This was a very old part of London, with such quaint street names as Seething Lane, Crutched Friars, and Pudding Lane, where London's Great Fire had begun, destroying much of the area around us. The streets were so built up now with houses and businesses, a hundred and so years later, that I would be hard-pressed to tell what had gone.

When we reached Lower Thames Street and I stepped down, Brewster had a word with the hackney driver, promising I'd pay him a generous tip if he'd wait.

"I'll have nothing left if I go on like this," I grumbled. I did so lightly, however. The allowance that Donata's man of business had insisted on made me a damn sight richer than I had been of old. Accepting the allowance had embarrassed me a bit but had assured Donata's solicitors that I'd have no need to rob Peter of his inheritance.

Brewster was in no mood for my humor. "You'll weather it."

He followed me into the Custom House, which was as teeming as ever. The din was deafening. I pushed my way through the long room toward the large clock, trying and failing to catch any clerk's attention.

"'Ere, you." Brewster simply seized a hurrying man with papers under his arm by the coat tails. "We want Mr. Seabrook."

The man glared at us, half-amazed, half-furious. "Make an appointment," he snarled. He yanked himself away from Brewster and was gone.

"They're customs officials," I said over the tumult. "Impossible to frighten them."

"Unnatural." Brewster feigned a shudder. "It's why His Nibs don't like dealing with them."

"Let us see what happens when we simply walk in." I led the way up the stairs I'd climbed with Eden, and to the office. The door was closed, and I knocked on it.

The spindly clerk who'd admitted us before stuck his head out, his expression turning more respectful when he saw me. "Mr. Seabrook is very busy, sir."

"Who is it, Bristow?"

"It's that captain from yesterday. And his … man."

"Ah, good. Send them in. I need a holiday from this mess. Captain Lacey." Seabrook stood as we entered, his piles of papers not noticeably diminished. "What brings you back to the Custom House?"

"A puzzlement." I accepted his offered seat, though Brewster decided to stand next to the door, glowering at Bristow, the clerk, until the young man departed, shutting us inside.

Seabrook frowned. "Explain?"

"I might have evidence of a man smuggling guns from Antigua. Or I might be jumping to conclusions."

Seabrook's eyes widened. "Do tell, Captain. If you have discovered something that heinous, you are obligated to report it."

"My thoughts precisely." I then related how Brewster had found the carbine stashed under Mr. Warrilow's floorboards and how Mr. Laybourne had reacted when I'd mentioned it. "What if Warrilow discovered Mr. Laybourne was bringing in a cache of weapons to sell, either here or on the Continent, took one as evidence, and threatened to report him? Warrilow might have decided to blackmail him instead of going to a magistrate, but in either case, Laybourne would have reason to kill him, or hire someone to kill him, before Warrilow could act on the knowledge."

Seabrook quietly took a seat and pulled out a paper and pen. He dipped the pen in ink and made a note. "This is dire."

"It is motive for murder."

"Quite." Seabrook shook his head. "This could be a very bad business, Captain. I thank you for alerting me. But I assure you, my men checked the cargo on the *Dusty Rose* thoroughly and found nothing of the sort."

"Perhaps the guns disappeared, just as other cargo on your docks has."

Seabrook grasped his pen between both hands. "A terrible thought. It is one thing to have crates of cocoa go astray, but not boxes of army carbines. Surely the captain of the ship would notice arms coming aboard." He trailed off thoughtfully. "Unless he is in on it."

"Not necessarily. Cargo is checked, but how thoroughly? Could a smuggler hide a few guns in boxes of, say, coffee? Layers of beans in the top and bottom, weapons in the middle? So that when a customs officer pulls off the lid and probes, he finds only the padding of coffee, or whatever the manifest shows the box should contain."

"Yes." Seabrook looked grim. "That has been done before, and we do keep a lookout for that, but some of these smugglers are dashed clever."

"Why bother?" This from Brewster in the corner. "Why try to hide such things among legitimate cargo? Be easier to hire your own ship, slip it into a hidden cove, and unload it under the customs officers' noses, with them being none the wiser ... Begging your pardon, sir."

The last was for politeness only. Brewster believed customs agents to be fools and had said so many a time.

"Such an endeavor would be expensive," Seabrook said, taking no offense. "One would have to be certain the captain one hires won't make off with the cargo and sell it himself. Brandy smuggling is rife and was uncontrollable during the war, but brandy isn't as perilous as a carbine in the wrong hands."

"Wouldn't smuggle guns, me," Brewster said. "Too dangerous by half."

"You are right, sir," Seabrook agreed. "One never knows if they'll be used to overthrow a king or simply to cause general mischief."

"The magistrates should know about Laybourne," I said. "If I'm wrong, then he'll be cleared."

"Of course." Seabrook nodded. "I'll send word at once, before he can flee to—High Harrogate, you said? Sounds as though once he sells his stash he will retire to blissful life in the country."

"He may have nothing to do with Warrilow's death," I said. "He was asleep at the time of the murder and has witnesses to say he took a dose of laudanum." I wanted to clear Eden of the crime, but I had to be fair.

"I will keep this in mind. Thank you for your candor, Captain."

The statement signaled that he was ready for us to go, and I rose. "One more question I have for you, Mr. Seabrook, while I am here. Your men seized an artwork from Mr. Fitzgerald, a painted box. Why did they?"

"Eh?" Seabrook's brow wrinkled a moment. "Oh, yes, that. I have chappies who are experts in art, and they wondered if Fitzgerald had stolen the thing. But Fitzgerald was able to produce paperwork that said it belonged to him.

He paid a man on St. Maarten three hundred guineas for it. Imagine."

"He must have wanted it very much," I agreed.

"That amount of money for a painted box, I ask you." Seabrook shook his head. "Well, I'm not much of a man for art. Commodities I understand. That is why the other fellows are in charge of looking at paintings and the like." He chuckled.

"So, you found nothing wrong with Fitzgerald's receipt?"

"No, all was legitimate. I charged him a duty for bringing an expensive luxury into the country, which he paid without fuss." Seabrook's eyes twinkled. "We customs men thrive on such things, you know."

I expected a response from Brewster, but he remained stoic, while I laughed courteously.

I had no more questions for the man and thanked him for his assistance.

"Not at all, Captain. I welcome the respite from the mundane tasks that fill my day. Drop in anytime. I enjoy chatting with those not in my tedious business."

Seabrook came forward and shook my hand. I thanked him again, and Brewster and I departed his office, much to the clerk's relief. Bristow slipped in to see his master as we left, carrying another ream of paper to slap on the overworked man's desk.

Brewster and I went down the stairs, navigated the long room, and made our way outside. The hackney waited, as promised, and Brewster hurried me toward it.

"That box is worth far more than three hundred guineas, guv," Brewster told me as the hackney driver took us toward Mayfair. He'd chosen to ride inside, likely to discuss this point.

"What did you say the artist's name was? Van ..."

"Van Hoogstraten. Probably is one of his. I'd need to have a look at it to be sure."

"Fitzgerald did say the man he bought it from was in need of money. Fitzgerald might have sensed this and driven a hard bargain."

"A very hard one. I think you should tell His Nibs about this."

"His Nibs made it very clear I was to stay out of his way," I countered.

"But he didn't know about this box then. He's keen to keep his eye on valuable artwork what comes in and out of the country."

"Why? So he can put his hands on it?"

Brewster shrugged. "Sometimes. And to make certain rivals aren't poaching his customers."

"Rivals such as Creasey?"

"Aye. Though Creasey might have nothing to do with Mr. Fitzgerald and his pretty box. But someone else might be using blokes like Fitzgerald to get pieces into England and on the market."

Cutting out James Denis and his high price for his trouble. I understood why Denis would wish to hear about such competition. I wondered if he'd take over the other fellow's business or eliminate it, and then decided I did not want to know.

"Seabrook found nothing wrong with the price," I said. "Thought it rather high."

"Begging your pardon, guv, but he's talking out his arse. His sort are happy to retrieve the fees, collect their pay for doing it, and go home, after cheating honest importers out of half their profit."

"He's only doing a job, Brewster," I said, amused. "Every man has to eat."

"He could take a different one," Brewster said stubbornly. "There's a reason His Nibs does everything he can to go around the customs agents."

More things I did not wish to know.

I wondered what Thompson had done with the carbine. I wanted to examine it again, as though it could give me a clue as to where it had come from. I thought of a man who might know. He was no longer in the King's army, but he remained close friends and cronies with those who were. He might be on half-pay, but he'd never truly left the military behind.

Brewster and I fell silent after that as the carriage took us back across London and into Mayfair to Curzon Street.

CHAPTER 16

*G*ibbons informed us coldly, when he at last opened the door to Number 45 a crack, that Mr. Denis wasn't seeing anyone. Only Brewster's insistence gained us admittance.

"I will inquire," Gibbons said in his chill tones. Several men hulked behind him, no trust in their eyes. "If he says he will not speak to you, you must depart. You no longer work for him, Mr. Brewster."

"Mayhap, but he'll not thank you if he finds out what we have to tell him some other way. So go on up, and be quick about it."

Gibbons had no fear in him. He gave Brewster a scornful stare and ascended the stairs, taking his time. He'd not ushered us into the reception room which left us waiting in the austere downstairs hall.

"Lewis," Brewster greeted another of Denis's men as he joined the first guards. "How goes the battle?"

Lewis, a smaller man than most Denis employed, shook his head. "He can't step out the door. We run off assassins every day. We've caught one or two." He closed his mouth and glanced at me as though not wanting to confess what they'd done to those they'd caught.

"He ought to go straight to Creasey and pull off his head," Brewster declared. "Enough of this."

"Creasey's well-guarded," Lewis said. "And he has magistrates and Runners in his pocket. Mr. Denis goes nigh him, he'll be arrested."

"Runners?" I asked. I thought of Timothy Spendlove, who'd do anything to get his hands on Denis. Would Spendlove partner with another known criminal to achieve his aims? I wasn't certain. As much as I did not see eye-to-eye with Spendlove, I knew he despised men like Creasey.

Lewis nodded at me. "You'd be astonished, Captain, at the goings on in high places."

I wasn't as astonished as all that. I'd lived in London long enough to understand that corruption was rampant.

"He'll see you." Gibbons's voice floated down from above. "For five minutes. Then you are to leave."

"Five minutes should suffice." I started up the stairs, my now-tired knee twinging. I reflected I might use up my entire five minutes climbing to Denis's study.

Gibbons showed us, however, not to the study, but to another room in the back of the house. Denis's bedchamber, I realized as we entered. A large bedstead with sumptuous velvet hangings stood between windows that overlooked the back garden — or would if the draperies weren't firmly closed. Candlelight from a single candelabra on a writing table lit the room, while a small blaze in the paneled fireplace lent the only warmth.

"You ought to leave London," I said to Denis as Gibbons shut the door and took up a place beside it. Another ruffian had been positioned near the windows. "It must be hell to live like this."

Denis, who was seated at the writing table perusing a paper, did not glance up. "I see no reason I should flee. I will prevail sooner or later."

"You are confident."

Denis at last laid down the page and pinned me with eyes that had grown even icier in the last days. "Tell me, if someone threatened to turn you and your family out of your grand house on South Audley Street, would you go? Or if they were bent on chasing your father-in-law off his land, would you blame him for staying on?"

"Of course not." Donata's relations had once been keen on getting hold of her son's estate, and I'd had them ejected. "Those are their homes."

"And this is mine. It is not simply a house to me, but a symbol of all I have achieved. The boy who slept in a dung cart is not about to give up his soft bed now."

"I do understand. But you can always return when it is over."

Denis's gaze held disdain. "You do not understand at all. If I flee London, it means I fear him, and then I am done for. Creasey is nothing to me. Will be nothing. I will win, Lacey, in the end."

His assuredness was unnerving.

"Very well, I will cease arguing with you. I am here at Brewster's insistence, though why he could not come to you with the information himself, I am not certain."

"Because you're honest, guv," Brewster said beside me. "Everyone believes you."

"I am not certain that is praise," I said. "However, it might be important."

I told Denis of my visit to Fitzgerald, the optical illusion box, and Brewster's certainty that it was an extremely valuable antique. I added Seabrook's information of Fitzgerald's receipt and what he'd paid for it.

Denis listened, Brewster and I remaining on our feet, as there was nowhere to sit. Denis frowned when I finished, the terrifying coldness in his eyes receding as interest replaced it.

"Mr. Brewster was quite correct. The boxes are rare and worth far more than the man paid for it. Fitzgerald's story of finding it on St. Maarten is unconvincing. What reason did he have for sailing there?"

"He was traveling through the islands, he said, but he did not say why. Perhaps looking for some way to make his fortune."

"If he sells this box he purchased so cheaply, he will."

"Could it be a forgery?" I suggested. "Perhaps that is why the Dutch fellow let it go so easily. Duping a foolish Englishman out of three hundred guineas."

Denis shook his head. "Even a forgery would be a masterwork. The boxes were painted with amazing precision, so that they could be viewed from several angles and yet have a perfect image each time. They were very fashionable in their day, but few survive. Once their popularity waned, those who inherited them did not understand them, and they were broken up or let go to ruin or forgotten. Such things are being discovered again — Bonaparte brought to light much artwork as he rode through Europe, robbing every city of its treasures for his museum."

"Some of that has been returned," I said. Or so Grenville, who kept himself informed of that sort of thing, had told me.

"Not all of it. Some owners had weak claims, or so it was said, and the art still resides in Paris. Or it is avowed that an artwork *did* go back to its former owner but has disappeared instead. This could be one such piece."

"The customs officials were satisfied with Fitzgerald's papers for it."

"Papers are easily forged. I would not be surprised if this Dutchman in reduced circumstances letting go an heirloom is a fabrication."

"Seems much trouble for bringing home one curiosity," I reflected.

"Unless this is not the only artwork he brought," Denis said calmly. "Perhaps it is the one he let the customs officials see, allowing them to seize it and check its provenance before returning it to him for the duty he paid. Mr. Fitzgerald has showed himself to be an affable if not overly bright collector, ready to help. If the rest of the cache is found, the magistrates will be more inclined to believe Fitzgerald when he expresses astonishment and declares it has nothing to do with him."

"Good Lord." My hand tightened on my walking stick. "If that is true, he is a very good actor. You certainly paint innocuous events as highly suspicious."

"Because my suspicions are usually correct. Such a ploy is one that an agent of mine might use—though Mr. Fitzgerald is *not* one of my agents. Until today, I'd never heard of the man. Depend upon it, he has brought in a hoard, and this is but the tip of it."

"When would he have done so?" I ran my hand through my damp hair. "Are you saying the entire time he lived in the Antilles, he'd been hunting artwork and shipping it home?"

"He might not have spent all his time there. Your friend, Major Eden, knew him only slightly, though the major lived four years on Antigua. You said Fitzgerald was unruly in his youth. Perhaps he was not as reconciled to being sent away as he has told you. A wealthy man's son could have easily traveled, especially during the chaos of the Revolution, the wars that followed, and Bonaparte's downfall, and found plenty to filch in Paris."

"Or he could have a hand in the cargo that's disappearing from the docks," I said, thinking hard. "Perhaps he ships his artwork disguised as more mundane items and then takes them once they are stored away."

"No, I believe Creasey is behind the stolen cargo," Denis said with conviction. "He'll have ships' captains in his pay, or the cargo masters, or both. They conveniently leave certain items off the manifest and quietly move them elsewhere. Then when those who have ordered the goods send for them, they've gone. The cargos have always been there, but by doctoring the cargo lists, they seem to vanish. I am certain that is what he did with the shipment from China he stole from me."

I would have to tell Thompson this theory. "Then you believe Fitzgerald is simply another smuggler, working on his own?"

"That is what I conclude from the information you have given me today."

I blew out a breath. "I wonder if anyone on that ship was not a thief or a smuggler."

"The passage to and from the islands holds much opportunity. Many will take advantage of it. I thank you for the story. I will try to discover if Mr. Fitzgerald is indeed an art smuggler and stop him. It is bad for business."

Denis spoke with an unruffled manner that belied the fact that he was hiding in his bedchamber, not allowing light to leak through the curtains.

"I can question Fitzgerald," I offered. "You have much to do."

Denis gave me a minute shake of his head. "He will only

lie and convince you otherwise. I can reach the truth. If he is innocent, then he is. But his is an unlikely tale."

"Very well." I did not like the idea of Denis pinning down the cordial Mr. Fitzgerald, but I had told Eden that I'd known congenial men who were the worst sorts of criminals. "I do dislike to see you cowed. Is there anything I can do to help?"

Brewster, Gibbons, and the other guard stiffened. Denis's expression did not change.

"My current circumstance is a precaution, not cowardice," Denis said. "I'd be foolish indeed to show myself in a window, when likely a sharpshooter has been placed in a house behind me, or on a rooftop. Mr. Creasey is thorough."

I glanced at the muffling draperies. "He would require a precise weapon for that distance."

"Such things exist. A crossbow, for instance, can be quite deadly and accurate in the correct hands."

I swallowed. I had not had to worry about such things as sharpshooters since leaving the army, and even then none of them had wielded anything as archaic as a crossbow.

"I hope you solve the problem soon," I said.

"I intend to. Good day, Captain. Please greet your wife for me and have a pleasant journey to Oxfordshire."

Denis wanted me gone, out of the way. One less worry for him. I would oblige him, whether I wished to or not. Brewster and Donata would make certain of it.

I nodded politely to him, and Brewster and I took our leave.

I SPENT ANOTHER PLEASANT NIGHT WITH MY WIFE AND daughter at home. After taking supper with Donata, I carried my books on chess from the library, set up the board in her

sitting room, and began working through various problems in
the tomes. One was in French, and I would have to brush up
on that language.

Donata watched me in part-amusement, part-alarm. "You
are not going to play that awful man again, are you?"

"I have no desire to." I studied a page then moved a rook
to box in a king. I remembered this play, I was pleased to
note. "But the match intrigued me, and I thought I'd find out
what I recalled. Perhaps your father will fancy a game."

"He might." Donata relaxed and went back to her newspapers. "Though I will declare both of you mad."

I thought of the chess-obsessed gentleman from whom I'd
taken lessons to pass the time in Pairs and conceded she could
be right. But then, Gabriella might enjoy learning to play, if
she did not know how already, and so might Peter. He was a
bright boy and would catch on quickly. I looked forward to
teaching him.

We retired to bed before long, Donata reposing with me
once more. I could grow used to having her at my side every
night, though I knew it was highly unfashionable for an aristocratic lady to share a bedchamber with her husband.

I was again in an amiable mood in the morning as I made
my way down to breakfast. Bartholomew served me, and
Barnstable set my correspondence and a morning newspaper
at my elbow.

I scanned the few letters I would read thoroughly later
and unfolded the newspaper. About halfway down the first
page, words in large type leapt out at me.

Murder in Cable Street.
Horrific death of a gentleman just returned from the West Indies.

CHAPTER 17

I had shoved a large hunk of toasted bread into my mouth, and I half choked on it. Coughing, I slurped down coffee even as I leapt from my chair.

Bartholomew, who'd lingered to see if the sideboard needed to be replenished, started back in alarm, the lid to a silver tray in his hand.

"Are you all right, sir? What's happened?"

I waved the newspaper at him. "They've killed Laybourne." My words were muffled until I gulped more coffee and cleared my throat. "The chap from Eden's ship. Where is Brewster?"

Bartholomew slammed the lid onto the tray of sliced ham. "I'll find him, Captain. Want a coach?"

"Please."

We dashed from the room, Bartholomew and his youthful energy taking him out ahead of me. He ran down the back stairs while I made for the front door, calling for my coat and hat.

A hired coach arrived as Brewster emerged from the outside stairs at the same moment I exited the house.

"Wapping Docks," I told the driver. "The River Police."

The driver pursed his lips but nodded, starting the horses the moment Brewster and I were aboard.

"I killed him," I announced.

Brewster's eyes widened in alarm. "Don't say such when you're near the River Police. Ye were in bed all night with your lady."

"I mean that my words killed him. I reported my suspicions to Seabrook, and Seabrook said he'd tell a magistrate. Whoever was working with Laybourne knew this and murdered him before he could be arrested and reveal his cohorts."

"Or a passing burglar did it. Mayhap there is a gang robbing houses in that area and knocking those in the head what try to stop them."

"Hardly likely, and you know this. Depend upon it, Laybourne was a gun runner, but only part of a gang. If he went before a magistrate, he might well decide to give up the names of everyone involved. What would he have to lose?"

Brewster grunted, but ceased arguing.

Thompson was in when we reached the house of the River Police and came outside to meet me.

"Bad business," he said, before I even spoke. "The Constable of the Tower has sent men to investigate, and so has Whitechapel. I heard this morning and went to the house in Cable Street. Mr. Laybourne's throat was slit."

I had perused the newspaper story while I'd waited for the coach and Brewster. The journalist had relished in the gore, talking about the blood splashed on the walls and the pools on the floor, though he'd likely not seen it for himself.

"Do they have any idea of the culprit?"

"None at all," Thompson answered. "The landlady heard nothing. Was asleep, she says. Her bloodshot eyes tell me she was inebriated, so I believe her. The front door was unlocked —anyone could have gone inside. But Mr. Laybourne was the target, apparently, as no other tenant was hurt, and nothing was stolen. None of the lodgers heard anything either."

Thompson's pained expression told me what he thought of these heedless lodgers.

"I believe he was the owner of the carbine we found at Warrilow's." I quickly told him of my visit to Laybourne yesterday, and what Denis had suggested about the stolen cargo. "I told the customs official who had searched Laybourne's ship. He reported to the magistrates."

Thompson's thin brows rose. "I'd heard nothing of this, but the other houses don't always share information. True, the murder might have to do with weapons smuggling, but one gun in pieces is not the same as finding a stash."

"If that stash can be found now," I said glumly. "I ought to have marched Laybourne straight to you or Sir Montague in Whitechapel instead of leaving him to his meal."

"You cannot arrest every man you speak to for showing fear. He might have been worried about something entirely different."

"Yet, it seems he was not."

"True, but now I and the other magistrates will be on the lookout. That carbine was new, not a collector's gun. And your Mr. Denis might be right about how the cargos are being stolen. Doctoring the manifests mid-voyage—perhaps taking out a page or two—is a clever way to go about it. When the ships are unloaded, all the goods are accounted for, and the extra boxes are carted away before anyone realizes it." He tapped his lips in thought. "Are these weapons part of that cargo? Perhaps loaded with some other goods and then that page of the manifest dropped overboard along the journey?"

"Can you question the ship's captain?"

Thompson pulled his threadbare coat tighter across his chest. "My job is to make certain thieves don't swarm aboard the ships as they lay at anchor and help themselves to goods. Or steal from the warehouses. Smuggling is up to the excise men and the company the captain works for. Not that we don't assist each other from time to time."

Thompson normally maintained a calm facade but I saw a spark of animation in his eyes. Catching a gun smuggler would bring him accolades.

"This is obviously a dangerous venture," I said. "I had the idea that Laybourne murdered Warrilow—somehow— because Warrilow had discovered the guns being transported and either threatened to expose him or demanded money for his silence. But now Laybourne is dead. Killed by the man he worked for? Perhaps the true gun smuggler heard Laybourne would be questioned and feared what he would tell. The same way he feared what Warrilow knew."

"Many speculations," Thompson said. "What we do know is that Warrilow had a stolen weapon and that Laybourne looked worried when you mentioned it."

"May I examine the carbine once more? I might learn more about where it came from—I used to shoot the things once upon a time."

Thompson shook his head. "I handed it to a commander in the Seventh Regiment. He confirmed it was indeed a new weapon and wondered where I'd found it."

"Where did the *smugglers* obtain it?" I asked.

"A question worth answering. The guns might originate here in England, might have been on the docks awaiting transport, and Laybourne and his colleagues stole them.

Might have had nothing to do with the ship Laybourne and Warrilow sailed on. Perhaps Warrilow was passing once they landed and saw them."

"More speculation." I fidgeted. Brewster, who never liked being near any sort of police, had walked down the docks. "Do you mind if I speak with someone from the army about it?"

"Not at all. Please share what you discover."

"I will, of course."

We shook hands, and I stumped away to find Brewster.

He was having a chat with a man fishing off the end of a wharf. Around us, the tall ships loomed, hulls like giant walls, bare masts reaching for the gray skies. I hadn't sailed in a ship like this since my journey to Egypt, which had been a fine one. I'd enjoyed the fresh wind in my face, the bright sun, and glimpses of faraway shores. Grenville, on the other hand, had been miserable with seasickness, poor fellow.

As I approached, Brewster gave the fisherman a nod and ambled toward me. "Always good to speak to the local folk," he said.

"Does he know anything about the murders?"

"Not really. Heard of them—everyone around here has. But he does know about what's on ships and where they come from. He fishes in that spot every day."

"Ah. Then he has solved the mystery of the guns and knows the mastermind?"

Brewster sent me a disparaging glance. "Very amusing, guv. But he watched the *Dusty Rose* unload. Sometimes, if he's near, he'll help lift a particularly heavy crate or extra box. He says before *Dusty Rose* docked, there were men extremely restless that the ship was late. Most of the dockhands are resigned, like, when a ship isn't on time—as many aren't. They just do the job when it's in front of them. These blokes were nervous and unhappy. When the ship finally came in, they leapt out ready to cart things off. Took off the first load—that is once custom agents were done nicking half of it."

"Were they upset about the customs men?" I asked. "If they were waiting for their contraband, I imagine the excise men crawling all over the cargo was terrifying."

"Fisherman didn't say. They just champed at the bit until the cargo master shouted they could start unloading, and then they dove in, grabbed crates, shoved them on carts and dashed off. Never came back. The other dock men had to do the rest of the unloading on their own."

"Had he ever seen these impatient men before?"

"He said not, but he couldn't be sure. But they weren't friends he's made over the years, and none greeted him."

"Thank you." I turned to Brewster as we approached our coach. "Very thorough questioning."

Brewster shrugged and steadied me with a strong arm as I scrambled into the carriage. "Watching His Nibs put people through it for so long, I learned the knack."

I WENT TO LAYBOURNE'S BOARDING HOUSE, THOUGH I knew I'd find nothing there. Indeed, when we arrived, the curious had flocked to the place, wanting a piece of stone or brick from the house where a murder had occurred. I pushed my way through, but the landlady refused to let me in.

"Go on," she shouted at me from the doorstep. "How do I know you ain't the murderer, come back to finish me off?"

"I assure you madam—"

"Be off with ya. And take that ruffian with you. Cook says he was downstairs yesterday, asking all sorts."

"Waste of me time," Brewster growled. "And not even a cuppa tea for me pains."

The landlady slammed the door. I waded through the crowd to the carriage, Brewster following.

Before I could ascend, I caught sight of Harry, who'd presumably come to view the scene as well. I waved to him. He hesitated, but when he saw Brewster with me, he slid readily through the throng to us.

"Another murder, sir," he announced when he reached Brewster. "We ain't safe. I told my gran she should move away, but she said that was nonsense."

I imagined Mrs. Beadle did not want to shut up her house and the income it brought her.

"I think I saw the murderer," Harry declared proudly to Brewster. "I didn't confront him or nothing. You said to only fight those what I was as good as. So I hid."

I opened my mouth to question him, but Brewster held up his hand, and I subsided. "Good lad," Brewster said. "Never start a fight ye can't finish. Who was it that you saw?"

"The tall, thin bloke I saw outside our house, before Mr. Warrilow was done over."

The tall thin bloke was probably Mr. Kingston, the missionary.

"Did he go inside?" I asked, unable to remain quiet.

"No. He knocked on the door, but the landlady sent him away."

"What time was this?" I went on.

Harry considered. "Maybe seven of the clock? Me gran sent me around to the baker's down this street for bread. He sells the loaves leftover for a lesser price. I was walking back with the bread when I saw him. Oh, and the major."

"Major Eden?" I asked in dismay.

"Aye, it were him. He were walking along, easy as

anything. He went around the corner yonder." The boy pointed to the east end of the road.

I stifled curses. What the devil had Eden been doing in Cable Street on a night a man who lodged there had been killed?

If Pomeroy discovered this information, he'd not hesitate to arrest Eden anew, and this time make it stick.

———

"WANT TO GO WRING THE STORY OUT OF MAJOR EDEN?" Brewster asked as we rumbled away in the coach. Harry had got another shilling from me for his information.

"I do, though there's also another visit I'd like to make. But I'll do that one alone."

Brewster regarded me in irritation. "No, you won't. I won't be explaining to your lady wife why I let you get bashed about because you insisted on being private. My life won't be worth a farthing. I'll go if I have to stand in the street to be run down by passing carts."

I hid a sigh. The errand would be taxing enough without having to explain to Donata why I'd gone. She'd have the truth out of Brewster quickly enough. There was no question which one of us he'd obey if pressed.

"St. James's first then," I said. "We'll find Eden and ask him what his business was here last night."

The task was not so simple. When we arrived in St. James's Place, Eden was out. His landlady had no idea where he'd gone or when he'd return. No, he hadn't moved out—all his things were still in his rooms, and he'd bade her a cheerful good morning as he'd gone.

I handed her my card. "Please tell him to call upon me at

his earliest convenience," I said. I touched my hat and departed.

"So polite we are," Brewster growled as we walked away. "*At his earliest convenience.* I'd say I'd pull all his teeth out if he didn't come to me right away."

"I doubt such a threat would frighten Eden. Besides, if you tell a man you'll pull out his teeth if he *doesn't* come to you, it hardly motivates him to find you."

"Yes, it do. Because he'd know if I ever found him again, he'd be gumming porridge the rest of his sorry life."

Statements like these made me realize why I preferred Brewster as a friend, not an enemy.

We emerged from St. James's Place to the corner where the carriage waited. "Brook Street," I told the driver.

Brewster was silent as we traveled the short distance northward into Mayfair, through Berkeley Square and on to Brook Street. Brewster offered to remain in the hackney, but I told him he might as well take some relaxation in the kitchen. Here, I knew, they'd give him tea, or beer, or whatever he liked.

I plied the knocker on the front door and was told by the cool footman who opened it that Mrs. Brandon was indeed at home and would receive me in her breakfast room.

CHAPTER 18

"Gabriel, how delightful." Louisa Brandon came to me in a waft of lemony scent and kissed my cheek. "Please, sit. Coffee, Albert." This last was spoken to another footman, who had the silver pot in his hand and was setting down a porcelain cup at a place opposite Louisa's before she finished her command.

I bowed. "Thank you for seeing me and rewarding my appallingly bad manners."

I took the offered seat, relaxing into its comfort. Louisa's room was bright and sunny—she loved yellow—filled with touches of softness, such as the cushions I reposed against and the thick carpet on the floor.

"Friends do not stand on manners. How is Anne?" Louisa sent me her warmest of smiles. "Is she not the most beautiful babe on this earth?"

One of Louisa's greatest regrets was that she had never borne children. Her series of miscarriages were responsible for the only lines on her face. She'd turned her attention to my children with great joy, reveling in details of Anne's babyhood and every change it wrought. She'd been thus with Gabriella as well, which had earned the great jealousy of my first wife.

"I will not argue about that," I said, my pride surging. "I am very sure she can say *Papa*, but Donata tells me I am dreaming this."

"It will not be long." Louisa thanked Albert for pouring the coffee and waved him off. He set down the pot, bowed, and retreated from the room. "Anne will be talking, and running everywhere, driving you spare, as your Mr. Brewster might say."

"I look forward to it. And I know she adores her Aunt Louisa."

Louisa sent me a shrewd glance as she lifted her cup. She drank tea, but she kept coffee for her husband or wayward guests.

"I will not press my way into Anne's affection. The last thing I want is to make Mrs. Lacey unhappy."

"Donata knows my fondness for you has taken on the ease of friendship." I sipped coffee, enjoying its rich flavor. I hadn't been this warm or comfortable since I'd left my house earlier this morning.

"That you love her distractedly is obvious," Louisa said. "I was thinking more of *my* foolishness regarding you. She knows all."

"It was a long time ago." Louisa had come to me once, begging me to run away with her. I had been sorely tempted, but we both had been glad I'd sent her home.

"Not all that long ago. I have come to my senses, but a wife is aware of a husband's past and never quite loses the worry."

I knew Louisa spoke not only of Donata, but of herself. Brandon had given her cause to doubt him more than once.

I let the subject drop. I wanted Anne to know the Brandons, who had been an important part of my life, but equally I did not want to upset Donata by forcing the matter.

"As enchanting as I always find your company, I actually came here to see your husband," I said. "Is he about?"

"He went to Tattersall's. It is hunting season, you know, and when we return to the country, he wants to put a new horse into the field. His usual mount is aging and will be retired to the pasture."

"Fortunate horse. If Brandon will return soon, I'll sit and enjoy the coffee. If it will be a long time, he can call on me, if he's able. I want to ask him about carbines."

Louisa's brows rose. "Carbines? You intrigue me. Truth to tell, I have no idea how long he will be. It is Aloysius, looking over horseflesh. He becomes immersed."

I understood this. All cavalrymen were horse mad.

"In any case, I will drink this excellent coffee and visit. We'll chat like old friends who haven't seen each other in years. Ah ... Miles Eden has resurfaced."

"Has he?" Louisa asked with interest. "He rather disappeared after Waterloo. He went to Antigua, did he not?"

"Indeed." I told her the tale, including the fact that our old friend Eden had been accused of murder. Louisa listened with rapt attention.

"Surely not, Gabriel," she said when I'd finished. "Captain Eden—Major Eden—was a bit reckless, but never murderous. Why would he creep into a gentleman's bedchamber in the middle of the night and bash him on the head? Still less, slit his throat." She shivered. "It's horrible, and Miles Eden is not a horrible man."

"I wish I knew why he'd gone to Cable Street last night. I couldn't find him this morning to give me his explanation."

"I admit that looks a bit suspicious, though he might have had a perfectly reasonable excuse."

"Will it be reasonable enough for Pomeroy?"

"Or reasonable enough for you?" Louisa took another sip of tea. "You seem to want him to be guilty."

I stared in amazement. "I do not. I like Eden. His high spirits helped me through many a battle and again when Carlotta deserted me. I fear he is responsible, rather. I do not want to let sentiment stand in the way of the truth."

"You are letting *worry* stand in the way of it. If he is guilty, then there is nothing more for you to do, and you walk away from the matter. A much more difficult task is to believe in him in spite of the evidence—or in spite of coincidences. You stood by Aloysius when no one else, including me, was convinced of his innocence."

"Because I know Brandon well."

"Because you did not want to deal with the aftermath, including his distraught widow."

I chortled at her demure glance over her teacup, consciously making light of the strained agitation we'd both experienced at that time. "Nonsense. I knew Brandon had done nothing more heinous than being a fathead, though it was devilish tricky to prove it. Eden might be just as much of a fathead as your husband."

At this auspicious moment, the door burst open and Colonel Brandon strode inside.

My former commander, who was as robust as when I'd met him twenty-three years ago, took in his wife and his one-time rival companionably sharing a beverage in her morning room. His brow clouded, then forcibly cleared, no doubt as he recalled that I'd married a beautiful society woman who held my devotion.

"Lacey," Brandon greeted me as I rose. "Just bought a fine hunter. Goes phenomenally well. Come riding with me when you return from the country, and I'll show him off to you."

"I will," I said. I was as mad about horseflesh as Brandon ever was.

"Now." Brandon threw himself into a chair and held out a cup for Albert, who'd rushed in behind him, to fill it from the silver coffeepot. "Why are you here irritating my wife?"

I waited until Albert had finished fussing around Brandon and departed before I leaned to him and spoke in a low voice.

"Why would new British carbines show up in Antigua, available for smuggling back to England?"

Brandon had been taking a casual sip of coffee. His face went purple, and he quickly set down the cup and swallowed.

"Where have you heard such rubbish?"

"Not rubbish. I held one such carbine in my hands, before I turned it over to Mr. Thompson of the Thames River Police. He said he gave it to the Seventh Regiment."

"It's a cavalry weapon," Brandon said. "Nothing to do with foot-wobblers."

"That may be, but Thompson isn't an army man. I imagine it's all the same to him."

Brandon scoffed, as though every person should be born understanding the contention between cavalry, artillery, and infantry.

"Are the regiments being rearmed?" I asked. "I must wonder how a smuggler came upon these weapons."

Brandon heaved a long sigh. He glanced sideways at Louisa, as though contemplating commanding her to leave, so the men could discuss important issues. She returned his gaze serenely, remaining in place.

"The weapons aren't British," Brandon said, resigned. "That is, they are not meant to be. The Spanish are losing their holds on the countries of South America. Those coun-tries—Venezuela, for instance—are pushing for indepen-dence. Almost no one is coming to their aid. But arms find their way across the ocean, though no one knows a thing about it, do they? Also, and this is something you will tell no man, Lacey ..." Brandon leaned to me and lowered his voice. "The regiments are on alert, with new weapons being made ready, in case the disaster at Manchester is repeated."

We descended into uncomfortable silence. Earlier that summer, workers in Manchester had gathered to listen to Henry "Orator" Hunt who was leading rallies, agitating for more of the laboring classes to gain the vote. On a hot day in August, hussars and local yeomanry were sent in to disperse the crowd in St. Peter's Field who'd come to hear his speeches, and arrest Hunt. Those gathered had resisted, and in the ensuing chaos, nineteen had died, and hundreds more, including children, had been hurt. The fact that many of these attacking hussars had been heroes of Waterloo goaded the newspapers to label it the "Peterloo Massacre."

The tragedy had been terrible, but the government had quickly brought forth acts banning all such meetings and allowed local magistrates to search homes for weapons. The memory of the revolution in France was fresh, and many feared such an uprising in Britain. Even the press had been gagged, though I scarcely saw any obedience there.

"So they are minting new weapons in case of an uprising?" I asked.

"That is what I hear." Brandon spread his fingers in a gesture of uncertainty. "The surplus goes to South America, via the Caribbean islands."

"Where the shipments are waylaid." I pondered. "Stolen outright, perhaps, and sold where a profit can be had. Shipped straight back through London and presumably to the Continent."

"There would be plenty of customers," Brandon said somberly. "The Greeks are working themselves up to battle the Turks. The Austrians are trampling over the Italian states, and anyone else who bothers them. Anarchists in France stalk the king's family, wanting no more monarchy. The absence of Bonaparte simply lets whatever his menace kept buried bubble to the surface."

"Bloody hell," I said softly. I glanced at Louisa to apologize for my language, but she appeared as unhappy about Brandon's story as I was. "I've not been paying much attention to the wider world, I admit."

"Best that way," Brandon answered. "Especially if you are prone to melancholia."

He had a point. There was little I could do about much of this. Better to be concerned with my daughter learning to walk and Peter going off to school than about who stole guns meant for one revolution and sold them to men planning another.

On the other hand, I certainly did not want my son and daughter to be hurt by all the machinations that might rise to engulf us.

"Gabriel fears that Miles Eden might be involved," Louisa said in her gentle voice. "I told him those fears are ungrounded."

Brandon did not dismiss them. "I knew Eden well. I can imagine his hand in this."

"Can you?" I asked as Brandon sipped his coffee. "Louisa has only finished convincing me he would never stoop to such a thing."

Brandon shot us both a dark look. "He was always a charmer, was Eden. A good man in a fight. But I noticed he never did anything that did not benefit himself in some way. Saved men in battle—then earned a medal, a promotion, more pay. Volunteered to join the regiment in Antigua, then left when drilling for nothing became dull. I correspond with the colonel in charge there, and he was disappointed in Eden. Eden found nothing in peace for heroics, so he bought a plantation and rescued the slaves working there. But if Eden was so adamant about saving the enslaved, he could work to ban slavery altogether, as others have done. But he does not. When he could not make a fortune in the islands, he came home—obviously. Perhaps he discovered the gun smuggling along the way and decided it was dangerous enough to interest him."

"That is possible," I had to acknowledge. Eden had always enjoyed charging into bad situations. I noted that when I'd first gone to see Creasey, Eden had immediately leapt in beside me to face him.

However, he'd vanished for my second encounter with Creasey, and I still did not know why.

"The murders were rather cold-blooded," I said. "Not like Eden at all."

"Were they?" Brandon asked. "Or were they the result of quarrels? A man refusing to … what? Give Eden his share?"

"Or, he was crusading *against* them," I said slowly. "Stopping the smugglers the most daring way he knew how—by confronting and killing them. Though I still believe Warrilow was a blackmailer, not a smuggler. He seemed to pride himself discovering the faults in others."

"*I* believe you both cast Major Eden in the wrong role," Louisa said. "I knew him as well, remember. If he wished to crusade, he'd have talked you into joining him, Gabriel. You also see yourself as a champion of the weak. I simply do not think Miles Eden has it in him to smuggle weapons and murder others to keep them quiet about it."

Brandon remained unconvinced, and I reluctantly admitted I shared his skepticism.

"I will have to find Eden," I said. "And persuade him to tell me what he is up to."

"Please leave him unscathed," Louisa said. "You were once very good friends, and he might be innocent of all this."

"I will be most happy if he is."

Louisa frowned at me, then she deliberately turned the topic to innocuous things—my upcoming journey to Oxfordshire and the subsequent one to Gloucestershire. Brandon expressed interest in Grenville's horses, speculating he'd have the best on the field. Which brought the conversation back around to his new hunter.

As we conversed, I recalled long evenings in the Brandons' tent in Portugal and Spain, when we'd recount the happenings of the day and speak of what we'd do in the faraway time after we'd retired. We'd been excellent friends, inseparable and devoted. It had been unthinkable that I'd have any time in my life when I'd not be with Louisa and Colonel Brandon, laughing and sharing troubles. They were the pair who'd helped me find an escape from my miserable upbringing, taught me to discover my talents, stood by me when I'd lost my wife and daughter.

Then Brandon had destroyed our complacent happiness with his jealousy and rage, and I'd destroyed it with my temper and frustration.

Much had happened since the day he'd sent me out to die and I'd returned to spite him. I believe now Brandon had been much relieved to see me, or at least had come to regret those rash orders.

We'd recovered our friendship somewhat, but as we chatted in Louisa's warm chamber, I knew the tension hadn't quite eased. Beneath our conviviality was a strain that might always have been there, though I'd been too absorbed in my own troubles when younger to notice it.

I had a feeling that tension always would be present, though I was glad that we could at least chat about inconsequential events and part cordially when the coffee was finished.

I'D HAD NO WORD FROM EDEN, I DISCOVERED WHEN I returned home. I took a small meal in the dining room, hungry after my truncated breakfast, trying to ignore the chaos into which the house was erupting.

We were vacating for several months tomorrow, possibly until after New Year's. Boxes, bags, crates, and baskets had sprung up in the halls and on the stairs, with servants dashing up and down to make certain we left nothing behind.

I had once expressed amusement at this procedure, as we usually traveled to furnished homes, such as Donata's father's, where they had plenty of bedding and foodstuffs. This had received disparagement from everyone from my wife to the boot boy. His little lordship and his mother could not travel like rustics with all their worldly goods in a small pack.

I'd decided not to explain that *I* could, but bowed out and left them to it.

Once Brewster had taken some food and ale in the kitchen, I resumed my quest. A footman began hammering a crate closed, the thunderous banging following me out the door.

Another hackney took us back to St. James's, but Eden had not returned. I chewed my lip, not happy with his absence. If Eden had nothing to do with the smuggling or the killings, then the true murderer might regard him as a threat who knew too much. That person had not shied from murdering the sickly Laybourne.

"Lambeth," I told the coachman. "A parish church near the Archbishop's Palace."

The driver stared down at me. Between his high hat and scarf over his face to keep out the rain, I saw only glittering dark eyes in a belligerent gaze.

"That's not an address, guv," he barked.

"Try St. Mary's," Brewster, a child of South London, said behind me. "Near Bedlam."

CHAPTER 19

The driver shook his head at the follies of gentlemen who wanted to go anywhere close to Bethlehem Hospital, but he waited for us to climb aboard, and we started off.

The coach trundled from St. James's Street along Pall Mall to Whitehall via Cockspur Street and Charing Cross.

We rolled past the Admiralty and the Horse Guards, and I wondered what either of them knew about men stealing British-made guns to sell to those rebelling around the Continent. Whatever went on inside the offices in those thick-walled buildings did not show on their facades.

The driver took Westminster Bridge across to Lambeth, the stench of the Thames rising to us. The cold and rain kept the smell dampened a bit, but only a trifle.

Beyond the bridge were open lots, the chimneys of a brewery wafting smoke not far away. To our right were a few small farms, still bright with greens. The pile of Lambeth palace lifted beyond them.

The driver turned south at a crossroads, toward the dark bulk of Bethlehem Hospital.

I hoped we would not have to inquire there. It was a prison for madmen, though they styled themselves as a place of respite. Bedlam took in the mad whose families no longer could care for them. Sometimes it imprisoned those whose families wanted rid of them—they'd coerce the courts to declare said member of the family insane. A person might go mad inside those crumbling walls, even if they had not been thus when they arrived. The hospital gained fees by opening the halls to ordinary folk, who could pay to see the poor souls screeching and muttering to themselves in their cells.

The driver halted at a small church a few yards shy of Bedlam's gates. I settled my hat and went around to the vestry, hoping someone would be in.

They were—the vicar, readying himself for an evening service with his choirmaster. Both assumed harried expressions when I asked about the Kingstons, but the vicar directed me to a small house around the corner. He was very polite, but his manner indicated he thought I ought to take myself a few paces down the road to Bedlam for asking for the Kingstons.

The house was a small cottage that had been squashed between larger buildings as this area developed. Only two stories, made of brick, it looked snug and quaint, with ivy growing over its front windows.

My knock was answered by a woman of unexpected tallness. She was almost my height, and I stand above six feet.

"Good afternoon, madam." I extracted a card. "I have come to speak to Mr. Kingston."

"My husband." The woman accepted the card, read the name, turned it over as though there might be surreptitious lettering on the back, and nodded at me. "Do come in. I have heard of you, Captain Lacey, from Sir Gideon Derwent, who is as godly a man as I have ever met. Have you come to aid us on our journey?"

"Journey?" I removed my hat as I stepped into a small, flagstone hall. Brewster was a step behind me, stubbornly refusing to leave my side. The woman did not seem to mind him. "I heard you just returned from Antigua. Are you setting off again?"

Mrs. Kingston laughed, a merry sound. I understood why Eden called her spirited. "Aren't you a one? I mean our never-ending journey to spread the word of the Lord. We can save as many folk right here in London as we can around the world. Though I have to admit that watching savages suddenly see the light is quite rewarding."

She beamed as she led me through the surprisingly deep house to a room in the back. "Mr. Kingston, we have visitors."

The chamber we entered was a cozy study filled with books, worn from use. A window showed a back garden with struggling greenery.

The man who rose from behind a desk was tall. *Stretched* might be a better adjective. He was extraordinarily thin, as though someone had taken him by the top of his head and pulled him upward.

He was not sickly, however, as Laybourne had been. This man was robust, with interested eyes, healthily pink skin under his island tan, and a straight back. When Mrs. Kingston stood next to him, she did not appear as tall. They were well matched in size, and I wondered if Kingston had chosen her as his bride so he would not have to stoop to kiss her cheek.

Not that either seemed inclined toward intimacy. They both wore severe black, the white stock around Kingston's neck a sharp contrast. Mrs. Kingston's cap was pale gray, and she wore a fichu around her collar of the same color.

Their somber dress did not make them somber people. Mrs. Kingston's manner was lively. "Just think, Mr. Kingston. This man is a friend to Sir Gideon Derwent."

Mr. Kingston brightened. "A blessed gentleman, is Sir Gideon. He bathes in sorrow because his wife will leave him soon, but please tell him to rejoice that she will be safe in the arms of Jesus."

I did not believe Sir Gideon or his family would like to be told to rejoice in anything, but I kept my opinion to myself.

"I am also acquainted with Major Eden, a fellow passenger on your voyage," I said.

Mr. Kingston began to answer, but Mrs. Kingston cut in. "Yes, Major Eden. Such fine manners. Quite gallant. Utterly depraved, of course, but perhaps he will come around in the end."

"Depraved?" Not a word I'd use to describe him.

"He does not follow the path of righteousness," Mrs. Kingston said. "I tried to help him. I can only hope my words went through, and he finds his way."

"I imagine he will muddle along," I said. "I came to ask you about Mr. Warrilow." I decided to dive in headlong. "You were seen visiting him the evening of the night he died." I directed the words to Mr. Kingston.

That man flushed. "Well, I ..."

"Of course Mr. Kingston was there," Mrs. Kingston broke in firmly. "Mr. Warrilow needed us."

I raised my brows, aware of Brewster, who'd remained silent, inching closer to me. "For what purpose?"

"To save him, of course," Mrs. Kingston said in triumph. "Oh, no, Captain, I do not mean to save his life. I mean to continue what we'd begun on board ship, the saving of his soul. I only hope my husband was in time."

"Why did you decide to go that evening?" I asked. "Did you make an appointment with him?"

Mrs. Kingston looked blank, but Mr. Kingston burst in, "He sent for me." He said the words rapidly, as though fearing his wife would answer for him.

I blinked in surprise. "Sent for you?"

"I do not know why. I was never able to speak to him. I was turned away."

"Because Mr. Warrilow refused to see you?"

"Indeed." Mr. Kingston nodded. "So I—"

"That's what the landlady said," Mrs. Kingston finished for him. "Though why he'd send for my husband and then not admit him is puzzling. But it is heartening that he wanted to speak to Mr. Kingston. Perhaps he knew somehow it was his last night on earth and wished guidance into the palace of the Lord." She clasped her hands.

Mr. Kingston was a bit more skeptical. "Before we left the docks, he asked me to visit," he said while his wife caught her breath. "He told me where he was taking rooms but never said why he wanted to see me."

"He had a premonition." Mrs. Kingston nodded with confidence.

Or, I thought, he wanted to confide in Kingston about the weapons and who had been smuggling them. Kingston, in Warrilow's opinion, would be honest enough to report it and respectable enough to be believed. But maybe Warrilow then had second thoughts about asking for Kingston's help and decided instead to blackmail Laybourne for whatever money he could obtain.

Then again, perhaps Kingston himself was the smuggler. What more innocuous guise for a gun runner than a pair of missionaries who irritated all with their proselytizing?

"I see," I said. "Why did you return to Warrilow's later

that night?" Harry had said he thought he'd seen Mr. Kingston in the street after Warrilow had gone to bed. "And Mr. Laybourne yesterday?"

Mr. Kingston blinked, and Mrs. Kingston turned to him in shock. "Mr. Laybourne?" she repeated.

"I did not." Kingston shook his head. "I never went back to see Warrilow, and I did not cross the river at all yesterday. I was assisting the vicar."

"I never saw you at the church." Mrs. Kingston's eyes narrowed.

"I assure you, my dear." Mr. Kingston flushed.

I did not pursue the question, but I wondered whether he lied, and why. "Thank you. I appreciate you admitting me into your charming home."

"It is good to be back," Mrs. Kingston said. "Though we'll be off to foreign parts soon enough. They need us."

"How well did you know Mr. Warrilow?" I asked. "Were you acquainted with him on Antigua? I inquire because none know of his family—none have come to collect his body or any of his things."

Mr. Kingston took a step forward, as though to block his wife from answering first. "We did not know him at all. Met him for the first time aboard, though I'd heard of him. He owned a small plantation. Not a kind person."

"But everyone is worth saving." Mrs. Kingston jumped in as soon as she was able. "I do not believe he had any family living, but not to worry. We will donate his things to our charities and see that he has a good Christian burial."

Brewster shifted. "Why would ye? If ye never knew him? And he was a right bastard, begging your pardon, missus."

Mrs. Kingston did not flinch at Brewster's language. "God welcomes even the direst sinners into his kingdom. It is obvious Mr. Warrilow had repented his evil ways and wanted

Mr. Kingston's help in his last hours. He is now with the Lord, the angels rejoicing that he came to them."

I could only imagine Mr. Warrilow snarling at these angels until they fled him, but I let Mrs. Kingston have her imagined happy ending. I recalled that Eden said the Kingstons had fought hard to put through anti-slavery bills, and I respected them for that.

"I bid you good day," I said, making another bow. "May you have safe travels."

"We always do, Captain," Mrs. Kingston said brightly. "The Lord keeps us well on the seas. He saved Jonah from the belly of the whale, did he not? I have faith he would do the same for us."

"You think they did in Warrilow?" Brewster asked as our hackney traversed the streets back to Mayfair. "Went 'round to see him, pretending they'd preach at him, then knocked him on his head? Maybe they are the gun smugglers?"

"It is a tempting idea." I idly spun the head of my walking stick. "Is Mr. Kingston lying about going to Laybourne's lodgings? Young Harry saw him."

"Missionaries don't lie," Brewster said with a straight face.

"I rather think they do," I said.

"Course they do." Brewster barked a laugh. "They're the biggest liars of all. Depend upon it, he's the killer. Or at least, has summut to do with it."

He might prove to be correct.

We returned to South Audley Street, I puzzled by what the Kingstons had told me and worried about Eden. Still no word from him, both Barnstable and Bartholomew informed me when I stepped inside.

I had intended to renew my search for Eden, but as Barnstable took my coat, a tightness around his eyes, I heard screams of agony stream down from above.

In alarm, I tossed my coat to Barnstable and leapt up the stairs, heart banging, barely feeling my protesting knee as I went.

CHAPTER 20

*A*s I reached the landing of the second floor, I met a strained Donata descending. Above us the screams grew more shrill.

"What has happened?" I bellowed. I imagined all sorts— Anne falling from a chair or her bed, grabbing broken shards of a cup or snatching at a bare knife, or attempting to climb on a shelf, windowsill, or table, and crashing down to the floor.

"It is temper, not distress," Donata answered, thin-lipped. "She is not pleased to be moving from this house."

Her glare told me she knew exactly from whom Anne had inherited her temper. I could not argue, but I knew exactly from whom Anne had her stubbornness and her spirit.

"She is not even two years old." I banished the visions of Anne lying bleeding on the floor, though my heart continued to race. "This is confusing for her."

"I do understand that, but she has been shrieking for an hour. Nothing will placate her."

"Let me see if I am able."

Donata clearly did not think I would be. She made an

exasperated noise and stormed into her bedchamber, slamming the door.

I reflected that Peter and I were the quiet ones as I continued climbing toward the nursery floor. The tumult increased as I ascended. I heard Nanny McGowan alternately scolding Anne and telling her sweetly that all was well, that we were off to see her brother.

When I pushed open the nursery door, I beheld Anne sitting in the middle of the floor, on a rug, her dress awry, and her dark curls standing on end. Her mouth was open, a pink oval in a scarlet face, her eyes squeezed shut. From this mouth issued a roar that rattled the windows.

"Good heavens, has Bonaparte escaped again?" I shouted the question. "Shall we saddle our mounts and meet him in battle?"

Mrs. McGowan, who'd been at the edge of the carpet, hands on hips, drew a breath to admonish me, but I waved her to silence.

The roaring abruptly ceased. Anne opened her streaming eyes and gazed up at me, her lower lip trembling. She let out another wail, as she had built up a momentum that she could not quench, but the cry had less power.

"Well, that is a relief," I said, my voice much quieter. "I thought we were in danger once more. Everything is well, my sweet."

Anne trailed down into curious sniffles. Her face was beet red, her nose running. Coupled with the mass of her hair every which way, I realized she looked much as I did the morning after a long night of revelry.

The nursery was in disarray with half-packed bags and boxes standing on every surface. It looked as though an army had been stowing everything they could lay their hands on, but fled when Anne began to scream.

"No wonder you're angry," I said, making for her. "Your brother vanished, your parents are rushing about without you, and your home is at sixes and sevens. Why don't you and I find something else to do?"

The cries had completely ceased, Anne regarding me with interest. She wiped her eyes, then emitted a halfhearted sob, as though remembering she ought to be weeping.

She reached for me at the same time I reached for her. I scooped her into my arms, kissed her mussed hair, and proceeded to kidnap her.

Mrs. McGowan rushed forward with a shawl. "She'll catch a chill."

"No, she will not." I took the wrap, snuggled Anne into my arms, and carried her down the stairs.

By the time I reached the floor below the nursery, Anne was playing with a fringe of the shawl and making burbling noises with her lips. Donata peeked from her bedchamber with an air of relief.

"Thank you, Gabriel." She paused to kiss Anne's cheek, making her smile.

The staff regarded me with reverence as Anne and I continued down the stairs and to the library. I closed the door on the lot of them.

Nothing had been disturbed here. My books and things were not considered essentials for a journey, and I agreed. Earl Pembroke had a massive library, and I looked forward to seeing how Grenville had stocked his.

Barnstable had found another, older chessboard in the attic, which he'd set up for me in this chamber, likely so I wouldn't wear out the fine ivory chessmen in Donata's sitting room. These pieces were made of wood, abstract carvings, one set of dark walnut, the other of ash.

I settled myself and Anne in front of the board and opened one of my books.

Soon I had an interesting game started, the walnut army surrounding the ash. Anne assisted by stealing my imaginary opponent's queen and trying to eat it.

I STAYED HOME THE REST OF THE AFTERNOON, ANNE AND I keeping out of the way. She was a lively child and did not drop off to sleep until well after dark. Even then, the packing continued, Donata having her lady's maid, Jacinthe, lay out her entire winter wardrobe.

"This will do until Christmas," I heard Donata say as I passed her door. I'd carried a sleeping Anne aloft and helped Mrs. McGowan put her to bed. "With luck, we'll be back soon after New Year's. I will be hopelessly behind on my spring frocks."

I found some aspects of life with a lady of fashion bizarre, but I'd learned to say little about it.

Brewster refused to stray a step while I was home, so I sent Bartholomew out to see if he could hunt down Eden. Bartholomew returned after I'd taken a hurried supper alone in the dining room to tell me he hadn't found him.

"Landlady says he did stop home for a few moments then went right back out again. Landlady gave him your message, at least."

I relaxed a fraction. "Well, he is alive, then. That is something."

Bartholomew followed me upstairs to my chamber. This room too, was a wreck, as Bartholomew had spent all day sorting my suits, surely too many for me to wear during our country visits. I sank into a chair to remove my boots, more than ready for bed, and Bartholomew continued my packing.

"I suppose you'll be happy to reach Gloucestershire," I said as he worked and I sipped a brandy he'd brought me.

"Sir?" Bartholomew glanced up at me as he folded clean cravats into a box.

"To be reunited with your brother. It has been a while since you've seen Matthias."

Bartholomew shrugged, continuing his task. "Suppose."

The answer lacked enthusiasm. "Is anything wrong, Bartholomew?" I asked in concern. "Have you quarreled?"

I could not imagine it. Bartholomew and Matthias, both very tall, very blond, and very energetic, rubbed along better than most brothers I knew.

"Not exactly quarreled." Bartholomew closed the cravat box and began sorting through my gloves. "But he's a bit jealous, like. I'm a valet, aren't I? In a viscount's house. While he's only a footman still."

"Footman to Lucius Grenville," I pointed out. "That must be equal to butler for anyone else."

"Mayhap." Bartholomew brightened. "Mr. Grenville's butler is getting on. Creaks about the place, barely able to climb stairs anymore. Matthias can try for that post when the man finally retires."

The result would be up to Grenville—or perhaps Marianne if he gave over the domestic staff to her. I had to wonder if he would. Grenville's staff doted on him and were proud to be employed by the most famous man in England, but I wondered if they'd respect Marianne enough to listen to her. I hoped there would not be troubled waters ahead for her.

I could do nothing about that or any other problem I'd been embroiled in at the moment. I could only help

Bartholomew pack, until he firmly told me to leave him to it and go to bed.

I HALF EXPECTED A CRISIS TO DELAY OUR DEPARTURE — another murder, Mr. Creasey breaking his word to me and trying to assassinate Brewster, a successful assassination of Denis, or Pomeroy coming to tell me he'd arrested Eden once more.

Nothing of the sort happened. I received a note from Eden telling me he was sorry he'd missed me but to hie off to Oxford-shire and not to worry about him. He'd lie low and hope the Runners, patrollers, and River Police found the murderer for us.

Had I not been leaving a bed of unsolved problems behind, I would have thoroughly enjoyed the trip to Oxford-shire. We had tolerable weather, meaning only spitting rain and a cool breeze, a comfortable chaise and four, and a clear road. An aristocratic lady could breeze quickly through the turnpikes unlike the coaches and carts of the ordinary folk who crept slowly forward to pass the gate.

We took the journey in easy stages so that Anne would not be too tired, but I confessed to myself that it was I who appreciated the many stops and the overnight stay in Reading.

The Thames River valley became greener and lusher as we neared Oxfordshire, the beauty of this country never failing to uplift me.

We arrived at Pembroke Court at nearly midnight, but the mansion was lit from top to bottom, candlelight in nearly every room. When we rolled through the gates to the front door, the servants rushed out to welcome the daughter of the house, Earl Pembroke's only child, back home.

Donata and Anne, who had recovered her temper during the long ride, were engulfed by them, and I limped along behind, unworried. I knew Donata and Anne would be protected in this place.

Bartholomew, who had the energy of an eager squirrel, had me in my warmed chamber to unpack before I could scarcely draw a breath.

Peter, who was supposed to be abed, charged into my chamber and flung himself at me. "Papa!" he bellowed. "You came, just as you promised."

"Of course, my dear fellow."

I lifted him and gave him a bearhug, carrying him across the room as I sought a chair. I sank into it gratefully—it neither swayed from side to side nor bumped painfully over stones.

I did not admonish Peter for leaving the nursery. He could hardly be expected to stay there while the rest of the household dashed about with so much fervor.

"Letter's come for you, sir." Bartholomew retrieved it from the footman who'd darted in and shoved it at him. "Arrived this morning, apparently."

He brought the missive to me, and I settled Peter on my knee. The letter was from Grenville. I eagerly broke the seal and read.

I read with great interest your description of your adventures in London, he wrote, after preliminary greetings. *Trust you to find excitement the moment I am rusticating in the country.*

I will bypass my usual pique about not being in the thick of things and answer the question you posed to me.

You inquired about Orlando Fitzgerald. He was indeed a friend of the Regent and Alvanley when they were young and feckless fools. I never knew Fitzgerald, as he is about ten years my senior, and by the time I joined in the revelries at Carlton House, Fitzgerald had already been banished to the colonies.

But I have heard a great deal of him. A charming man, knowing exactly how to speak to whomever is before him. He comes across as harmless, so says Alvanley. Brummell always said so as well. Fitzgerald never tried to be the best in say, fashion, or gambling, or imbibing, or whatever they decided was their raison d'etre for the day, conceding to the winner without rancor.

However, Fitzgerald apparently could become enraged, especially when one stood between him and something he truly wanted. That might be a lady, or a horse, or an artwork, or a house. Never mind he might not be able to afford the horse, artwork, house, or dare I say it, the lady, but he'd go after it with obsession. Anyone who thwarted Fitzgerald was subject to a barrage of abuse, which is why gentlemen called him out. If he wanted a lady, he was happy to shoot the man to whom she was devoted or even wed, to obtain her. Fortunately, no one actually was murdered ... but shot, yes.

The Regent claims he was ready to eject Fitzgerald from his circle, but Alvanley says the Prince never mentioned it until Fitzgerald was in disgrace and sent away. In any case, there was a collective sigh of relief when the man was gone. Some regret, as he was usually an affable chap, but when he exploded, one tended to flee until the tempest had died down.

Is Fitzgerald capable of murder? I believe he would be, for the right reason. Although I had the idea from Alvanley and others that he was not a confrontational man himself. Rather, he'd infuriate others until they came after him.

In your scenario with this Mr. Warrilow, it could be that Fitzgerald went to him—for whatever reason you will no doubt by now have uncovered—and provoked the man into attacking him. Whereupon, Fitzgerald struck out to defend himself, and felled him.

I am not certain of this, of course. Fitzgerald preferred duals, where he could claim to have settled the argument honorably. Afterward, he'd be quite pleasant to all, apologizing to his opponent and footing the doctor's bill for whomever he shot.

I know of no one in Antigua who was acquainted with him. Once Fitzgerald's father, finally tired of his embarrassing son, sent him off, no one heard of him again. He did not correspond with Alvanley, Brummell, or any of his friends. He simply vanished.

You say he was companionable and hospitable when you visited him. Also much more rotund. He apparently cut quite a dash in his day. But we all thicken as we age, do we not? And perhaps a long time in the tropical heat has mellowed him.

I will be interested in what else you have learned from him and about the rest of this business. When you arrive, we will have a very long talk. No matter that I have about twenty-five guests arriving for a hunt—we shall snub them and closet ourselves to thoroughly hash out this problem. I will tell Gautier to decant plenty of the best brandy.

The letter turned from the topic after that, telling me that Marianne was settling in nicely and savoring her new role as lady of the manor. Grenville closed, expressing delight we'd be arriving soon, and I folded the letter.

Peter was asleep in my arms. I carried him to the nursery and tucked him in, then returned to my own bed. I half-hoped Donata would join me, but she'd been subsumed into her family, and I doubted I'd see much of her in the coming days.

LATER I REALIZED HOW MUCH I ENJOYED THAT RESPITE IN Oxfordshire. My cares fell away, and contentment set in. I continued to worry about Eden—both wondering if my old friend had turned criminal or whether he would be the next victim—and about Denis and his war with Mr. Creasey.

I had given Denis his wish—I was well out of his way. Brewster was on hand to look out for me, but he had an easy time of it here, as I stayed home in the earl's great house if I wasn't out riding.

I'd tried to convince him to bring Mrs. Brewster along, but *my Em,* Brewster said, expressed horror at being exposed to the countryside, and had moved in with a friend in Islington until Brewster's return.

Brewster had messages during our sojourn from his cronies in London that Denis was keeping himself out of sight. However, both he and Creasey were fighting each other in myriad ways. One of Creasey's purloined shipments from the London docks vanished from under his nose, and rumor had it that Denis had seized those goods and already sold them on through his networks.

Denis had been very calm when he'd explained to me how Creasey was robbing cargo, which I now believed meant he'd already been planning his vengeance. I hoped that the two men would leave some parts of London standing.

Those worries became faraway and small as our visit commenced, receding to the back of my mind. I concentrated on riding with Peter, who was a natural horseman, and fearless. Anne took her first steps not long after we arrived, excitedly rushing toward Peter when he and I returned from a gallop. To the delight of her parents and grandparents, she toddled three paces before she collapsed to her backside, laughing in excitement. Donata's mother, the cool Lady Pembroke, who let little disturb her sangfroid, gathered up Anne and told her she was a clever, clever child.

Donata's father, a warm-hearted and intelligent man, which I'd discovered after I ceased being intimidated by him, indeed indulged me in the occasional game of chess. I used these matches and the two books I'd brought with me to refresh my memory of the game, and taught Peter the basic moves. As I'd suspected, he caught on quickly.

A few weeks passed in this golden haze, then we departed for Gloucestershire. Packing for this move was not as arduous, as we would stay only a short time at Grenville's and then return to Oxfordshire after Gabriella's arrival to remain until after the New Year.

Grenville's home near a village called Stow-on-the-Wold was far closer to Oxford than Oxford was to London, and we reached it after an easy day in the Breckenridge coach, driven by a careful Hagen.

We rolled up before a large house that was modest for a country estate. We'd passed the road to Blenheim Palace on the way, the vast pile of the Dukes of Marlborough, which Donata considered pretentious and overblown.

Grenville had opted for subdued. Built of stone during the days of the Stuart monarchs, the house had two gabled wings flanking the front door and a third wing to the right, making the home charmingly asymmetrical. An abundance of ivy and climbing roses growing over the three-story structure rendered it even more picturesque.

It was like Grenville to opt for understated elegance. His Mayfair home sported a fairly plain facade, as though its owner eschewed the grandeur that other men of wealth sought. No one would ever call the house we halted before a palace, but it was an attractive abode that spoke of friendly comfort.

The interior was as I'd expected—seemingly simple with whitewashed walls and dark wood paneling, but filled with inviting chairs, soft carpets, reading nooks, and large windows overlooking a lush garden, appealing even as cold weather set in. A large stable could be glimpsed down a hill, with horses wandering a pasture beyond.

"It is splendid," I declared to Grenville as we gathered for a late supper. He'd showed me all over the house after we'd arrived, with the same pride Brandon had for his new hunter.

Peter and Anne were already tucked up for the night, and Grenville's anticipated guests had not yet arrived, and so Donata and I, and Grenville and Marianne, were free to take pleasure in one another's company.

"Very happy you like it." Grenville, as resplendent as ever in a fine suit, one relaxed for country living, raised a glass to me. "I stumbled upon the house while visiting an old friend earlier this autumn, and happily, its owner was amenable to selling. He longed to retire to a village on the coast with his daughter and was pleased with the price I offered him. We moved in as soon as we were able."

"There are a few draughts here and there, but we shove newspaper into the holes," Marianne added.

She had been transformed. Marianne wore a blue gown tonight that was not quite matronly, but it hid much more of her limbs than had her frocks of old. A matching cap covered her golden curls, which had been tamed into a knot, a few strands of hair leaking out to retain her girlish appearance.

But her change hadn't come from the clothes alone. Marianne had relaxed—her tense, feral demeanor had faded. She no longer feared, I could see, that anything she had would be snatched away on the moment, no longer pridefully disdained all offers of assistance.

She must have finally realized, as I had, that Grenville, beneath his elegance and man-about-Town facade, possessed a truly kind heart. If Grenville liked a person, he did so without reserve and without expectations of anything in return. That he loved Marianne wholeheartedly, I did not doubt.

Over the next few days, as I observed Marianne talking easily with Donata, befriending our children, and hostessing our visit with aplomb, I discerned that her adeptness in becoming mistress of the house was more than simply playing a role. I had never received a straight answer from Marianne Simmons about her origins, but as she moved about Grenville's home, assuming her place as its lady, I saw an effortlessness in her that made me wonder if she'd returned to her natural situation.

Peter and I rode every morning. Donata used the opportunity for languor, indulging in long mornings in bed, gossiping with Marianne, or writing letters. Whatever business she'd conducted in London, she'd finished off in Oxfordshire, and now she relished her leisure. Anne was a constant companion, which neither Grenville nor Marianne complained of.

Grenville and I had long conversations about the murders of Warrilow and Laybourne, as well as the carbine Brewster had found, perhaps pointing to gun running, and Fitzgerald as a possible art smuggler. We also speculated on what would happen between Denis and Creasey. We talked long into the night, putting forth or rejecting theories, fortified by the promised brandy. Then in the morning, I would ride off my night's imbibing, with Peter enthusiastically at my side.

There was plenty of good riding near the house—rolling hills, twisting lanes, and hedges to jump. The enclosure acts had reached the farms here, but we still found plenty of open country through which to have long runs.

Grenville's guests began trickling in over the week. I noted that he'd been very careful, inviting only the most congenial of gentlemen and their ladies, with a mix of the aristocratic and genteel-born intellectual and artistic friends. None were scandalous, though some were unconventional, but no one would create any dramatic scenes at this gathering.

They'd been chosen because they'd not condemn Marianne nor snub her, I concluded. Grenville was canny enough to keep the guest list small, so that the fashionable would hear of this exclusive party and put aside their shock at his marriage to try to gain admission to future gatherings. Grenville was making Marianne interesting, an introduction to her something to be sought after.

I chuckled at his ploys but admired his wisdom. I let him play congenial host while I mostly kept to horseback, honing my son's already excellent riding skills.

On a brisk October day, Peter and I took a trail that led along a descending fold between hills. Peter cantered his horse ahead of mine, disappearing around the hill's bulk.

I followed more slowly, delighting in the view before me. The land receded into the distance, a blue haze swallowing it as it reached the gleam of a faraway river. If I were an artist, I'd paint the scene.

I continued riding around the gentle hill, expecting at any moment to find Peter.

I did not. I reached a gate in a grassy field, but it was shut. Deciding Peter must have leapt his horse over the low wall next to it, I turned my mount in a wide circle and jumped it across, landing on a downward slope.

At the bottom of that slope, in the waving grass, I saw a horse. It had no rider.

My alarm growing, I urged my mount forward. I rode a fine stallion, and he took me easily down the hill to the horse that skittered away from us.

Something had spooked him. I scanned the ground, but nowhere did I see Peter's small body lying with broken limbs.

I gazed about, becoming more frantic by the moment. "Peter!" I shouted.

I heard no small voice calling back to me, no answer or cry for help.

"Peter! Damnation, where are you?"

I guided my horse forward, circling Peter's mount in ever widening swaths, my gaze everywhere. I saw and heard nothing but the wind in the grass, the sharp cry of a sparrowhawk.

Mouth dry, I returned to the horse, walking mine slowly to keep Peter's mount calm. Once I was close enough, I reached over and caught its reins. The horse trembled but did not attempt to bolt.

It was then that I saw the paper peeping out from under the saddle's pommel. Speaking soothingly to Peter's horse — which was a feat, as my voice cracked with panic — I withdrew the page.

On it was a simple sentence.

Bring me Denis, and you will see your son again. Creasey.

CHAPTER 21

The note balled in my fist, I rode to the top of the nearest hill, desperately scanning the horizon. I saw no one, not a party of horses or a carriage taking away my son.

There were no hiding places to my eyes either. The abductors had planned well, likely scouting the area long in advance. I'd made no secret that I would visit Grenville at this time, and I'd come to Gloucestershire in the innocent belief that here, we'd be safe.

I knew Creasey did not mean I should fetch Denis and bring him to some hideaway in the Cotswolds. He wanted me to return to London, truss up Denis, and carry him to Creasey's warehouse by the wharves.

Tears wet my face as I turned my horse toward Grenville's home, leading the second horse behind me. I now had to find Donata and tell her I'd lost her son.

Brewster panted up to me on foot as I moved down the trail. "Guv."

"Did you see?" I demanded. "Where did they take him?"

"That way." Brewster stretched out his broad arm to the south. "They circled the hills, but they're on fast horses. They outran me." He leaned his hands on his knees, dragging in breaths.

"It was Creasey," I said grimly. I handed him the paper.

Brewster smoothed it out and read it, his breaths slowing as he took it in.

"What will you do, guv?" The question held worry.

"Exactly what Creasey wants. Give him Denis and rescue my son."

"You walk into Creasey's lair, he'll murder you too, depend upon it. Let me round up some good men and we'll give them chase. I'll storm that warehouse and get his lordship out."

I wanted more than anything to charge directly after the abductors, never stopping until I caught them, but I also knew they'd evade me. They'd planned this for weeks.

Peter was a viscount, a fact that might save him. Creasey wanted Denis, an even more important reason to keep Peter alive. Creasey would do nothing to the boy until I came to them with Denis in tow.

Then I would kill Creasey.

"Round up everyone you can," I ordered. "Hunt them. If you can find them, for God's sake do nothing that will make them hurt Peter. Meanwhile, I'm off to London to deliver Denis."

Brewster's eyes narrowed. "Have ye run completely mad? His Nibs will never let you, not even to save the lad."

"He will." The hard note in my voice made Brewster back a step.

He studied me a moment then gave me a nod. "I'll do as you like. If ye need me to knock His Nibs to the ground and tie him up, I'll do that too."

"Good." I tossed him the reins of Peter's horse, then

turned mine, and rode without further word back to Grenville's.

Donata had risen and was in her bedchamber with Jacinthe, discussing what she'd wear for the day. When I burst in, my riding boots coated with mud, she started up in surprise.

"What do you think, Gabriel? The green?" She held out a gown that shimmered in the light. "I think it a bit much for morning, but ..." She at last noted my expression, and her words died. "Gabriel, what is it? Peter—"

The fear in her eyes cut me. I saw that she thought him dead, thrown from his horse in a wild ride.

"Creasey has him," I said in clipped tones.

"What?" Donata stared at me, the gown falling from her nerveless fingers to land at the feet of a white-faced Jacinthe. A terrible silence followed.

Then Donata screamed. She came at me, fists flailing, beating my chest as she cried out. I gathered her up, she striking me again and again, her face red, tears streaming.

"I will bring him back," I promised as I held her. "I will find him, Donata, and bring him home. I swear to you."

"Damn you!" Donata broke from me, pounding me with both fists. I scarcely felt the blows. "You did this ..."

"I know." I caught her hands. "I know. If you want me gone, I will go. But first, I will retrieve Peter."

My quiet determination broke through her hysteria. Donata gulped, her breath coming in sobs. "What will you do?"

"Throw Denis at Creasey and shoot them both."

Such was my rage. Donata caught my arm. "Make certain Peter is out of danger first."

"Of course."

I turned away, preparing to mount a fresh horse and ride forth at once.

"I am coming with you," Donata announced.

"Lacey?" Grenville appeared in the doorway, flushed and out of breath. "Good Lord, what the devil has happened?"

I explained in a few words, and Grenville's bewilderment changed to cold fury. "Dear God, the man has gone too far. Do not worry, Donata. We will find Peter, and then London will be too hot to hold Mr. Creasey and those like him."

"I agree." The icy control Donata had learned during the years of her unhappy marriage descended on her. "But I am coming along."

"Of course, dear lady," Grenville said. "My carriage is at your disposal. I shall have it brought 'round at once."

Already I was striding past him out of the room. "I won't wait for a carriage."

"No, you and Brewster ride for London. We will follow you and meet at South Audley Street. Then we will plan our attack. I will send messages to your magistrate friends and the Runners—every patroller will close in on Mr. Creasey. He'll not last the night."

I continued down the stairs, never feeling my injured knee, barely realizing I'd left my walking stick in the stables.

I made no comment on Grenville's plan. He took over with the smoothness in which he commanded everything, and I knew he'd execute his schemes perfectly.

Meanwhile, I'd ride straight to London and continue with *my* plan.

Brewster, who hated horses, climbed into the saddle of one without fuss and turned it behind me. I would ride hard, and I could only hope he'd keep up with me.

I REMEMBER LITTLE OF THE JOURNEY TO LONDON. WE rode straight through, halting only at posting houses to acquire fresh horses. I could barely speak to the ostlers, and it was Brewster who explained that our original mounts should be returned to Mr. Grenville, Brewster who paid over money for the best horses for hire.

Everywhere we searched for Creasey's men and Peter. Brewster's searching near Grenville's home had revealed nothing, and he concluded that the abductors had immediately made for London. We asked at the inns if any had seen them, but none had. They must have ridden cross-country or changed their horses at private houses, or perhaps paid the posting innkeepers handsomely to keep quiet. I did not linger to question them closely but hurried on.

When we reached London, I did not stop at home but rode straight to Curzon Street. It was very late and even the denizens of Mayfair who kept long hours had retired. The streets were quiet, the clopping of our horses' hooves loud in the stillness.

My face was rough with beard, my coat dirt-spattered and rent, my hat lost, my boots caked with mud. I swung down from the horse, barely able to walk now, but I managed to reach the front door of Number 45 and pound on it with my fists.

I continued to pound until the door opened a crack. I saw the butler's face behind it, but I did not wait for him to inquire what I wanted. I slammed my shoulder into the door and forced it open.

Brewster rushed in two steps behind me, drawing a knife as Denis's men surged forward to intercept us.

"Get him," I bellowed at the butler.

Gibbons's hard face reminded me that he'd once been a

ruffian of the violent sort. Before he could open his mouth to argue, Brewster stepped up with his knife. "Do it."

We'd have to begin battle, I could see, as none of the men moved. They were poised to seize us and toss us out, no matter what.

Denis himself materialized on the upper landing. He was fully dressed, including his greatcoat. I wondered dimly whether he'd been going out or coming in.

"What has happened?" he asked in his cool tones.

"He took my son." Rage boiled out of me. The tight calm I'd maintained when explaining to Donata what I'd do and the rigidness that had sustained me through the ride fell away. "He took my *son*. He wants you in exchange, and I will give you to him."

Denis gazed down at me from two flights above, his eyes in shadow. The hand that touched the railing did not move.

I could barely remain still. Seven men blocked my way to the stairs, but I would barrel through them if I had to. Brewster stood by me, his knife held competently.

Logic told me I'd lose the battle, but I could not afford to. I must deliver Denis for Peter, and this I would do.

Denis lifted his hand from the railing and started down the stairs. "Very well. We will go."

I rocked back, uncertain I'd heard correctly.

"Begging your pardon, sir," Brewster called up to Denis. "But if you run in with your army, Creasey might dispatch the lad right away."

"I do know that, Mr. Brewster." Denis continued down the stairs like a chill fog lowering. "Captain Lacey, you will take me in as though I am your prisoner. We will retrieve Viscount Breckenridge, and then you will leave Creasey to me."

"Fine," I turned. "Let us be gone."

"We'll go in a carriage." Denis's cold tones stopped me. "You must have patience for a few more minutes."

"I have no patience," I snarled. "He was taken because of you."

"I understand this, Captain." Denis reached the ground floor. His blue eyes met mine. In them I read—regret? I could not say.

"'Tis a mad idea," Brewster argued. He slid away the knife but kept his hand on it under his coat.

"It is the only idea," Denis countered. "We need to invade his stronghold in order to reach his lordship, and this is the best way. Creasey wants my head so much that he will risk springing a trap."

Several bodies stood between Denis and me, so I could not seize him and shake him. "You do *nothing* until Peter is safely away with me. Nothing."

Denis gave me a nod. "Of course."

After my wild ride across country and through the sleeping city, I chafed to wait one more moment, but it was not long before Denis's carriage rolled to a halt at the front door. He had been murmuring to his men at the end of the hall, just out of my hearing, and now joined me to leave the house.

Even now, Denis exercised all caution moving from door to carriage. His men surrounded him, and me. He climbed into the carriage first, then Brewster shoved me inside behind him, and hauled himself in to land beside me.

None of the other men followed. They dispersed, flowing to do whatever Denis had instructed them.

"When we reach the wharves," Denis said as the carriage jerked forward, "we will descend there, and you and Mr. Brewster will walk me the rest of the way. Creasey might simply hand over his lordship, or he might try to hold on to him longer. Regardless, you take him and go, with Mr. Brewster to guard the pair of you. No argument."

"Agreed." I folded my arms, the one word sufficient.

"His mum is coming," Brewster said to Denis. "She wouldn't stay behind."

Denis acknowledged this with a nod. "By the time she arrives, she should be reunited with her son."

I said nothing. Donata might take Peter from my arms and shut the door in my face. I would not blame her. I knew that if I'd extricated myself from Denis years ago, his enemies would not have used my family to snare him. Likewise, if Denis had not required me to deliver the white queen, Creasey might never have paid attention to me.

If Donata turned me out, I'd retreat to Grimpen Lane. I would not disgrace her with a divorce if she did not want that, but she'd never have to see me again.

My heart burned somewhere beneath my fury and fear, but I would have to face one emotion at a time.

Because the streets were deserted, the morning deliverymen just beginning their rounds, we reached Lower Thames Street fairly quickly. The closer to our destination we came, the more I wanted to fling open the door and drag Denis out, hurrying the rest of the way on foot. Only Brewster's bulk next to me, solid and calm, his shoulder against mine, kept me in place.

At last the carriage halted before the Custom House. Brewster was the first out, reaching back to help me down. He handed me a walking stick I did not recognize, but which made Denis's eyes flicker. Filched from Denis's house while we waited, I presumed.

As my stick was in Gloucestershire, I accepted the purloined one without question. Though it had no sword inside it, it was solid oak with a heavy gold head and would make a good weapon. I hefted it as the carriage moved off to await my return with Peter.

Denis would walk between Brewster and me into the lane. We'd guard Denis from anyone shooting at him from the windows—I did not want Creasey to kill him and then decide he had no more need for his hostage.

"Lacey?" A voice rang behind me before we'd reached the mouth of the lane. "What the devil?"

Eden rushed to us from the direction of the Custom House. The question of why he'd been there or in this area at all so early in the morning tickled the back of my mind, but at the moment, it was not important.

"Creasey has my son," I said as Eden reached us. "This is James Denis. I'm exchanging him for Peter."

Eden looked Denis up and down in amazement while Denis stood tolerantly still. Then Eden's mouth flattened.

"Right then. Let us get on with it."

Brewster cleared his throat. "Might not be the place for you, guv."

"Rot that," Eden snapped. "Creasey has seen me—he knows I'll champion Lacey. Another pair of fists, not to mention the knife in my boot will help things along and keep *this* one from running." He jerked a thumb at Denis.

Denis did not bother explaining that he had no intention of giving himself up to Creasey. "He is right," Denis said. "Follow behind us."

Eden nodded and took his position as rearguard. "Should we bind his hands?"

"Best not," Brewster answered. "When we have the lad, you make sure the captain runs with him, eh? Don't try to stay and fight."

"Understood," Eden said.

Eden would not have to bother. I would take Peter and go, and to hell with the rest of them.

We marched in close formation around Denis along Hill Lane, Denis's greatcoat swirling. His tailored ensemble with hat and gloves was incongruous with my travel-stained clothing, Brewster's working man's attire not in much better shape, and Eden's sensible suit, worse for the wear of a night in it.

Down the lane we went. No one tried to assault us or shoot from on high. We walked unchallenged to the door where Creasey lodged, and I rapped upon it with the walking stick.

The door opened, and the thin lackey who'd greeted us the first time peered out. His eyes widened when he saw me with Denis.

"I've brought him." I stepped up to the man. "Tell Creasey to send Peter out."

"No, guv." The lackey opened the door wide. "You're to come in. If ye want t' see your stepson alive, ye bring Mr. Denis upstairs."

CHAPTER 22

I gazed into the chill, dark interior of the warehouse, knowing that if I went in, I would be hard-pressed to escape.

On the other hand, Peter was in there, or so I was to believe. I could not chance that Creasey wouldn't send out his body if I refused, so I planted the walking stick on the threshold and crossed it.

Denis came behind me, removing his hat as though he were making a formal call. He did not offer to fight or argue, said nothing at all. Brewster flanked him, and Eden kept an eye out from behind.

The lackey seemed a bit surprised that I'd readily obeyed, but he bolted the door and led us across the large empty space toward the stairs at the back, the lantern he carried a pinpoint in the darkness. I was aware of watchers in the shadows, hulks of Creasey's men staying just out of sight.

The stairwell was as filthy as ever. I used the walking stick to balance myself and noted that Denis kept to the middle of the steps, not letting his greatcoat touch the walls.

Upstairs was dark, the lackey's lantern barely cutting the gloom. I sensed more watchers here, and the hairs on the back of my neck prickled.

When we arrived at the office door, the lackey reached for the handle. I pushed him aside and opened the door myself.

The cluttered room was full. Creasey had brought in guards, all large and powerfully built. That each was armed, I had no doubt.

Creasey sat behind his desk. On a chair beside him, hands tied with a thin rope, a dirty gag in his mouth, was Peter.

He'd been crying, and his face was dirty, but I saw no bruising or abrasions. Peter met my gaze as I came in, his glare reminiscent of the late Lord Breckenridge's.

My heart beat thickly, and my legs threatened to buckle. Peter was here, and alive.

"I've brought Denis." My words cracked as I jerked my thumb behind me. "Give me my son."

"I will, in time." Creasey had the audacity to send me a smile over his laced fingers.

I lunged at him, brought up short by four men who held me hard. "Now," I said, my voice strengthening. "That was the bargain."

"Yes, but Mr. Denis has not kept his part. His toughs are surrounding my house even now, ready to battle it out. He has used my summons as an excuse to put himself in a position to best me, and he knows it."

"Whatever our differences are." Denis's tones were frigid. "They have nothing to do with Lacey and the boy. Take that rag out of his mouth and hand him over."

Creasey signaled to a man standing behind Peter. The man cut loose the gag and pulled it away. Peter tried to bite him.

I raised a hand in a calming gesture. "My friends and I

will take my son and go. You have Denis. That should be enough."

"Unlike you, I have no trust in him," Creasey said. "I apologize for the gag. The boy has a foul mouth and a vile temper. I'd watch that, were I you."

"Come, Peter, we are going."

"Now, now." Creasey lifted a finger. "I do not trust you either. But I know you are a man of honor. You wear it like a cloak. What I propose is this." He folded his hands once more. "You were an interesting opponent in our game of chess. You and I will have a match. If you win, you take your son and leave unheeded. Your friends and Denis and all his men will be free to as well. We withdraw to fight another day."

"And if I lose?" I asked tightly.

"You and your son will still be released. But all the others, including your army friend and your lackey, stay with me. To dispose of as I see fit."

"This is not their fight." My voice took on a growl.

"I could kill all of you on the moment." Creasey ceased smiling, the steel in him coming forth. "Gratify me on this one point, and you and your boy, at least, will live."

I drew a long breath. The chessboard lay waiting, the pieces in their rows. He'd planned even this, no matter that he pretended the proposed game was a spontaneous whim. He knew he had to let Peter go or risk the wrath of every magistrate and the entire House of Lords and most of the judiciary. But he could humiliate me and take his revenge on Denis at the same time.

"Major Eden has nothing to do with this," I said. "He should leave now."

"He made his choice," Creasey said. "Now you must make one. Decide."

The game? Or take our chances battling our way back to

the street? And then every moment after that until Creasey was dead.

I tapped my way to the game table, which remained alone in its corner. "I have the advantage of moving first?"

"If you like." Creasey pried himself to his feet and made his way to the board, guarded at every step.

I glanced at my friends. Brewster tried to signal me with agitated eyes not to accept. Eden's brow furrowed in concern. Only Denis remained implacable, his expression a careful blank.

I'd seen Denis face his enemies before, outwardly calm, but inwardly raging. This time, even his eyes showed nothing. He protected everything from Creasey, including his true thoughts.

I pulled out a chair and sat down. "Then let us begin."

"I will make it easier for you," Creasey said as he seated himself. "We will play not just one game, but three. Whoever wins two of them will be declared the victor. That way you may learn from your mistakes."

I did not want to learn a thing from this man but how loud he screamed when Brewster broke his bones. I removed my ruined gloves and set them on my knee.

"Very well," I answered.

I immediately lifted a light jade pawn and moved it two squares forward. Creasey drew a breath at my abruptness but countered by bringing out his king's knight.

We shifted the pieces one by one. Creasey expected me to pause and study before making each decision, so when I simply fanned out my pieces with decided clicks, he blinked a little.

Soon I had my pawns in a guarding line and had castled to move my king to a safer position.

Creasey formed a pawn chain of his own, taking control of

a long diagonal. I moved my rooks to one corner, readying them to swoop. Creasey placed his queen to block this setup, and I took it with a knight.

While another man might curse at this loss, Creasey simply took *my* queen with his bishop. He was setting up to check my king, and I sacrificed a pawn to prevent him.

Creasey took the pawn with delight. He obviously did not expect much from me, even with the resolute way I was playing tonight, and he sucked in a breath when I rained one rook down and took a pawn in his chain, threatening the entire line. He brought over his rook to defend, but I moved my second rook all the way to his king row, putting him in check.

Creasey blinked again, then his lip curled, and I knew that from now on I'd have to fight for my life.

Anger made him a tad careless, however. Creasey lost a rook to my bishop before he took my bishop with a pawn. After a series of flurried moves, we were left with only a few pieces on the board: He a rook, pawn, and king, me with a rook and king.

I noted the room had grown very quiet. I was fairly certain not all the men around us were familiar with the game, but they'd drawn close to watch this battle in miniature.

Creasey thought he had me. My rook was a few squares from his king, but his lone pawn protected it. If I took the pawn, he'd take my rook, and then I'd be dead in the water.

I moved the rook swiftly to his end of the board. Creasey tried to counter by checking me at my end with his rook, but in a few moves, I'd made him put his own pawn between my king and his threatening rook, and moved my rook to check his king.

Creasey gave me a look of fury. "It will be a draw," he said.

"I agree. Stalemate."

Creasey snatched up the pieces and proceeded to set out a new game. "You must win two. Draws do you no good."

"I understand."

Again, he let me open, but I believe he was beginning to regret this generosity. Creasey was a seasoned player, and I'd only been relearning the game in the last weeks, but as I faced him now, the words of my old teacher brushed the back of my mind.

Pawns are the soul of chess.

I played my pawns as he'd taught me, setting them up to block while at the same time, letting my own pieces through. I was particularly fond of rooks, because while they could not move as powerfully as the queen, I had two of them. When I paired them or set them one behind the other to break through Creasey's wall, I felt a tingle of satisfaction in my fingers. The rooks reminded me of Brewster, all bulk that could smash through anywhere they wanted to go.

I had to relinquish my queen because I needed to stop one of his pawns that had made a slow march to my end of the board. Once a pawn reached the opponent's king row, it could turn into any piece its player wanted. Creasey would invariably choose a queen, and with two of those in play, he'd crumble my defenses to dust. I knocked down the pawn, and Creasey seethed even as he snatched up my queen in retaliation.

Focus on controlling a pivotal square.

I put all my effort on the space before Creasey's king, ensuring he had nowhere to run. He of course piled his pieces on to defend that square, but I maneuvered the diagonals.

His queen began her assault on my king, but I moved another bishop, and then a pawn, cornering his king. Creasey smiled as he took one of my knights. I countered by taking his, and then his queen was in jeopardy.

Creasey tapped his lips as he studied the board, his face tightening. He moved his queen one square down, a move that did nothing but purchase him time. I slammed a rook in front of it.

Certain I'd made a blunder, Creasey snatched up my rook. But I'd lured the queen from guarding the square that was my goal, and I moved my second rook to take the pawn protecting his king.

"Check," I said quietly.

His king could not capture my rook without coming under fire from both my bishops, so he leapt the king one square away. I backed the rook off.

"Mate in two," I announced.

Creasey worked it out. If he moved his queen to block my assault, I would simply take it with my bishop, leaving the king completely unguarded. If the king moved from the corner of the board, my rook would return with a rush and end him.

Creasey slammed his king to its side. "Best of three, I said. Your luck has run out, Lacey."

I said nothing as I set up the pieces. The trouble with men like Creasey was that they could not believe anyone might possibly be as clever as they were. A country-bred army captain, who'd spent his years directing real battles in the heat and mud of the Peninsula, could never truly understand a sophisticated game like chess. It never occurred to him that I could read, study, practice, and pursue lessons when the game caught my interest during my year in Paris. The game had been a lifeline to distract me after Carlotta had gone.

Creasey also thought he could prevail against Denis, who'd been holding him on a loose rein for years. Denis had let Creasey alone for the simple reason that he hadn't wanted Creasey's business. Now Creasey believed that his superior forces would prevail.

He ought to know that James Denis would never, ever come unarmed and unaided into an enemy camp, no matter what that move would gain him. Denis had a plan — probably more than one — working behind that expressionless face of his, though I could not imagine what.

Nor did I care at the moment. I was one game away from taking Peter home. Creasey had promised the two of us could go even if I lost, but I did not trust him to keep his word. Once this game was done, Peter and I would run.

Peter had already worked himself free of his bonds. The men around Creasey were so focused on the game, they hadn't noticed. They weren't paying much attention to Denis either, which was fatally foolish.

Creasey proved he'd been holding back during the previous games by charging forth with an all-out attack. However, I had learned in my cavalry days, that one could charge too far. If a commander led troops too swiftly through the enemy lines, those troops could be surrounded and cut down.

Chess and real battle were of course quite distant from each other, but I taught Creasey a lesson about hurtling himself too far. I surrounded his army of pawns while I sent one of my own pawns marching resolutely to his end of the board.

The fight became vicious. Creasey hurtled his queen into the melee, capturing my knights and bishops. He'd not let me control the diagonals again. My queen went next.

But as I said, I was fond of the rooks. I found an open file and stood them one behind the other, a solid menace. Using these rooks, I took pawn after pawn, then his knights, and finally, his queen.

End game. Creasey and I faced off, I with a pawn and a rook guarding my king, and he with the same.

My pawn was a step away from being made a queen. Creasey couldn't stop it, so he checked my king with his rook. I calmly moved my king one square aside. He chased it, checking again and again, until my king stood in front of my pawn.

One more check, and then I moved my rook one square in front of my king, blocking any more checks. Creasey roared his rage. No matter what he did, I'd move my pawn to the last square, make it a queen, and then have no mercy on him.

"Mate in four," I said.

He tried. A reasonable player would resign, shake my hand, and send me off. Creasey decided to try to run his rook around mine and bring his king into the battle. I picked up the white queen, deciding not to comment on the irony that I'd brought him a white queen to signal Denis's challenge weeks ago, and set it on the board in place of my pawn.

In three more moves, I had his king cornered, while his rook desperately tried to defend.

He lifted my king and hurled it across the room.

"Checkmate," I said softly.

"How?" Creasey's face was red, his mouth quivering. "When you first played me, you made mistake after mistake. How did you become a master in so short a time?"

I shrugged. "I was humoring you. I feared that if I played like a true opponent, I would anger you, with dire consequence to me. Also, it was true, I hadn't had a game in a long time, and I wasn't certain I remembered the strategies correctly. Since then I have studied to refresh my memory."

"But you could not," Creasey bellowed before he forced

himself to calm. "No one can move from rustic bumbler to expert in a matter of weeks. No matter how many books you read."

"That is so." I leaned back in my chair, resting my hands on the stout walking stick, feigning relaxation, in spite of my pounding heart. "Have you heard of Monsieur Philidor?"

"Philidor?" Creasey asked in amazement. "Of course I have. I've watched him play, in Paris and in London, at Parloe's chess club. None could touch him." Creasey's eyes widened. "Are you saying *he* was your teacher?"

"Not at all. I was at Cambridge when he died as an émigré. I joined the army soon after that. Six years later I was in Paris. My teacher was one of Philidor's pupils. The chap knew everything Philidor did, but he was hard up—it was difficult to make a living as a chess master at that time. To pass the hours, I let him teach me." Eden handed me the king Creasey had thrown in his pique and I stood the beautiful jade piece on its home square. "I let him teach me everything."

"You lied to me."

"Not at all." I rose, hoping I hid my trembling well. "You assumed, and I did not correct you."

"Man of honor, *pah*."

"I always keep my word. Now, we agreed that if I won, I and my son and my friends were free to go. That you would withdraw for now."

"Oh, yes. So I did."

He would not let us leave so easily, I knew. I was poised to tear across the room and snatch up Peter while Brewster cleared a path for our escape, when the door flew open.

On the threshold was Lucius Grenville, pistol in hand. With him, to my immense dismay, was Donata. Behind the two of them were a contingent of Denis's men, grim-faced and ready for battle.

Peter saw Donata. "Mum!" he shouted.

No one could stop her. Donata was through the crowded room and to her son, gathering him in her arms.

"Peter, love. It's all right. I'm here."

Creasey's men regarded Donata in some awe, probably shocked she had the temerity to invade this place. Donata straightened, holding Peter, and sent Creasey a gaze that could scorch him to nothing.

"As for *you*," she said in her clear voice. "I will have the law on you, for kidnapping, holding my son hostage, and any other crime I might think of. You will never, *ever*, touch any of my family again."

Donata was usually cool as an icicle, but when she became enraged, lesser men fled out of her way. Creasey was a hard being, but even he regarded her with his jaw slack, uncertain how to respond.

I moved from the game table to the door, which Brewster had sidled toward while we'd played. He'd let none prevent us from leaving.

Donata did not wait for me. She marched out, Grenville behind her like a sentinel.

"You made one mistake," I told Creasey in a mild tone. "You upset my wife. She is a very powerful woman, connected to still more powerful men. There will not be many places you can hide from her. The queen, you know, is the strongest piece on the board. Good morning, Mr. Creasey. Thank you for the match."

I was proud of the little speech and made certain not to ruin it by immediately departing. Eden came behind me.

"Good Lord, Lacey, I thought you'd have us all killed."

"And we might still be if we do not make haste," I said. "Brewster," I called softly behind me.

I heard voices inside Creasey's office, Denis discussing

something with him. I wondered if Creasey would reinstate his truce with Denis if we actually escaped this building.

Brewster did not follow until Denis exited the office unimpeded. Denis's men surrounded him, enclosing him like pawns around a king.

Creasey's men let us pass. The sun had risen, and the dim light from the end of the building showed us a horde of them, poised in the shadows. But we moved through and down the stairs without hindrance.

On the ground floor, Denis, striding swiftly, caught up to me. Grenville and Donata, slower with Donata carrying Peter, were just ahead of us.

"Thought I'd soil myself when you took him up on the game," Brewster said. "You're a dark horse, ain't ye, guv?"

Denis moved past us. "We can discuss it later, gentlemen. For now we should move quickly. Quite quickly."

My heart constricted. "What did you do?" I asked.

Denis did not answer. He hastened his steps, and around us, his men broke into a run.

I hobbled forward as fast as I could. Denis joined Grenville, wrapping an arm around Donata and pulling her onward at a faster pace. Brewster did the same with me, nearly carrying me by the time we burst out of the dark warehouse and into the morning light.

"Do not stop." Denis kept hold of Donata, who was being very quiet. Peter was too, sensing the danger.

"Better do as he says, guv." Brewster dragged me onward. Eden took my other arm, the two of them almost pulling me off my feet.

As soon as we reached the mouth of the lane, a huge explosion sounded behind us. The draft shot us out into the road, bricks and pieces of board hurtling toward us and flying along the cobbles.

I turned. Black smoke poured from the building that had housed Creasey, and flames sprang up behind the windows. Screams and shouts erupted from Lower Thames Street, and then the common folk of London rushed toward the conflagration, joining to form a bucket chain to squelch the fire as swiftly as they could.

CHAPTER 23

*D*enis's coach waited for us well away from the tumult. Denis assisted Donata inside and Grenville handed up Peter as Denis climbed aboard.

"I'll leave you here, Lacey." Eden glanced into the coach. "Not enough room for me. You had me worried, but I might have known you had a trick up your sleeve. What the devil caused that blast?"

I knew exactly what had but decided now was not the time to enlighten him.

Grenville, who also had guessed, answered. "You never know what has been stored in these old warehouses. Gunpowder, rum, brandy. The old Custom House exploded a few years ago, and papers from it were found all the way to Hackney."

"Indeed?" Eden asked, intrigued. "Hmm, well. It was a pleasure to meet you, Mr. Grenville." Eden stuck out his hand, and Grenville, well-bred, shook it. "I hope to make your acquaintance again, under better circumstances."

"Quite." Grenville gave him a polite bow. "You are at Brooks's? I shall look you up there."

Eden, gratified by this exchange, bowed to Donata, waved to me, and scurried off into the crowd.

I wondered anew what had brought Eden to the Custom House in the dark hours of the morning, but for now, I was anxious to take Peter home. Grenville assisted me into the coach then clambered in after me, and Brewster slammed the door. The carriage listed as Brewster took his seat on the back.

Donata, next to Denis and across from me, had gone silent, her arms around Peter, who sat on her lap.

"All right, Peter?" I asked.

Peter's face bore lines of exhaustion, his eyes red-rimmed. But he nodded. "Yes, sir."

"You are a brave lad. Very brave." I patted his knee, careful not to touch Donata.

"Indeed," Grenville said. "You showed remarkable sangfroid, Peter, in the face of danger. That is a fine thing."

Peter sent him a grave nod. "I thought of how brave Papa was when the Frenchies caught him. I pretended I was he."

I'd given Peter a truncated version of the ordeal that had shattered my leg and left me lame. His answer made my eyes sting.

"You're a good lad." My words sounded inadequate. To save myself the embarrassment of weeping in front of them, I turned to Denis. "Ridgley?" I asked.

"Yes." Denis answered without inflection. "He was not here, but I instructed my men to bring one of his devices."

"I see." Ridgley was a cold-blooded maker of incendiaries, two of which had nearly killed me in the past. I'd wondered whether Denis had rid himself of the man, and he'd now given me the answer.

"It was the only way," Denis said. "He'd not have ceased otherwise."

"He might survive it," I pointed out.

"He might." Denis gave a nod. "Though I doubt it. It will teach him to leave me be."

My anger rose. "You had that device put into a building that held my son and my wife."

Denis stirred impatiently. "I had assumed you would leave immediately with the boy. Agreeing to Creasey's game to satisfy his vanity was foolish, but I admit, I enjoyed seeing him bested. I had no idea that Mr. Grenville would bring her ladyship."

Grenville sent us a weak smile. "She rather insisted."

"Of course I did," Donata said, some of her imperious manner returning. "I am a mother first, gentlemen. And I would have had the Runners on Mr. Creasey as soon as I had Peter safely home. There was no need for theatrics." The icy stare she turned on Denis made me swell with pride.

"Forgive me, your ladyship, but it was necessary," Denis said without heat. "Creasey would have found a way to elude the Runners. He has a few in his pay, and he is careful to eliminate any evidence of his deeds. I am right that he would have continued to try to kill me, possibly using you, or your son, or even your daughter as another hostage. I decided to end it. I had planned to do so another day, but Captain Lacey brought me the immediate opportunity."

"Opportunity, you call it." Donata's ire rose. "He abducted my son."

"A poor choice of words. I planned to make certain his lordship was well and safe before springing my trap."

"It's all right, Mama," Peter said, patting Donata's arm. "Papa came for me, as I knew he would. He saved us all."

Donata's eyes were flinty, but she did not correct him.

Grenville chuckled. "He did, indeed. Your papa has hidden depths."

Donata turned on Denis. "*Your* foolishness caused my son to be put into grave danger. I would put the Runners on to you as well, but I know it would be a futile gesture." She subsided. "Besides, I do not like that Mr. Spendlove."

"I will do my best to make it up to you, your ladyship," Denis said.

"See that you do."

Donata turned away from us, staring resolutely out the window. At least her first incoherent terror had gone, and she could hold Peter and give a silent prayer of thanks that he was well.

DENIS TOOK US TO SOUTH AUDLEY STREET. GRENVILLE descended with us, wanting to see us inside and to make certain we were well.

Before I could enter behind them, Denis stopped me and spoke to me in a low voice. "This time, I owe *you* a debt, Lacey. When you have need of anything, send word to me, and I will do all I can."

I gazed at him in frank astonishment. "I thought you preferred to keep all your acquaintance under your firm thumb."

"I do. But I also know when a debt has been paid and exceeded. The advantage is to you." Denis paused. "But never ask me to play chess. I am exceedingly bad at it."

I looked for amusement in his eyes but found none. If he made a joke, he would not let me know.

Denis bade me a formal good morning, then ascended into his carriage once more.

"I'll be off, meself," Brewster said. "Now that Creasey is dust, I'll tell Em to come home. Would be fine to see the old girl."

"I may still have need of your help," I said. "I have not yet cleared Eden, and he is becoming even more evasive." I gazed up at Donata's home that stretched high above me. "I will let him go for the moment. Now, I will rest—or perhaps hunt for somewhere else to live. My wife is not happy with me."

"She'll come 'round," Brewster said with confidence. "Now that the little lordship is safely home, and all is well."

"That remains to be seen. Donata was correct when she blamed me for this."

"If you don't mind me saying so, your lady is much more sensible than you. She'll work things out." Brewster shrugged. "You can always go back to your old rooms. Lucky you kept them, innit?"

With that cheerful observation, he trudged away up South Audley Street to make for St. Giles and home.

I entered the house. Barnstable had been caught in his shirtsleeves, polishing silver in the dining room with the footmen. He now stood in the hall, mouth open, holding a rag in a gloved hand.

Donata was busily giving him orders to have fires laid in the bedchambers and a cot made up in her room for Peter. Mrs. McGowan had remained in Gloucestershire, and Donata did not want Peter sleeping in the nursery alone.

"Can I sleep in Papa's chamber?" Peter asked. "His snoring don't bother me."

The footmen, who'd lined up behind Barnstable as he struggled into his frock coat, barely hid smiles. Donata glanced from her hopeful son to me, her gaze frosty.

"Very well. Barnstable, please have the cot readied in the captain's chamber."

She stalked upstairs, leaving the rest of us behind, back straight, poise unaltered.

Grenville touched my sleeve. "Why don't you clean yourself up, Lacey, while Peter and I find some grub? Mind if we invade the kitchen, Barnstable? We're too hungry to wait to be served, I think."

Peter brightened at this chance to go down to the kitchen with the great Mr. Grenville. I knew Barnstable and the cook would minister to them both, and I truly was appallingly dirty.

I left them to it and ascended to my bedchamber. A footman brought me hot water and helped me peel off my clothes. Fortunately, some of my belongings had been left here, and I was able to dress in a fresh suit.

I was exhausted, my eyes grating, my legs too shaky to support me. I had kept hold of the walking stick Brewster had taken from Denis's house, but I would ask Barnstable to return it when we made once more for Gloucestershire.

If we did. Donata might simply remove herself and Peter to Oxfordshire on the morrow and fetch Anne, uncaring what I did with myself.

I moved through my dressing room and entered Donata's bedchamber, lightly tapping on her door before I did so.

I found her flung across the bed, sobbing.

"Love." I sank next to my wife, my hand on her hair. I did not know if she wanted me to touch her, but I could not leave her distraught without offering comfort. "Peter's home. He's safe."

Donata continued to weep. I leaned down and kissed the top of her head. "I'll go, if you like," I whispered.

Donata started up, nearly colliding with me, then she threw her arms around me. "Do not dare leave me. Do not dare."

"No." I soothed her. "I'll stay." Something inside me

unclenched, though I knew we were a long way from reconciliation. "I agree that I am to blame. I have allowed Denis to pull me into his machinations, when I should have torn myself from him long ago, no matter what he threatened."

Donata raised her head and wiped her eyes with the back of her hand. Even with her face splotchy and tear-streaked, she was beautiful. "You are *not* to blame. If you had defied him as you say, perhaps he might have threatened Peter, or me, to keep you tame. Denis plays his own games. In this one, you simply happened to be in the way."

"I'd like to believe I have my own will," I said with feigned indignation. "Though I am happy you are not angry with me."

"Oh, I am angry." The flash in her eyes told me that. "I will be for a long while. But I realized, as Grenville and I rode from Gloucestershire, that you were powerless. Mr. Creasey was a terrible man, and the blame rests squarely upon *him*."

"It does. I am appalled at Denis's methods, but I am glad I will not have to deal with Creasey again."

"Mr. Denis was correct that it was the only way. Killing him, I mean." Donata shivered and laced her arms around me. "Let us return to Gloucestershire, and Anne, and forget all this." She rested her head on my shoulder, and my heart warmed. "Where is Grenville, by the bye?"

"Having breakfast in the kitchen with Peter."

"Grenville is all a gentleman should be." Donata raised her head, her faraway smile one that would have made me mad with jealousy before I came to understand her. "He is a reason I turned my rage from you to Mr. Denis and Mr. Creasey. He put forth a logical argument that you were coerced by both gentlemen, even one that reached through my worst fears."

"I owe him much, then," I said.

"You can thank him when we are back in Gloucestershire. His house is quite cozy. We'll leave tomorrow."

The commanding woman had returned. "Will you give me time to find Eden again? I want to locate Warrilow's killer, and I am certain Eden can tell me much more than he is saying."

"Perhaps one more day," Donata said. "I can do some shopping."

She'd give me no more, I knew. I gathered her against me, my lips in her hair, and we rejoiced that Peter was safe and well.

I SLEPT A LONG TIME, ALL THROUGH THE NIGHT AND INTO the next morning. Peter was curled up on a cot at the foot of my bed, the boy worn out. I'd feared he'd have trouble sleeping or experience nightmares once he did, but Peter had dropped off quickly and was still asleep when I rose. I bade a footman watch over him while I went down to find a meal.

Grenville, who had accepted Donata's invitation to be a guest here so he would not have to open his own house, had gone out, Barnstable informed me.

"Mr. Grenville slept only a little," Barnstable said as he served me coffee and a light breakfast in the dining room. "He is a most energetic gentleman. He said he had things to see to this morning."

I ate hungrily, agreeing with Barnstable. Grenville suffered only one malady, motion sickness, but he quickly recovered from it once he was on his feet again. I admired him for bringing Donata from Gloucestershire in one go. He must have been in a bad way on that journey.

I'd have little time in London, and I must make the most of it. I would find Eden and shake out of him what he was keeping from me. It might have nothing to do with Warrilow's murder, but I had a feeling it had everything to do with it.

Now that the threat of Creasey had been removed—even if he'd survived the blast, he would not likely be in position to retaliate right away—I had time to think about Eden's conundrum.

I called for pen and paper and listed out my thoughts as I ate.

My theory was that Warrilow knew about the smuggling —both the guns and Fitzgerald's artworks. He was apt to dig into everyone's business and upbraid them for it. I suspected he tried to blackmail both Laybourne and whoever had killed him. If Warrilow had been an upright man, he'd have gone straight to the Thames River Police or a magistrate or the customs men with his knowledge. Instead, he'd hidden the gun and admitted a late-night visitor to his rooms, getting himself murdered for his pains.

I had thought the carbine a key to the murder when Brewster found it, but there was another possibility. The gun had been in pieces, well hidden. The killer obviously hadn't known it was under the floorboards, or he would have taken it away with him. In that case, perhaps Warrilow had been struck down because he'd known about the *art*.

I could imagine Fitzgerald, smiling and agreeable, calling on Warrilow, perhaps making an appointment to meet him that night. Warrilow would not be on his guard with Fitzgerald, as he sneered that he knew all about Fitzgerald's smuggling. I could also imagine Fitzgerald, a large and strong man, silencing Warrilow with one blow of the washbasin's heavy pitcher. There had been no blood on the pitcher that Mrs. Beadle had noticed, but perhaps he'd cleaned it and replaced it carefully before he'd gone.

Fitzgerald would have no need to search the room for the

missing carbine, because he was only interested in smuggling his artworks. He'd have gone, dusting off his hands.

Why then, would he have killed Laybourne? I made another note.

For the same reason, I imagined. Perhaps Laybourne, while offloading his contraband weapons, had found Fitzgerald's pieces. Laybourne had been waxing nostalgic about returning to the affluent spa town at the edge of the Dales. Had the threadbare man been paid handsomely by Fitzgerald to look the other way? And Fitzgerald, fearing Laybourne would not keep silent, killed him.

Whose carts had the fisherman seen surreptitiously take away a few loads? Fitzgerald's I wagered.

It must have been unnerving for both Fitzgerald and Laybourne when the customs agents were crawling all over the ship, randomly seizing goods. The customs men had already been alerted about missing cargos and were carefully examining everything.

Then there were the Kingstons. Harry, the boy from Warrilow's lodgings, had said he'd seen Mr. Kingston attempt to visit Warrilow, and Kingston had admitted he'd been there. His story that he hoped Warrilow had made an appointment with him so Kingston could save his soul was thin. Harry had again seen Mr. Kingston outside later that night, and then the next day near Laybourne's, though Kingston had denied that.

Then again, *Mrs.* Kingston was tall, though not as slender. I had noted that their heights were not too far apart. If she dressed in her husband's clothes, she might pass for him in the darkness.

I drew another sheet of paper to me and wrote a note to Sir Montague Harris, suggesting that he investigate a man and wife by the name of Kingston, recently returned from Antigua, missionaries from Lambeth. Brewster was correct that missionaries could easily move about the world, in a prime position to smuggle goods. Port authorities and customs officials might dismiss them as unthreatening. Or, when the Kingstons began to preach at them, wave them through to be rid of them.

I'd sent this letter off with one of our footmen and was finishing my breakfast when Grenville returned.

He was flushed, agitated. "Excellent, you are awake." Grenville slid out of the greatcoat Barnstable reached to take from him. "I called in at Brooks's to see if Major Eden might be there. I agree we need to speak to him most pressingly. He'd anticipated my arrival and left this."

Grenville shoved a folded paper at me. Barnstable slid out a chair, trying to coax Grenville to sit, but he remained standing, leaning his fists on the table.

I opened the paper and read.

Mr. Grenville,

Forgive my rudeness, but please pass word to Lacey to meet me at once at Number 25 Wellclose Square. I fear much and need his help.

Eden

CHAPTER 24

*B*arnstable had Grenville's carriage, driven by his coachman, Jackson, ready for us in a flash.

I asked Jackson to take me first to St. Giles, where I would retrieve Brewster. While we crossed the city, I told Grenville what I'd been mulling over breakfast, and we speculated on my ideas.

I was very glad to sit across from Grenville once more, discussing an investigation. His quick mind complemented my plodding one, his diplomacy, my frontal attacks.

"Major Eden is ready to confess, is he?" Brewster asked when I summoned him from his house. Mrs. Brewster was there, greeting me cheerfully as usual, and pushing her Tommy out to help me once more.

"That remains to be seen." The carriage could not come into the warrens, which suited Jackson, and so we walked through the awakening slum to meet the coach and Grenville at the church. "He is agitated enough to send for me."

"Or he could be luring you into a trap, as Creasey did."

"That is why I am bringing you along," I said.

Once we were aboard, Jackson turned the coach along Holborn then south on Fetter Lane to Fleet Street and east until we were again past the Tower and into the once-elegant Wellclose Square.

The house Eden directed us to was on the east side of the square, around the corner from Warrilow's lodgings. The home's three stories rose to a series of dormer windows, again reminding me of Parisian residences.

The door was opened to our knock by a handsome, black-skinned woman with large dark eyes, whom I guessed to be in her thirties. She wore a trim gown of blue-and-white cotton stripe with a white lawn cap.

"Good evening, madam." I greeted her with a bow. "I was told I'd find Major Eden here?"

"You must be Captain Lacey." The woman exhaled in relief and opened the door wide. "Yes, please, come in."

She spoke with the liquid accent of the West Indies, one I'd always found musical and soothing. At the moment, the woman showed much distress as she led us into a sitting room in the back of the house.

"He's here," she announced.

Eden rose from a chair near a cheerful fire. "Ah, thank God. We're in a bit of a dilemma, Lacey. I see you found my note, Mr. Grenville. Excellent."

"Grenville?" The woman looked Grenville up and down then pressed a hand to her chest. "Oh, my heavens. You *are* Mr. Grenville. I've read all about you in the newspapers."

Grenville, nonplussed, removed his hat and bowed. "At your service, madam." Though Grenville had traveled as hard as I had from Gloucestershire, he was dressed impeccably in a well-fitted suit and a brilliant white cravat, unsoiled gloves on his hands.

"Forgive my manners," Eden said. "I am too distracted for

formal introductions." He swept his hand around the room. "Captain Lacey, Mr. Grenville, Mr. Brewster. Mrs. Davies."

Mrs. Davies curtsied. "Pleased you have come, gentlemen. Major Eden says he relies on you. I'll hunt up some tea. Won't be a tick."

Charmingly blending her West Indies accent with London cant, she moved smoothly out of the room.

"Lovely woman," Grenville said. "Who the devil is she?"

"Er, well ..."

"I was right," I said in triumph. "You did spirit her away across the seas."

"Not exactly. I am ready to confess, Lacey. No, not to murder." Eden laughed breathlessly. "But all my sins. The trouble is, I'm afraid I'm about to be arrested."

"By Pomeroy?" I asked in alarm. "Does he want to pin Laybourne's death on you as well?"

"Eh? No, not the Runners," Eden said. "Customs and Excise."

"Customs and Excise?" Grenville broke in. "Can they arrest people? For what?"

"Smuggling, of course," Eden said.

"What were you smuggling?" I asked sternly. "Artwork?" Had he been in league with Fitzgerald all this time?

Eden started. "What? No, no." He swept his hand to a shadowy corner next to the fireplace. "Him."

I gazed to where he gestured and saw a pair of eyes about three feet from the floor staring out at me, glittering in the thin light.

"Don't be afraid, Robbie," Eden said. "These are my friends. Come and say good morning."

A small boy peeled himself from the wall and hurried to Eden's side. His clothes were new and fashionable—trousers, shirt, and coat—though like most boys, including Peter, he'd already managed to wrench them awry. He had black skin and the same round eyes as Mrs. Davies.

"Cor," Brewster said. "You smuggled *'im?*"

Mrs. Davies returned bearing a tray, which Grenville instantly took from her to set on the wide tea table.

"He did." Mrs. Davies sent a glowing smile to Eden. "Just as he promised."

Eden's flush rose. I recalled now that he not only blushed when he lied but also when caught out doing a good deed.

"Perhaps we should have that story now, Eden," I said sternly.

"Not much to it." Eden waved us to chairs as Mrs. Davies sat and poured tea.

"Major Eden doesn't like to talk about his kindness," Mrs. Davies said serenely. "I worked on his plantation, you see." She poured with grace and handed us delicate porcelain cups with a steady hand. "He bought the place with everything in it and everything on it from a gentleman who was selling up and going back to England. When Major Eden took over, he freed all of us. There was nowhere in Antigua for me to go, so he made arrangements and sent me here, legally, finding me respectable work so I could pay my way."

I recalled Eden telling me that if he had rescued a woman from Antigua, he'd free her first and have her ride a ship as a legitimate passenger. He'd already done so, damn the man, admitting to his actions without betraying himself.

Mrs. Davies's mouth turned down in sadness. "The only thing I could not do was bring my son."

Robbie was about ten if I were any judge, the same age as Mrs. Beadle's grandson, Harry, and a little older than Peter. He had taken a seat next to Eden, his small legs swinging above the floor. He stared in blatant fascination at Brewster, who balanced his tiny teacup on huge fingers.

"Meaning young Robbie here wasn't free to go?" Grenville asked.

"He belonged to Warrilow," Eden said.

"Ah," I took a sip of very good tea. "I begin to see."

"Mr. Warrilow had sold me to his neighbor when Robbie was about six summers," Mrs. Davies said. A spark of old anger rose. "He refused to let Robbie come with me, saying he was useful for work in the garden. It was not so bad—Mr. Warrilow's plantation was close, and I visited Robbie whenever I could." Her stoic words belied the anguish I saw in her eyes. She'd faced her pain with a courage most men I knew, including me, would lack. "When Major Eden freed me, I told him about Robbie. Major Eden promised he'd fetch him, and we'd be together always. I didn't quite believe it." She sent Eden a radiant glance.

"As you might guess," Eden said. "Warrilow wouldn't sell. I tried everything to talk him into it, even offering him an exorbitant price, but he would not budge. He knew I wanted Robbie badly and delighted in being intractable." Eden shrugged. "So, I stole him."

Robbie flashed a huge grin. "It was brilliant."

Eden laughed with him. "Robbie is a born actor. I managed to speak to Robbie when I came to badger Warrilow, and told him exactly what he needed to do. Robbie never breathed a word to anyone, turned up to do his work in the gardens as per usual that day. He then walked off to eat his lunch in the field—as per usual—but he kept on to the windmill on the edge of the plantation, where I was waiting. I swept him up, and off we went. I'd already booked passage on the ship, and we boarded the next morning. I had no paperwork for the lad, nothing to say I owned him legally or that he was free to depart Antigua." Eden rubbed his forehead. "So I had to smuggle him."

"I hid in his trunk," Robbie burst out. "He gave me things to eat and drink and said I had to be very quiet. I'm good at that." His voice filled the room now, but when we'd come in, I'd never seen nor heard him by the fireplace.

I remembered the box with the key Eden had carried away from the Custom House. It was large enough for a small boy to hide in. That day Eden had also left me to Creasey, claiming to Brewster that he had an appointment. He'd likely been coming here, to check on Mrs. Davies and Robbie.

"He is a very good boy," Mrs. Davies said with pride. "He did exactly what Major Eden said, and here he is." Her happiness rolled from her, filling the cozy room.

"I did not keep him in the trunk the entire voyage," Eden said hastily. "So, please do not look so appalled, Mr. Grenville. Once we were well out to sea, no turning back, I would have spoken to the captain and had the quartermaster fix a bunk for him. But, I am ever unlucky." Eden sighed. "Warrilow decided at the last minute to sail to England, and ours was the only ship going that day."

"Robbie is why you went constantly to the hold during the voyage," I said, the pieces falling into place.

"Of course. I had to feed the poor mite, and let him walk about and relieve himself. One of the sailor boys was pleased to help and keep it quiet—he despised Warrilow too."

"Did Warrilow discover you? After all, Robbie disappeared, and you, who'd tried avidly to buy him, left for England at the same time. Did Warrilow put the two events together?"

Eden made a noise of derision. "Do you know, he hadn't

even noticed Robbie was gone. When I came across Warrilow at supper the first night, he crowed that he'd thwarted me from purchasing the lad, and said obviously I could not now, as I was heading for England, never to return. At first, I thought he had found me out and was taunting me, but no. He had no idea."

"How did you spirit Robbie away once you landed?" Grenville asked. "The customs agents were everywhere, you say, and they took your box."

"That actually was easy. The sailor boy lent Robbie some of his clothes, and Robbie simply walked off the ship with him. No one pays much attention to boys. I did nearly have apoplexy when the customs officials said they were taking my baggage, but the sailor lad managed to get Robbie away while the men were searching the cargo. I thought all was well."

"But?" I asked as Eden paused. "Why did you really look up Warrilow that night?"

"Because I saw him here in Wellclose Square. I met up with Robbie on the wharf and brought him to this house, which I'd leased a year or so ago, for Mrs. Davies. And there was Warrilow, walking into a house on the adjacent side of the square. Not terribly surprising, as there are only so many places in the area a man can lodge, but my bad luck again. I went to make certain that he hadn't, in fact, seen Robbie, and also whether he'd be leaving London soon. But, as I say, he was in bed when I called. I'd planned to return the next day, but ..." Eden threw open his hands.

"Then you never were found out," Grenville said. "Why do you believe the customs agents will arrest you now?"

"Because Robbie has seen them flitting about near this house," Eden said. "Tell them what you told me, lad."

"I did see them," Robbie said stoutly. "Wandering across the road near the church. I remember them from when they came down to search the hold. I had to hide until they were busy looking through the boxes, and then Jacko—he's the one what gave me his clothes—led me off and showed me where to wait for the major."

Robbie's words put things together in my mind, all that I'd debated with myself whenever I pondered Eden's problem, and what I'd been trying to sort out this morning.

"What else did you observe while you were in the hold, Robbie?" I asked. "When the agents were there?"

"The fat man giving them money," Robbie said promptly.

"Fitzgerald," I said.

"Precisely what I thought when Robbie told me all this today," Eden said. "I imagine he's the villain after all."

I leaned to Robbie, trying to use my kindest voice, though my heart was beating swiftly in excitement. "What did the agents you saw across the road look like?"

Robbie considered. "There's three of them. Two are ordinary—I saw them in the belly of the ship. The other was tall and very thin. Like that missionary chap."

Well, well. I turned to Eden. "Why do you suppose they had anything to do with you? They might be searching for the gun smugglers."

Robbie shook his head. "They were staring straight at this house. Watching it, like."

Mrs. Davies' hand trembled as she set down her cup. "Can they come and take him from me? My Robbie?"

Grenville, master at soothing troubled waters, answered. "I shouldn't think so. Slavery is illegal by the laws of England and the acts abolishing the international slave trade, so the boy should be free on this soil, which presumably was Eden's thinking. No, I'm wondering if they aren't afraid of what Robbie might have seen in the hold. They probably thought him of no consequence if they glimpsed him there, but if they ever saw you with him, Eden …"

"My thinking too, Mr. Grenville," Brewster said. "Someone likely followed you here, Major, maybe caught sight of young Robbie, and worked it all out. What with you always down in the hold, they might think you saw other things too. If the customs agents were taking bribes, they'd not want anyone to find that out."

"They are clearing up loose ends, you mean," Eden said in alarm.

"Warrilow was a loose end," I said, surprisingly calm. "He knew, with his way of ferreting out men's secrets and berating them, about the smuggling and the bribery. I still make him out to be a blackmailer, but he was a threat."

"Jove." Eden swallowed. "Laybourne was a threat too, wasn't he? Poor fellow. I imagine he only wished to retire, as he said."

"And they killed him for it," Brewster put in. "He knew too much about the goings on."

I glanced at Mrs. Davies, who'd followed the conversation without surprise.

"Oh, I've told her all," Eden said, catching my look. "She had it out of me after Warrilow was killed, and I came to her, so very upset."

"It was a terrible thing," Mrs. Davies said. "Even if Mr. Warrilow was a very bad man. I wager you are right that Mr. Warrilow took money for his silence, Captain. He did the same with others on Antigua."

"It's Fitzgerald doing this then?" Eden asked. "He bribed the customs men to be able to offload his artwork without hindrance, and then shut up Warrilow. Laybourne too, because Laybourne must have known about the bribe—since he was paying one as well. A pity. I rather like Fitzgerald."

I set down my cup and rose abruptly. It was time to put a stop to this.

"I believe we should visit the Custom House itself, gentlemen. Put forth all we know, and let them and the magistrates take care of the villains in their midst. I'd like Robbie to come with us, Mrs. Davies. I promise to return him very soon, and unscathed."

CHAPTER 25

I wanted to bring two more people with us. One was
Harry, whom I borrowed from Mrs. Beadle. The
two boys, about the same age, and dwelling in close proximity,
already knew each other.

"Mornin', Robbie," Harry said as Brewster lifted him into
the coach. "Where we going?"

"Custom House," Robbie said. "Wherever that is."

"I know it." Harry spoke with the confidence of the
London-born. "Mornin', Mr. Brewster. You wouldn't have a
flask on ye, would ye?"

"I would," Brewster said as he shut the coach's door on us.
"But the captain and your grandmum would break me bones
if I gave it to ye."

He chuckled as he turned to climb onto his perch in the
back.

I asked Jackson to make one more stop on Wapping
Docks before he took us to the Custom House.

Always easygoing, Thompson did not question me when I

hurried into his office and asked him to accompany us. He chose to join Brewster on the back of the coach, his slim build fitting easily onto the seat with him.

We piled out at the Customs House and went inside, making our way to the long room. Eden led the way through the crowd there, the rest of us trailing, as Brewster held firmly to each of the boys' hands.

When we reached Seabrook's office, I halted. "There won't be much room inside," I said. "Brewster, will you look after the lads? I'll want them to speak to him, but I doubt we can all squeeze in at once."

Brewster nodded, cheerfully telling the boys they'd hunt up something interesting to do.

The clerk, Bristow, recognized Eden and me but was doubtful at our reception. "He is ever so busy, Captain. There was an explosion near here yesterday, and a fire. It's put out now, but the warehouses on that lane are being gone through, and it's a job."

Seabrook wouldn't be sorting through whatever ruined goods were found, I reasoned, but dealing with all the reports. I pictured the piles on his desk growing taller.

"We'll not take much time," I said.

"It's devilish important," Grenville put in.

Bristow studied Grenville, evidently a wealthy man, possibly a powerful one. One who might give him a good tip, I saw him conclude.

"Right then. This way, sirs."

He tapped on Seabrook's door and opened it at Seabrook's invitation.

The customs official stood up with an expression of gladness when he saw us. "Excellent. I needed an excuse to lay down my pen." He dropped it on the tray with a clatter.

"What can I do for you today, Captain? Major Eden?" He glanced with interest at Grenville and then Thompson. "Aren't you a Thames River fellow? Yes, I think we've met once or twice."

"Peter Thompson." Thompson peeled off one fingerless glove and shook Seabrook's hand. "This is Mr. Grenville."

"Oh-ho." Seabrook grinned. "What has brought the famous Mr. Grenville to the Custom House? To rescue some very fine brandy?"

"Hardly." Grenville shook his hand and gave him a friendly nod. "I purchase mine legally, I assure you."

Seabrook chuckled. "Please, sit down, gentlemen, if you can find space. What brings you here? What can you tell me about the warehouse that blew itself into powder?" His sage expression told me he believed I'd been involved somehow.

"I am here to explain what happened on the *Dusty Rose*," I said. "The ship that brought Major Eden to England."

"Yes." Seabrook nodded. "That cargo was finally cleared, although as I say, we have not found what was stolen."

"I do not think anything was actually taken from the ship," I said. "But it was used to smuggle expensive, and possibly stolen, artwork, and shipments of guns. Carbines and possibly more."

"Ah, yes, the carbine you found." Seabrook sifted through papers on his desk and extracted one. "I have my notes on it. Did you discover any other weapons?"

"Not yet. Mr. Laybourne likely knew where they were. But let me give you a sequence of events as I believed they happened."

I glanced at my friends. They nodded at me to continue, though Eden appeared apprehensive.

"The *Dusty Rose* sailed with cargo and several passengers," I began. "Major Eden, Mr. Warrilow, Mr. Laybourne, Mr.

Fitzgerald, and the missionaries, Mr. and Mrs. Kingston. Warrilow was a passenger of the sort most people dread, arguing over every point in a conversation, prying into their business. He was suspicious of Eden, who visited the hold to check on his belongings, and also of Laybourne, Fitzgerald, and the Kingstons. The Kingstons seem to be exactly what they are, zealous missionaries. I've met them. But a little too zealous to be true perhaps?"

"Ah," Thompson murmured.

"I am also interested in Kingston because he is tall. I will come to that in a moment." I rested my hand on the gold head of Denis's walking stick. "The voyage continued without much drama, except Eden and Mr. Warrilow resorting to fisticuffs at the dining table. But once the ship landed, there was plenty of drama. First, the ship was delayed. They had to sit downriver for a long time until they were able to inch up to the wharves to unload. This worried men who had many surreptitious things to do. Finally, the ship docked.

"As usual, customs officials boarded the ship first, consulted the cargo master, and then went below to search the hold. Mr. Fitzgerald, who had gathered stolen artwork—I am afraid I don't know what, but I will leave that to Mr. Thompson—slipped down to the hold and paid the agents some coin to leave his things alone. He then had the items unloaded to waiting carts, which slipped off in the night. Fitzgerald allowed the customs agents to take one object, his painted box, for which he did have paperwork of a sale. This paperwork might have been forged, or perhaps his tale of buying it from a man on St. Maarten is true. Mr. Fitzgerald then disembarked with the other passengers and made his way to White's to take rooms, like the very respectable gentleman he paints himself to be."

Seabrook's face had gone wan. "He bribed my men? Bloody hell. I know corruption goes on, but *my* men?"

"I believe Warrilow witnessed this exchange of money take place, or he guessed. Possibly Fitzgerald visited him that night and paid him to keep his silence."

"And killed him," Eden said with conviction.

"No." I shook my head. "Not Fitzgerald. He is guilty of smuggling artwork, possibly stolen ones, but not of murder. That was someone else. I haven't come to Mr. Laybourne. It was he who brought a stolen cache of weapons from the islands to England. I believe it is part of a ring—the weapons are seized on their way from Britain to South America. I imagine the smugglers take only a part of each cache and send the rest on, to avoid an intense hunt for the missing weapons. Mr. Laybourne was in charge of the boxes that went to England on the *Dusty Rose*.

"Mr. Warrilow found him out somehow, and took one of the carbines as evidence, perhaps to use it to blackmail him once they'd landed. Laybourne was seen speaking to Warrilow in Warrilow's lodgings, though Warrilow would not let Laybourne into his room. Perhaps Warrilow extracted money from Laybourne at that time, or perhaps they arranged to meet later for the exchange—we likely will never know. Mr. Laybourne was awaiting his payment for ferrying the weapons, enough money for him to contemplate golden retirement near the Yorkshire Dales. I say waiting, because if Laybourne had already received the money, I imagine he'd have lived somewhere other than the dreadful boarding house I found him in. He was most relieved that someone had killed Warrilow, which saved him from having to pay out in blackmail."

"But then Laybourne was killed too," Eden said.

"Another reason I've dismissed Fitzgerald as the murderer.

He'd have had no worry about Laybourne. Fitzgerald had managed to cart away his artwork, but Laybourne was doing something even worse, smuggling weapons. Laybourne would not be a threat to Fitzgerald, but perhaps the other way around, if Fitzgerald saw the wrong thing at the wrong time. No, Laybourne was killed because of the gun smuggling. He knew too much—who was doing it, and how the weapons were taken off the ship and transported on, and to whom. Dangerous knowledge."

Thompson tapped his fingertips together, his only sign of excited curiosity. "And how was it done? Who took the weapons from the ship?"

"The customs agents," I said without hesitation. "Who is better able to take whatever they wish from a ship and store it wherever they like for however long they want? The customs agents, who go through the hold and seize goods until duties are paid or owners can prove they are bringing the things into the country legally. The agents who boarded the *Dusty Rose* went straight to the boxes of the guns and carted them off, making certain to also take with them plenty of other innocuous things, which they brought to the Custom House as suspected contraband. Customs agents do this last all the time. The agents likely didn't expect Fitzgerald, who almost got in the way with his smuggled artwork, but why not make a few coins by accepting his bribe? Laybourne, who knew who the customs agents were—probably had worked with these men when he'd been a customs agent himself—had to be killed."

"Why?" Eden asked, perplexed and horrified. "Isn't that like killing the golden goose? He'd just brought them valuable cargo."

"Because Laybourne was retiring. We can't ever know, I suppose, exactly why they did it. Perhaps he tried to blackmail *them*. Perhaps they simply could not risk him telling anyone how things were done."

"Good Lord." Eden blinked.

"Likewise, Warrilow was murdered because he'd spoken to Laybourne, revealing that he knew about the guns. Whether he understood the entire business or simply knew Laybourne was involved, again, I do not know. But the agents could not take the chance that Warrilow would not divulge all."

Thompson nodded. "Gun running is a bad business, conducted by bad men."

I continued. "What the customs agents also did not expect to find in the hold was a small boy. A stowaway, who'd sought freedom in England. This boy had seen the agents take things away—would he understand what he'd observed? Or would anything he had to say be dangerous? He was just a child, after all. But then they noted the boy in the company of Major Eden, who was also on the ship and might well put two and two together. That same boy has seen these agents lurking outside his home, and I believe the lad to be in great danger."

"Not if I have anything to say about it," Eden declared.

Seabrook took all this in, his jaw slack, distress in his eyes. He rose to his full height, thin-boned fists clenching. "Who are these agents, Captain Lacey? I will have them arrested at once."

"I suppose we must ask our witnesses." I nodded at Grenville, who stepped to the door and opened it.

Brewster, at a signal from Grenville, ushered in the two boys, one from across the sea, the other London born and bred.

Both gazed at Mr. Seabrook looming over us, their eyes going wide.

"That's 'im." Harry pointed a stubby finger. "That's 'im

what I saw lurking outside me gran's the night Warrilow was done. And then going into Mr. Laybourne's house."

Robbie moved closer to Brewster's thick leg. "He was outside our house, by the church."

"Are you certain?" I asked. "This is very important lads."

Seabrook backed a step. "Nonsense. I never went near Wellclose Square."

"I saw him on the docks when I ran from the ship," Robbie said in a near whisper. "He was taking boxes away."

My friends were now on their feet. "I thought that was Kingston," Eden said in confusion. "Tall and thin. Harry heard his name."

"That were a different bloke," Harry said. "Depend upon it."

"Kingston did visit Warrilow," I said. "He and his wife claim it was to pray for Warrilow's soul. But who knows why Warrilow truly asked to speak to him? To confide in him what he knew about the guns? But Kingston was turned away, and so was Major Eden, with Laybourne fobbed off after a few words. Then Warrilow, who'd made an appointment for later that night, one he believed would bring him much blunt, pretended to retire for the evening. He rose and dressed again once all else in the house were asleep, and admitted Mr. Seabrook himself. But Mr. Seabrook had come to kill him. Perhaps he hadn't intended to, until he realized Warrilow's demand for money would never cease, and knew the man had to be silenced. The pitcher in the washbasin was handy. One blow, as Warrilow turned away, perhaps to fetch the carbine, perhaps to count the money Seabrook gave him. It felled him. Seabrook then wiped the pitcher clean or clean enough, and returned it to the stand. Mrs. Beadle, in her zeal to scrub down the room for the next guest, took the pitcher away and washed it, never noticing, completing the erasure of the blood."

Seabrook's face was red, and he retreated another step. "The devil I did any of this. You have no evidence. None."

"I know," I said.

Thompson wore a grin of delight, an expression I'd never seen on him before. "Never mind that. I'll be happy to spend time talking with you, Seabrook. We can discover much about the deeds you've done before I hand you over to the magistrates. Why don't you come with me now, and we'll have a chat?"

Seabrook tried to run, but he was hemmed into the room behind his wall of papers, and we were between him and the door. He moved to the window in a flash, but the sash was stiff, and Brewster was on him before he could budge it.

Mr. Thompson grabbed my hand and pumped it up and down, happier than I'd seen him in a long while. He let Brewster help him take Seabrook out, the man protesting his innocence all the way.

THE CLERK BRISTOW'S TRUE SHOCK WHEN BREWSTER AND Thompson dragged Seabrook away told me he was innocent of his superior's machinations. The other clerks gained great entertainment watching Brewster strong-arm their overseer down the stairs.

"He is not going quietly," Grenville remarked. "The other agents involved will be forewarned, and attempt to flee."

"True," I said. "But I imagine Seabrook will give up his accomplices to Thompson, and I trust Pomeroy to resolutely track them down. Catching a gun smuggler will be a large feather in Thompson's cap, and I'm certain the reward for the many convictions will be enough to satisfy even Pomeroy."

I led the way down the stairs, through the interested throng in the crowded room, and out to the damp, chill air.

"Why the devil did you believe it was him and not Kingston the boys saw?" Eden asked once we'd emerged. The two lads, excited by the encounter, began to run about the wide space before the Custom House, causing men and women to shout curses at them. "I had concluded it was the irritating Kingston murdering these gentlemen, if it wasn't Fitzgerald."

"I believed it was Kingston as well," I admitted. "Until I reasoned out the easiest method for transferring the weapons. The customs clerks took them from the ships and hid them, and either sent the weapons on to the Continent or received the payment from the buyers, or both. Ordinary customs agents would be hard-pressed to run this scheme without being caught, but if a supervisor were in on it, things would run much easier. Kingston is quite tall and thin, but so is Seabrook. Much more probable that a customs official who was always near the wharves ran a weapons-smuggling operation than a missionary from Lambeth, who'd be instantly noticed as out of place. Seabrook knew where Warrilow and Laybourne were housed, as his men had questioned both of them before they left the ship, just as they'd questioned Eden. And then I told Seabrook my suspicions of Laybourne smuggling weapons." I sighed. "Which I suspect is the main reason Laybourne was killed. Seabrook knew that if Laybourne went up before a magistrate, he'd confess all," I finished glumly.

I'd blithely told Seabrook that Laybourne was a threat to him, believing myself to be helpful.

"Well, at least you saved me from the noose." Eden settled his tall hat. "Now, shall we return these lads to their homes?"

I let out a whistle that I'd used to signal my troops across the battlefield—the boys ceased their games and came running. This time, I let them sit up top with Jackson as we trundled our way to Wellclose Square.

"I suspected you were doing a good deed, Eden," I said as we rolled along. "I simply didn't know *what* good deed." I sent him a look of exasperation. "Why didn't you tell me what you were up to?"

"Because I'd promised the boy's mother," Eden said simply. "She was terrified that her only child would be snatched up and either sent back to Warrilow's plantation, or far worse. So I gave her my word I'd tell no one until I was absolutely certain Robbie was safe. You must also realize that Mrs. Davies and Robbie had motive for murdering Warrilow —what if Warrilow had discovered where Robbie was? Living just around the corner from him? Juliet is a strong young woman. She could easily have hefted a pitcher at the back of Warrilow's head. I did not want you and Pomeroy rushing in and arresting the poor lady, Lacey. She's had a hard enough life without landing in Newgate on a charge of murder."

"I see." I stretched my knee, which was beginning to cramp. "You and your damned honor. I begin to understand why others find mine a nuisance. You could have trusted me completely, but I suppose you could not know that."

"I soon realized you were a stickler for justice," Eden countered. "You always have been, Lacey. But if you believed that Juliet, or even Robbie, who's a wiry lad, had killed Warrilow, you'd have had them in the dock."

"Perhaps," I conceded. "But I am just as pleased they had nothing to do with it."

"Juliet?" Grenville asked, his lips twitching.

Eden's color rose. "Mrs. Davies's Christian name. Lovely isn't it?"

"So is the lady," Grenville said.

"A lady who gazes at you with great admiration," I put in. "You have given her back her son, on top of freeing her from a life of servitude."

"Is there a Mr. Davies?" Grenville asked.

"No," Eden answered quickly. "I confess, I am not certain who fathered young Robbie."

"Warrilow?" I asked gently. "That would explain why he was so adamant about not selling the lad to you."

Eden shook his head. "I do not think so. I believe she would have told me that, and Robbie does not have the look of him, thank heavens. No, I suspect she loved his father and that he is dead or out of her reach. As you point out, Lacey, Juliet's life was not her own. I won't hold that against the poor woman."

"I am certain you will not." Grenville let his smile come. "Mixed marriages are not uncommon these days, you know. I followed my heart, and it has brought me great happiness thus far."

Eden's brow furrowed, and he gazed from Grenville to me in bewilderment. Then he let out a hearty laugh.

"Good Lord, gentlemen. You believe me smitten? I am fond of Mrs. Davies, it is true, and young Robbie, but marriage?" He laughed again, the sound deep and loud. "I have told you many times, Lacey, I am an avowed bachelor."

To the rumble of his laughter, we rounded the corner into Wellclose Square and to Robbie's and his mother's home.

WE SPENT ANOTHER PLEASANT HOUR WITH THE LOVELY Mrs. Davies in her parlor, explaining to her what had happened. She applauded in delight when we described the villain being taken away.

"You should have no more worries, dear lady," Grenville assured her.

I would not be as sanguine until all parties were locked away. I would ask Sir Montague to either send patrollers to guard her house or contact his cronies in the Tower to do the same.

Eden decided to remain behind with Mrs. Davies when we departed. We pried Harry from the rear yard where he was teaching Robbie the boxing moves Brewster had showed him and returned him to his grandmother. Mrs. Beadle was surprised to learn the identity of the killer, but relieved he'd been arrested.

"None want to stay in a boarding house where men are murdered in their bedchambers," she declared. "But if it had to do with the excise men, then there's no worry. No one likes *them*," she finished with conviction.

I bade Jackson return Grenville and me to the Thames River Police. Once there, Thompson thanked me for this coup and told me he'd given his prisoner to the Constable of the Tower, who had jurisdiction over Wellclose Square and its environs.

"If he's convicted, it might well be treason," Thompson said. "Stealing weapons from Britain and supplying them to other countries." He shook his head. "I'm sure it was bloody lucrative. He already gave me names, which I have passed on to the Runners. I may have hinted to Seabrook that his charges might be reduced to smuggling and theft, rather than treason if he assisted me." Thompson shrugged, his worn coat swaying. "Don't know what the judges at the Old Bailey will decide to convict him on."

"Where has Brewster got to?" I asked after we'd said our farewells. A swift glance around told me he was nowhere in sight. "His wife will want him home in one piece."

"He said he was going back to the warehouse that burned yesterday. He gave no reason. I bade him a good day."

He had me curious, but I thanked Thompson for the information. Thompson waved me off. "If you ever wish to lay a gun-running ring, an art smuggler, and the answer to stolen warehouse merchandise at my feet again, please do." He turned away, whistling.

"I must fetch Brewster, if you do not mind," I said to Grenville as we ascended into the carriage once more.

"Not at all. Then we will retire to South Audley Street to sup, drink wine, and regale Donata and Peter with our adventures."

"Donata will be relieved it is all over," I said as the carriage started forward. "I think she will not want me pursuing villains for a long time to come."

"Perhaps. Perhaps not. I do have a proposal for you, Lacey, but I'll not make it until we are with Donata. Marianne already knows about it."

"Leaving me to stew in curiosity?"

"I am afraid so."

Grenville's expression was amused, and I did not pander to his vanity by begging to know what he meant.

Jackson let us out in front of the Custom House once again, and Grenville and I trudged down the lane to what was left of Creasey's warehouse.

I imagined the bodies had been taken away, and I wondered if any of Creasey's men had survived. We would know, in time, I supposed.

Brewster stood near one of the blank brick walls in the middle of the ground floor of Creasey's warehouse. The blown-out windows let in far more light now that the filthy panes were gone. Glass, bricks, and wood had been strewn thickly across the floor, the shell of the walls still standing.

Brewster held a sledgehammer in his strong hands, and as we entered, stepping carefully, he bashed it into the wall beside him.

"Brewster," I called. "What the devil are you doing?"

Brewster pounded the hammer through bricks and the plaster behind them, then withdrew it and wiped his brow. "Oi. There ye are, guv. I was pondering, if I'm honest, where Creasey's stolen goods had got to. None's been found, I'm hearing, and now that Creasey has met his maker, he can't tell us, can he?"

"You believe them behind the wall?" Grenville scanned the long line of blackened bricks. "Are you certain?"

"Why would the man live above empty storerooms?" Brewster asked. "Unless they weren't truly empty. I came back here and measured the inside versus where the walls should fall on the outside. Came up several feet shy. It's an old trick, and Creasey was an old thief."

Before we could comment on that, Brewster hefted the sledgehammer and continued his bashing. He and his cronies had done the same to my house in Norfolk once upon a time, searching it for stashes of stolen paintings. It had been the first time I'd met Brewster, in fact.

"Aha." Brewster cracked bricks that were not as sturdy as they appeared, and they and the sooty plaster backing them fell away.

There, between studs of a false wall, lay a neat line of crates and wooden barrels. Brewster dropped the hammer and used a pry bar to yank the lid off a crate.

"Ah, now that's a fine sight to see," he declared.

Grenville and I crowded around. Inside, nestled in a bed of straw, gleamed objects of gold, many of them. I made out the shape of a dog-headed Egyptian statue.

"Lucky thing these were shut back here," Brewster said. "Saved them from the blast."

I had to wonder if Denis had thought of that.

"I'll take these to His Nibs," Brewster said with a grin. "He'll be chuffed."

I had to agree that he would be.

CHAPTER 26

We helped Brewster load the crate he'd opened into the carriage. I wanted to alert Thompson and Sir Montague about his find, but Brewster forestalled me.

"Let me retrieve all His Nibs' things first," Brewster said. "Deliver that box to him and tell him to come identify the rest. Then ye can bring Mr. Thompson in. He's a good bloke, for the law."

Brewster was correct that once the magistrates seized these goods, the chances of Denis recovering his shipment was low. The items would be held as evidence and only slowly returned to whoever truly owned them—if that could even be determined.

We left Brewster happily tearing through the rest of the walls and returned to Mayfair.

"Do you think Eden and Mrs. Davies will make a match?" Grenville asked as we rode. "Despite his denials?"

I shrugged. "Eden has always been carefree, and I haven't seen that change in him. But who knows? Mrs. Davies is beautiful and grateful, and her home is pleasant. I suspect

Eden will drift more and more to that house, and one day never leave it."

"I wish him well." Grenville gave him an imaginary toast. "He seems a good man."

"He is. And rash, impetuous, and a poor liar."

"Hmm." Grenville eyed me, then shook his head and gazed out the window.

We arrived in Curzon Street as thick clouds covered the sun and a heavy October rain began to fall. We found Denis reestablished in his upstairs study, though his guards were in evidence throughout the house and outside it. One never knew.

Denis received the box of Egyptian treasures with a nod and ordered Gibbons to send others to assist Brewster.

"Will anything be left in that warehouse when they are finished?" I asked him.

Denis answered with one of his minute shakes of the head. "The shipment I lost was substantial."

I chose not to argue. Nor did I protest too much when Denis lifted a bejeweled golden scarab from the crate and offered it to me. Donata would be pleased with it, I decided.

I left Denis to his stratagems. When we alighted at South Audley Street, Grenville declared himself quite fatigued and retired to his chamber for a nap. He closed his door before I approached Donata's sitting room.

Donata was there, once again writing letters at her desk. I crossed the room, laid the scarab before her, and kissed the top of her head.

Donata took up the scarab, enchanted. "Good heavens, Gabriel, it is lovely." She glanced at me as I hovered behind her. "Is this a peace offering?"

"It is a beautiful trinket I thought you would like," I said quietly. "I believe Denis's intention is a peace offering. Or a step toward the debt he says he owes me. He likes to have things in balance. Usually tipped in his favor."

"That is true." Donata admired the scarab once more and gently laid it on the writing table. "Thank you."

I laid my cheek against her hair. "You are welcome." I drew a breath. "I can never bring the balance between us aright again. I know that." I rose, stepping back. "I accept that."

"Gabriel." Donata turned in her chair. "Please, do not go."

The words made my throat tighten. I drew a chair beside hers and sat down, taking her hands. "Never. Until you send me far away."

"I do not wish to."

Her words were soft, her eyes holding pain, but also hope. This was a lady who'd been through much. Her life, which was the envy of many, had been hard enough to toughen her into steel.

"I do not wish to go either," I answered.

Donata rested her hands on my shoulders. Her answer, without words, eased my heart. It was a long time before we adjourned to find supper.

BARNSTABLE SERVED US AN APPETIZING MEAL SEVERAL hours later. Donata, Grenville, Peter, and I relaxed in the dining room, discussing all that had happened.

A smaller mystery had been solved when I received an answer from Sir Montague about the Kingstons. He'd sent his best Runner, Mr. Quimby, to Lambeth to chat with Mr. Kingston, Mr. Quimby quite good at extracting information.

It turned out that Kingston did have an alibi for the time of both Warrilow's and Laybourne's murders. When I'd spoken to him, he'd claimed to have been helping the vicar, and Mrs. Kingston had said with some suspicion she'd seen him nowhere near the church.

In truth, he'd been not far away from home, at a local pub, indulging in a pint of ale and friendly conversation. Mrs. Kingston highly disapproved of public houses and taverns, but her husband apparently found them a peaceful retreat from her zealous and never-ending chatter.

I read the missive out, a lighthearted note after so much direness.

After we'd laughed and continued our meal, Grenville laid down his fork and cleared his throat.

"My proposal, that I mentioned to you, Lacey, is this," he said. "I have a villa not far from Rome. Perhaps not a villa, but a large house with a pleasant view. I have thought about withdrawing there with Marianne for some time, until others grow used to our new arrangement."

"Sensible," Donata said. "Bask in private enjoyment to fortify yourself for coming battle."

"Yes." Grenville took a long sip of wine. "I am afraid this Season will be one continuous battle. Our current house party is going well, but that is because I handpicked the guests. When the *ton* bears down on us come spring, it will be a different situation. But if I invite the correct people to visit us in the beautiful Italian countryside, and they report in London what bliss we live in, so much the better."

I lifted my glass. "Sound thinking. I wish you well."

"The villa is not far from the excavations in Pompeii and Herculaneum. I will assume you'd like to come and view them, Lacey? As well as the splendid ruins in Rome?"

"Ah." My breath quickened. Peter, who had been good about letting the adults converse uninterrupted, bounced in his seat.

"Would I come too?" he asked.

"I extend the invitation to the entire family," Grenville said. "The ladies may sun themselves and shop to their heart's content while we gentlemen prowl the buried cities."

"It sounds an excellent sojourn," Donata said with a decided nod. "Provided we spend the Christmas season in Oxfordshire, with Gabriella. My mother is rather insistent."

"Of course," Grenville said. "We'd go in early spring. It is much warmer there than in beastly England, and we'll return at the height of the London Season. Gabriella should come, along with all your children. It will be a family outing."

"Excellent," Donata said. "Then I will begin plans to remove there."

That was settled. I raised my glass. "To a Roman spring."

Donata and Grenville followed suit. "A Roman spring."

"Will there be room for me, guv?" Brewster stood in the doorway, Barnstable quivering near him in disapproval.

"Undoubtedly," Grenville said. "I will rely on you to keep Lacey from trouble, as usual. Your lady wife should come as well."

"I'll ask her." Brewster wrinkled his forehead doubtfully. "Though Em's not much for foreign parts." He turned to me, his expression troubled. "His Nibs was grateful for the return of his trinkets."

I regarded him in surprise. "Is that a cause for glumness?"

"He offered me my old place back. Said I'd redeemed meself, like, for finding his treasures."

"Ah." My heart sank. I'd miss Brewster if he went, and surely he'd want to. Denis paid his men very well. There was nothing to say Denis would assign Brewster again to watch me, and in that case, I'd see little of him. I tried to sound encouraging. "Well, I suppose I wish you the best."

"Fing is." Brewster hesitated, moving uneasily.

"Do say what you mean, Mr. Brewster," Donata said. "Do not leave us dangling."

Brewster cleared his throat. "Fing is, I told His Nibs I didn't want to go back to him. I'd rather keep *this* job. That is, if you'll have me, guv."

My dismay fled as Brewster sent me a defiant glare. I recognized that it had been very difficult for him to come to me, hat in hand, as it were, and ask if he was wanted.

"I'd not have it any other way, Brewster," I assured him. "You are most welcome to stay. Would you care to sit and toast your decision?"

Brewster glanced around the dining room, where silver gleamed in the candlelight, while Barnstable attempted to not look too appalled.

"I won't, if it's all the same to you. Too much in here tempting for an old thief. I'll say my good nights and go back to my Em."

"Your good health, Brewster." I raised my glass of wine. "Please give my best to Mrs. Brewster."

"I'll do that." Brewster gave the room one last glance and shook his head. "Off to run over buried cities. I can't imagine what sort of trouble you'll find yourself in there, guv. You'll need me looking out for you, no mistake."

ALSO BY ASHLEY GARDNER

Leonidas the Gladiator Mysteries

Blood of a Gladiator

Blood Debts

A Gladiator's Tale

Captain Lacey Regency Mysteries

The Hanover Square Affair

A Regimental Murder

The Glass House

The Sudbury School Murders

The Necklace Affair and Other Stories

A Body in Berkeley Square

A Covent Garden Mystery

A Death in Norfolk

A Disappearance in Drury Lane

Murder in Grosvenor Square

The Thames River Murders

The Alexandria Affair

A Mystery at Carlton House

Murder in St. Giles

Death at Brighton Pavilion

The Custom House Murders

Kat Holloway "Below Stairs" Victorian Mysteries

(writing as Jennifer Ashley)

A Soupçon of Poison

Death Below Stairs

Scandal Above Stairs

Death in Kew Gardens

Murder in the East End

Death at the Crystal Palace

Mystery Anthology

Past Crimes

Contains

Blood Debts

A Soupçon of Poison

The Necklace Affair

ABOUT THE AUTHOR

USA Today Bestselling author Ashley Gardner is a pseudonym for *New York Times* bestselling author Jennifer Ashley. Under both names—and a third, Allyson James—Ashley has written more than 100 published novels and novellas in mystery, romance, fantasy, and historical fiction. Ashley's books have been translated into more than a dozen different languages and have earned starred reviews in *Publisher's Weekly* and *Booklist*. When she isn't writing, she indulges her love for history by researching and building miniature houses and furniture from many periods, and playing classical guitar and piano.

More about the Captain Lacey series can be found at the website: www.gardnermysteries.com. Stay up to date on new releases by joining her email alerts here:

http://eepurl.com/5n7rz

$$\begin{array}{r} 1.8 \\ 20\overline{)37.0} \\ \underline{20} \\ 170 \\ \underline{160} \\ \overline{10.0} \end{array}$$

Made in the USA
Monee, IL
11 November 2020